How Much Wine Will Fix My Broken Heart?

BOOKS BY KRISTEN BAILEY

Has Anyone Seen My Sex Life?
Can I Give My Husband Back?
Did My Love Life Shrink in the Wash?

KRISTEN BAILEY

How Much Wine Will Fix My Broken Heart?

bookouture

Published by Bookouture in 2021

An imprint of Storyfire Ltd.
Carmelite House
50 Victoria Embankment
London EC4Y 0DZ

www.bookouture.com

ISBN: 978-1-83888-977-7
eBook ISBN: 978-1-83888-976-0

For Grace Green
1992–2016

PROLOGUE

Gracie,

If you have this letter then I am afraid the worst has happened and I'm not here any more. I don't want to use the d-word so I will paraphrase in the best way possible: my body has literally given up on me. Stupid body. It's quite a thing to have to write this letter before the event, to stare down this very possibility myself, but I don't want to be gone and, basically, not have the final word. God, that's awful to write, eh? I don't want to be lying on my deathbed and forget to tell you something.

There's only the one letter. I won't spring these on you once a year or send Christmas cards from beyond the grave. This is it. I may come back and haunt you, though. Once I cross over to the other side, I'll enquire about how I can make that happen. Fear not, it won't be like a horror film. I won't stand in dark corners and hide under the bed in a freaky haunted doll way. I'll be a friendly ghost like in a BBC sitcom. I'll be very benign. I hope I might have the ability to fly through walls. That'll be handy as I have a feeling you'll still need me to put the bins out.

I'll just appear when you're brushing your teeth, give you the occasional fright. Boo! Remember me?

There are so many other things to tell you. I feel I need to give you lists of PIN numbers and passwords. Grace2000 is the password for most of my things. But for my email, it's monkey-balls1992, which I hope will make you laugh. What else? Make sure you give my clothes away. Don't keep them because that's sad. What are you going to do with them? You could wear all of them at the same time and just lie in bed and pretend I'm there. Or make a patchwork blanket out of all my best hoodies. Don't frame the clothes.

Also, while I have this platform, it's important for me to say the following. Herbs and spices don't have expiry dates. Those are best before dates. Don't hate me but I think you waste a lot of money replacing your paprika every year. When it comes to tea, I also don't know why you put the milk in first, with the teabag. It's not the way to do things. It does affect the taste because the water isn't the right temperature to absorb the tea through the bag. And I haven't made that up. You called it my strange tea science but it's truth, which is proven by the fact that my tea was always far more drinkable than yours. There are probably a million other things I need to say that are more important than that but those are the ones which come to mind at this very precise moment.

Next: try not to cry too much when it happens. I mean, cry a bit because if you don't shed a tear then people will think you're some sort of psychopath. Just don't over-cry and I say that with the very best of intentions because, when you over-cry, you don't use the good tissues and you get that rash around your nose where the skin flakes off. I'll say it now because, hey, I'm dying, but it's pretty grim. Maybe put some Vaseline around there to smooth out the edges. Hay-fever season, you look pretty monstrous most of the time. The things you can say to a spouse when you're dead, right?

I don't know why I'm joking as this still feels like the unfairest thing in the world, the rudest of interruptions. This has to be the final word as, while my ego would love you to mourn me forever, in black lace, shrouded in pain like Queen Victoria, building shrines in my honour, I don't want you to do that. I don't want my wonderful beautiful girl to die too. When the pain has subsided, let people in, date again. Date someone interesting and significantly better looking than me, of course. I've looked into single people around our age. At the time of writing this, the following people are single: Henry Cavill, Neymar and Drake. If you're bringing Drake to your next family Christmas then record the moment your mum meets him for the first time. 'Your name is Drake? Like a duck?' I will come back and haunt you if you replace me with someone dull. You don't go from me to James from the Home Counties who drives a Škoda Fabia, drinks Foster's and supports Manchester United even though he's never even been to Manchester.

Promise me you won't regress, Gracie. That's what I worry about most. You've always been mildly serious about life, and I love that about you. It is wildly endearing. You've always had a plan. But I suspect me leaving the mortal realm is not in your plan so my one big fear is that I won't be there to balance you out. It is why we are so good together: you give me reason and order, you pull my feet back to the ground when I'm off in the clouds, you make sure that all my big dreams and ideas are possible in real-life situations.

Me: I want to go and build a school! I want children to think big! I want to create a system of education for all where no one is left behind!

You: You can't today, it's Sunday. You'll need planning permission first. And willing children.

In return, I hope I added a certain zest and unpredictable quality to proceedings. I love that feeling of yin and yang, of a relationship built on this giant melting pot of qualities and facets. It makes me ache to think what our children would have been like. They'd have been all the best parts of us. I mean, they possibly would have had my weak-ish chin and the boys may have suffered the indignity of a premature receding hairline. Still, they would have had your meticulous nature and my robot dancing skills, meaning they were never destined to fail.

You are so earnest, you put heart and thought into everything you do, every word and action. I teased you about it. I joked about it all because I always thought you took everything too seriously. I guess the final joke's on me. I should have listened to you when you first told me I needed to check things out. It was my health. It was serious. And all those nonchalant jokes I made about being young enough to fight this, thinking we had forever. I am sorry for all of that. I am sorry I thought we could exist without these things happening to us. I am sorry for not being more you. I am so very sorry.

Urgh, I didn't want this letter to get sad and philosophical. I wanted it to be droll. Has it made you laugh? I've deleted a crapload of clichés already. Life is short. That's a good one. I was going to have that printed on a wall sticker as a parting gift. I did think long and hard about a suitable parting gift, actually. Maybe something that has a lock of my hair in it. Did you know you could do that? I could weave you a friendship bracelet made of hair. I decided against it. It has a serial-killer quality to it, though it's useful if you want to go down the voodoo route.

Instead, I thought about what I want for you when I'm not here. I don't want you to sit still. You won't be alone. You've never been alone with all your sisters around but remember to let people in too. You are hard to penetrate (and not like that, that bit was easy and that was an awful joke, sorry) but allow people in so they can help you with this. Keep moving. You do get into the habit of sitting still, of making plans, and with those plans come lists and spreadsheets and it all gets a bit static, you know? You must move on.

So, this is my way of making sure that you do. You must, Gracie. You must promise me this one thing.

Enclosed with this letter is a round-the-world ticket. It allows for five stops and, to narrow down the infinite choice of possibility (because I know you'll pick places based on their tourist theft rates and currency values against the pound), I've selected those stops for you. All these destinations are countries I visited during my travels after university. Those three years when I was a selfish prick and left you to go travelling. Our limbo period. I know those places, they know me. I've attached lists of names and numbers of people to look up and some recommendations for things to do. I've also made the ticket completely non-refundable. I did this to ensure you go because you'll make excuses not to go. If I've spent money on this then you will feel fiscal guilt so this will force you to make this trip.

Travel, Grace. Just keep moving. Raise a glass or five to me in different continents. After we left university and we had all those years in relationship limbo, I don't think you ever understood why I went, why I left you. Hopefully, this fills in the gaps. At worst, you'll be distracted from the fact that cancer came and made me its bitch. At best, you'll move in the right direction, you'll see a sunset or learn a new language and understand that the world is still new, it's still turning, how this life malarkey isn't totally awful even though I'm not here.

I will always regret the things we never did together. We never got to live in Paris above a bakery where a man called Jean-Luc would keep us in fresh croissants. We never rode a tandem. I probably never held you enough or sang enough songs about how much I fucking adored you. But no regrets. Just to have had you in my orbit for what time we had was perfection. I keep thinking back to the time when we first met. It was that dodgy nightclub in Bristol, do you remember? I was so drunk. It was a Dynamite Boogaloo night and I knew all the words to every song and you looked at me like I was mental while I was doing my strange disco jogging moves. When I told you my name was Tom, you asked me which one. Everyone's called Tom. Major Tom, I said. And you asked why and then I told you my dad used to sing me that Bowie song all the time. And you didn't sing the song back to me like most do. You apologised because you noticed that I'd spoken in the past tense. That's what my Grace does. She's there for the details. And I don't remember half of what I'm supposed to in life but, man, that memory is etched into me.

I'm happy I have that memory of you in that shit club, your purple eyeshadow, your bra straps on show and your face gleaming with kindness. That is enough for me. It was always enough. What we've had was everything. Yet for you, this is not the end, not the past tense. You have a future so you must keep on. You must live for me. To not do so would be breaking my already broken heart.

I need to say my last words now, eh? My Grace, I could write books. I could write letters of no end that just describe all the words and feelings that line my brain. You know me. Teaching made me a wordy bastard. I am so scared. So scared to leave you, but I'll stop here. I used to tell you every day that you were magnificent and you are. It's been a pleasure, an honour and a gift to be your husband, to have loved you, to have been loved by you.

I love you so very much, Grace Callaghan. That I do.
Major Tom x

Chapter One

Gracie, I don't know if this internet will work so I'll make this short and sweet. I am in Ghana. Actual Ghana. Not that there's a fake Ghana but it's mental. The city literally beats with life. On the trip over here I seemed to make friends with everyone who sat on the bus. I seem to have a gift for it, don't I? I just make friends everywhere I go. Everyone is smiling and interested in me, my life, they welcome me into their homes.

I adore it. I adore you.

Love you, T x

Carrie Cantello has a Harry-Potter-themed front room. I don't know how old Carrie is but I'd put her around the late thirties mark. This wizard stuff is kind of everywhere, from the stuffed, boss-eyed owl that looks at me from the bookshelves to the monogrammed throws. There's a framed picture of the whole family on a themed ride at Universal Studios where they're all wearing matching Harry specs.

I'd really like to look in the cupboard under her stairs. Crap, she's also got Harry Potter mugs. Carrie, I feel like you need some sort of intervention. I bet you wear a cape to bed. Please let there be Potter-themed sex where she utters fake sex spells and talks about her husband's wand. *Penum Erecto*. Don't laugh, Grace. The husband has re-entered the room. Don't think about his wand.

'Ross, I said biscuits,' Carrie barks at him. She definitely orders him around the bedroom, doesn't she? I bet she refers to it as her golden snatch. Do. Not. Laugh. I bite on my lip and pretend I'm deep in concentration writing down the numbers. *Join the Parent Teacher Association. Surround yourself with people. Get out there, Grace*, Emma said. *Are you on the PTA?* I asked my dear sister. *No. My one's run by power women nut jobs. They're not all like that*, she told me.

Except they are. Carrie Cantello is the chair of The Downs Primary PTA. She possesses all the confidence and none of the charm and orders us around like her minions. She also doesn't use emojis so I can never determine the tone of her messages. Is that sarcasm? Or do you hate me? She has bushy dirty-blonde hair, though I wonder if that's to make her look like Hermione. Her skirting boards are super clean, like shiny clean. I imagine her scrubbing the skirting with a Potter film on, wearing her cape obviously. To cement her power in the school, she nominated her own husband to be governor. It's very conspiratorial. Ross is harmless but writes a lot of tweets dissecting football matches that are of no interest to anyone but himself.

To Carrie's left is her number one henchperson, Liz Boucher. Do you know how to pronounce that surname? No one does. It's French so she always reels it off with an accent like she's continental but really it means 'butcher' so it just suggests her ancestors were good with meat. Liz is the secretary because she has the iPad with the good apps for taking notes and making newsletters. She also loves a laminated sign for the noticeboard where she overuses exclamation marks. *Tuesday! 8.30 p.m.! Support the School! Do it!* Carrie and Liz like to go on girly days out to spas and call themselves besties on social media. They stand around gossiping at the school gate.

'Oh, I don't let my Josh play with him because I think he's possibly on the spectrum. His mum should really get him assessed.'

'I always have the time to at least *iron a uniform?'*

'That teacher does not invest enough of her time into my Ava. What a complete amateur.'

And most of us let it slide because it's not worth our time or energy. We're glad we're not like them. We're grateful they're in the minority. The rest of us are a motley crew that make this whole enterprise more endurable. Paula likes a wide-leg jean and a floral print blouse and carries her everyday belongings in a Bag for Life, Tina doesn't get any of the jokes but once got drunk at our Christmas shindig and told us her husband is only allowed one blow job a year (his birthday), and we all know Georgia, who comes with tales of her recent divorce and how she had her first orgasm at thirty-eight years of age using something called a Clitty Clamp. But can we sell these at the next Christmas Fayre, Georgia? Can we?

I am the treasurer. I'm an accountant by trade so it made sense. It means I'm doing my bit and I get to feel important by carrying a cash box around at school events. I'm getting out there and throw-ing all this positive energy into the world so it can come back to me in kind. Would I prefer to be at home under a blanket, eating pretzels on this cold January evening, binge-watching *Criminal Minds*? Yes. We could have done this by Zoom or email but then Carrie's cleaned her skirting boards. How else would she be able to show off her Harry Potter memorabilia? The owl on her shelf is looking at me, like I'm in his tree and he wants to peck my eyes out.

'So. Much. To. Talk. About.'

I really hope there isn't, Carrie. Just go through the agenda as quickly as humanly possible. There are ten of us squeezed around her living room on an assortment of dining room chairs, piano stools and an outdoor camping bench. This evening was not built for comfort.

'So, apologies for absence?' asks Liz.

'Kay Holland can't be here because her lot have the sicky bug,' says a voice from the back.

'Remind me to keep my kids away from hers then,' Carrie mumbles. 'Right, first things first: the Christmas Fayre made £3546, is that right, Grace?' I nod. I won't mention the fifty-two pence she's excluded from that figure. 'Seriously, pat yourselves on the back, please. Stellar work. We are *such* an amazing team.'

Oh, we're actually patting ourselves on the actual backs, as instructed. Carrie looks like she's performing the Heimlich manoeuvre on herself.

'I told you all that the photo booths were the way forward,' Carrie says. Liz claps, nodding. Except she didn't. To my left is Helen. It was all Helen's idea; she sourced the props and painted a Christmas backdrop complete with snowballs. Helen is possibly the only person I'd categorise with the 'friend' label here. We both have kids in the same classes and I've gravitated towards her sturdiness, how she doesn't seem to give a flying fish finger what people think. I'm eagerly waiting for the moment it will come to a head between her and Carrie because it will be worth all those nights sitting at a computer filling in invoices and Excel spreadsheets.

'All your idea, was it?' Helen suggests.

'Well, I approved it,' Carrie says.

'That's like saying you wrote Harry Potter because you like magic.'

I smile. I'm not the only one who's noticed.

'Being an amazing team is also ensuring people get credit for their contributions,' Helen adds.

'Well done, Helen,' I add. 'We got some really good feedback for that.' She turns to let me pat her back. I do so, laughing.

Carrie is less amused. 'When you're both quite done. Maybe we'll set up something similar for the Easter Eggstravaganza.'

She announces that in accentuated tones because she's come up with that name herself. Liz is clapping again and a few mums smile tiredly over their cups of tea and garibaldi. She hasn't even provided biscuits with chocolate.

'I've already booked in the petting zoo for that. Despite what happened last year, they realise it was not our fault.'

What happened last year is someone left a gate open and a three-year-old got run over by a sheep and a dad kicked said sheep in the head. There was also an incident where a child tried to feed a carrot up a particularly hairy guinea pig's bum because they couldn't work out which end was its face.

'And Ross has agreed to dress up as the rabbit this year. The actor we hired last year was farcical. He couldn't even hop.'

Helen twists her lips around, trying to stifle her giggles. Don't. That shit is contagious. I look over at the owl. That doesn't help.

'The actor was pants because the kids chased him around the field, tackled him to the floor and robbed him of his sweets. Feral little fuckers,' Helen adds. I grin because I was there. Though to see Ross Cantello chased and attacked by children may become a year highlight.

'Treasure hunt would be much better,' Helen suggests. 'The Twenty-Four-Carrot Fun Day. Find all the carrots and the children get an egg. I don't like mine getting all these random sweets and then they're off their tits on sugar. The parents hated us after last year.'

'I like that idea,' I say. 'From a money point of view, we'd have to spend less from the outset.'

Carrie glares at me. There's the murmur of approval from the other mothers in the room. I give Helen a cheeky elbow and she winks at me.

'But Eggstravaganza... it's an excellent play on words,' Liz adds.

'My lad's in Reception and he can't even say his own name,' Helen adds.

I take a sip of tea to hide my smirk. Keep prodding, Hels.

'Well, I'll think about it,' Carrie says, drawing that conversation to a close. 'We also had a plan for the end of the month. We don't normally put on extra things but I thought it'd be a really good idea to have a Chinese New Year event.'

Liz, stop clapping.

'Like a normal quiz night,' she carries on, 'but Chinese-themed for the end of January. We could get Chinese food in, perhaps some decorations, and I found a company who could print fortune cookies and fans for us.' My heart drops. I sense Helen taking a deep inhalation of breath.

'Oh my days, I know somewhere we could get straw hats,' Liz says. 'I have a kimono I could wear, it'd be a riot…'

I wait for it.

'What do you think, Grace?'

It was coming. Shitsticks.

'I think there are possibly better ways of making money for the school. A raffle maybe?' I mutter.

Carrie stops to study my pained expression. 'I thought you'd like that idea, what with your girls?'

All the eyes of the room fall onto me. Oh dear, I have to do this, don't I?

'My girls are not Chinese. They're Vietnamese.'

'Oh, well, it's all the same, no?'

'It really isn't,' I reply. Crumbs, Carrie. It's late. There's no alcohol here. I don't want a conversation about cultural appropriation and your lack of understanding of world geography.

'Then what about their father? Their Asian roots? I think they'd appreciate the fact we're trying to celebrate the diversity of our school?'

I pause for a moment. Carrie has never asked me about my family, my life, or my husband, which is really just typical of her self-obsessed personality, but Helen knows and I feel her body lean into mine.

'Maya and Cleo are adopted.'

'Oh,' Carrie says bluntly without a hint of an apology. 'You'd never tell. They speak English so well.'

I inhale sharply to cut off my words.

'I never see your husband about so I assumed he was the Asian one. Maybe he works all the time so is less involved in your family life.'

Deep breaths, Gracie. Deep deep breaths.

'He's less involved because he's dead. My husband passed away from testicular cancer three years ago.'

The room goes quiet. Not even quiet. Dead. As dead as this owl next to me. As dead as Tom. He'd have laughed hard at that joke. He'd literally have wet himself over the owl.

No one is speaking. When I throw that bomb, I never quite get why everyone goes silent. Is it the testicle bit, the cancer bit or the death bit? All three are the most loaded conversation-killers you can get.

'I… I didn't know that.'

'Well, you do now. The girls actually never knew him. I went travelling after Tom passed away and I adopted them during that time.'

The room take stock of that story. Some look down, some shake their heads, others you can almost hear the awkward sound of them swallowing and it hitting the pits of their stomach.

'And you should also know we have a huge mixture of kids from the South East Asian diaspora in our school. Blake in Year Four has a Cambodian mother and the twins in Year Six are Filipino. If you want to label some crappy quiz event as representative of all these different families and their cultures by wearing straw hats and dicking around with chopsticks and bad chow mein then you're just going to insult a load of people. Kimonos are also Japanese.'

If Helen could dance now, she probably would. She would actually twerk.

'So you're a single mother?' asks Carrie.

That's all she got from that? Yes, I am raising two sisters of Vietnamese/French ethnicity. On my own. In Bristol. In a house. And I am also sitting here with my pen poised ready to stab you through your jugular and tell you your Hogwarts-style living room is really quite the embarrassment. You have Hagrid coasters.

'I am. And a widow, I guess.'

It's like she doesn't understand that. How am I supposed to look? Am I supposed to be a pre-teen single mother? Am I supposed to look sadder? Dressed in black? Do widows wear denim? Carrie scans the ring on my finger, ready to spread this information around the playground. This is a variation of her life that she just doesn't understand and, for one small moment, I pity her.

'Well, it was just an idea. I don't want people being *sensitive* about it.' That smidgeon of pity evaporates pretty quickly.

'What about your Pancake Day idea, Carrie?' Liz suggests animatedly, trying to mend the mood.

'The Great British Toss Off,' Helen mumbles. A few mothers in earshot snigger to themselves.

'What was that, Helen?' Carrie barks back.

'Nothing. I likes a good toss. Can we dress Ross up as a lemon? He'd look good in yellow.'

They glare at each other. An event with you two, frying pans, fire and hot batter in the vicinity? When can we vote on that?

*

I get home that night at 10.36 p.m. after Carrie tore apart the quality of the school uniform (*Why are we letting girls wear trousers!*), the school teaching (*No child learns through play*), and Ross may have actually farted at one point as there was definitely a smell that weaved itself around the room that Carrie tried to ignore. It could have seriously started fires.

I shouldn't have walked. It's too cold for walking but if I'd driven I'd have lost my parking space at the front of the house, the securing of which is something I plan in far too much depth. Guarding parking spots and observing the correct bin days: that is my life. I fumble about in my bags for the keys as I trudge up to our terraced home with its bright yellow door. Yellow. It was supposed to bring me joy but on a cold February night like this, as the wind bites at my skin, it simply makes it easier to find which is mine. In the front bay window, Maya's Sylvanian Families are lined up ready to picnic along with an assortment of crayons and pens. I put the key in the door and let the warm glow of the house rouse me. A head pops out from the kitchen.

'Hey. How was it?' Sam asks. He's got a tea towel in his hand. He's done my washing-up? Gold star for you.

'Like pulling teeth. Carrie Cantello really is an awful human being.'

'That's not a huge surprise. What's she done now?' he asks.

'She outed me for being a widow. For having kids that don't look like me. It was a fun evening.'

'Wow.' You can tell he's not too sure how to soothe my soul. 'Tea?'

Good try. 'Something stronger? I have a bottle of Pinot Grigio in the fridge.'

'Excellent.'

He escapes into the kitchen while I take my boots and giant coat off by the front door. If I'm going to do cold weather, I'm going to do it cocooned like the warmest of caterpillars. I unwind the scarf from my neck and catch my reflection in the mirror. 'Ruddy warm' is the term. In the kitchen, Sam's not found any wine glasses so pours the Pinot Grigio into mugs.

'That's a good hat.'

I pull it off my head and feel the static of my dark brown hair clinging to my face. 'It's my favourite. If you're going to wear a bobble hat, the bobble should be the size of a doughnut.'

He pushes the mug in my direction.

'Thanks, Sam.'

Sam, one of my few school-gate friends, leans against my counter and holds the mug up to me in an attempt to offer his cheers. He's in his regular outfit of Levi's, hoodie and chestnut walking boots, with stubble lining his chin and creeping down his neck.

'Was Orlagh there?' he asks me.

I shake my head. 'She doesn't really do PTA any more. Not since…'

I daren't say the words out loud, but not since their recent divorce. Sam was, up until recently, married to Orlagh and they have two sons at The Downs Primary. It was a public split so she started keeping her head down, mainly because a lot of people knew about what was happening before Sam did. According to Orlagh, she just fell in love with someone else but, to all who knew the real truth, she met Jordan on a mums' night out in a local nightclub and apparently had sex with him in an alley. She continued this affair and we all had to play along with the charade, seeing Sam at the school gate and awkwardly waving at him like we knew nothing.

I befriended Sam after the divorce, at the Christmas Fayre that raised £3546.52 when we both ended up pulling a shift on the sweets stall. He's a lovely bloke, warm, extremely tall, questionable taste in music (country leanings), but he's in IT so has sorted my Windows for me. He brings the boys around for chicken nuggets. We chat. He rings me up in panic when he forgets Roald Dahl Day. Orlagh remains fresh in his mind so the whole experience is still very wounding. Even the mention of her name now renders an expression on his face like he's trying to pass a kidney stone.

'We have to do parents' evening next week and I don't know what to do,' he mumbles.

'Be civil? Clench and grin?'

'Perhaps.'

I am reminded of an assembly one month ago when Orlagh showed up with Jordan in tow and Sam went cranberry-coloured at the gate. He told me he then ran back to his car and sat there quietly for fifteen minutes, sobbing. Now, he stares out of my kitchen window into the darkness.

'How were the girls?' I ask, trying to change the subject.

'Not a peep. Do you drug them?'

'They swim on Thursdays. Tires them out. Thank you for looking after them. My usual sitter's not well.'

'You know me, nothing else to do. It was this or get a chip supper and stalk Orlagh on social media.'

'I hope you do that in your pants, in a low-lit room.'

'In front of a poster of her and then I cry on my own and rock on the spot.'

I take a big sip of wine. We can laugh about his breakdown now but, when he first separated from Orlagh, there were tears. Big tears. He cried them in my front room once over tea and I hugged him, not knowing what else to do but feed him entire packs of chocolate chip cookies. He misses her, like I miss Tom. We are both grieving something and I'm the first person to tell you there's no right way to grieve.

In fact, confessing the super sad details of my life to Carrie and a crowded room tonight has brought all that grief fizzing to the surface. Tom would have been a great rabbit. He wouldn't have let kids beat him up. He'd have started some dance-off with them to use up all that sugar-hyped energy. Hip-hop. Look, it's the hip-hop bunny dad. He'd have been at that meeting tonight and charmed everyone with his stories and made a comment to Carrie about the Harry Potter theme that would have been jovial without being offensive. I still insert him into every situation, imagining him there, because Tom made things better. And these feelings are still there. They're always there to be honest; it's often just a case of how well I can keep them submerged and out of my regular consciousness. Sam takes long noisy sips from his mug. It's not the best wine. I think it's been in the fridge for five days but, hey, alcohol. We're both firm believers in its magical healing powers. There's something else that works too.

'Do you want to stay tonight? I could do with the company,' I tell Sam.

'But… the girls…'

'You'll have to be quiet?'

He takes off his hoodie in one swift motion. I'll take that as a yes then.

The thing is, next to sorting my Windows, Sam is also more than a new friend. He is sorting much more. After our shift on the sweet stall, we met for coffee and both of us realised we were both consumed by solitude, hidden sadness and busy family lives. I wasn't looking for a new husband. He'd just had his heart ripped out of his arse in quite a public and humiliating way. But we both needed more beyond that. So we offered each other a warm body to lie next to: sex, comfort, company. It passes the time; it's a way to be connected to another human being. Is he good at the sex? He's not awful. He lacks stamina and sweats a lot. He's also fond of calling me 'baby', which I just think sounds wrong. But there is something to be said about having his weight on top of mine. He's also helped considerably with my insomnia. It's a mutual agreement of sorts. It saves us having to go out into the world and experiment with people who'd want more and misunderstand the emotional impact of everything, and it means we aren't masturbating into the night on our own.

'Here?' he asks. He puts his hands to my kitchen table to see if it'd take our weight.

'Christ no, it's cold in here. Too much tiling. I have throws in the living room… I could start a fire?'

'That's borderline romantic.'

'Don't read into it. I'll put the telly on. We can watch *Newsnight* at the same time. Do you have a condom?'

'I do. Was that presumptuous of me?'

'It means your mind is on safety and I find that erotic.'

'Oh, OK then.'

I walk over to him and give him a kiss on the lips. He can at least kiss. The stubble is an irritant, but I like how he appreciates good dental hygiene.

'Shall we?'

We laugh and I lead him to the living room where I close the door softly, putting my finger to my lips to remind him we will have to stay quiet. My girls would sleep through asteroids coming through the roof anyway but discretion is key here. I kiss him, gently backing him into some wall space. He's a bit quick off the mark tonight and has already undone his belt but, hell, that just makes my life easier. I reach down into his underwear and move my hand over him. He moans softly.

'Yes… yes, Orlagh.'

We both pause for a moment.

'Can you pretend you didn't hear that?' he whispers, his body tensing up.

'I've been called worse.' I laugh, trying to lighten the mood. It is what it is. Just don't call me by your bitch ex-wife's name again and I'll try not to call you Tom. I look him in the eye.

'Can I also be a complete dweeb and keep my socks on?' he asks.

I shrug. 'It's February. I'm keeping mine on too.'

Chapter Two

G, Can you do me a favour and check in on my mum? I'm in South America at the moment and she keeps forwarding me messages about cartels and how I can get beheaded and sold for my organs. Just go and have a cup of tea with her or something?

I'm passing through Venezuela and it's frigging ace here. Like, the heat is filthy, I get through about ten T-shirts a day so I smell. I don't think you'd fancy me much with my body odour. I'm digging the music here, there's an amazing new-wave/Latin-reggae thing going on and there's such an eclectic, cool vibe of people. Tell my mum it's all good.

T x

I am not sure what this school form is for but I have to put my marital status on it. I thought this was about school lunches? Oh no, it's vaccinations. I'm glad I didn't write that we're not keen on the chicken curry in the comments. It's not even curry. It's a stew, according to Cleo, and the rice is not to standard. I scan down the categories on the website. Well, I am widowed but also single.

Where is that option? And yes, I am white but the kids are not. How do I put that in? I might just put us all under the 'MIXED, OTHER' bracket. It's not half wrong.

'Mummy, where are my shoes?' Maya asks me. She's dressed herself this morning so the tights sit in ripples around her ankles where she's not pulled them up properly. She also has crusty bits of milk or possibly drool around the sides of her mouth.

'By the back door. I gave them a good clean and brush last night.'

Maya walked through dog poo yesterday on the way home, which made for an eventful moment when I was crouched on a grass verge trying to clean her shoes in the rain. There is a special place in hell for people who let their dogs crap within a hundred metres of a school. She hugs my midriff and goes off to find her shoes. This is Maya's first year in school but she's a summer baby so she's always felt tiny, especially because she scampers everywhere like a gnome. I notice she has handfuls of toast crusts in her palms.

'Where are they going?' I ask her.

'For the birdies. Grandpa says the birdies and the squirrels like them,' she tells me. I smile. Dad did say that and, with Maya so desperate for a pet, this seemed like a good way to attract wildlife. That said, knowing Maya it'll probably attract an urban fox that she'd try and domesticate. I'd most likely find it tucked up in a laundry basket one day and he'd then eat my face. I watch as she puts on her coat and shoes and skips out onto the grass, throwing bread in the air and calling out for birds to come get their breakfast, looking confused that they don't descend from the sky immediately.

Distracted by the doorbell, I leave the littlest to make her bird friends. I sneak my head into the living room to see if Cleo is ready.

Of course she isn't. This one is two years older than her sister so has a more relaxed take on her mornings, thinking the time constraints suddenly don't apply to her. She likes a leisurely piece of toast with her cartoons and to recline on a sofa with her hand propping up the side of her head.

'Half an hour until we leave…' I say, clapping. 'Chop-chop…'

'Hmmm…' she replies. 'I never get why you say that. It sounds violent. Like if I'm not quick then you're going to chop my head off.'

'Well, I wouldn't but I don't know what the school may do…'

'Someone's at the door.'

'I know.'

I go to answer it, clearing the mail from the doormat, and the person behind steps over the threshold animatedly. I hope I know this person otherwise Hermes are getting an angry email.

'Grace! Oh my! Come here!'

I hug back tightly, smiling broadly.

'Joyce. What on earth are you doing here? It's eight in the morning.'

'Best time of day, roads are empty.' She stands back to study my face and then looks over my shoulder as Cleo cranes her head around the door.

'Aunty Joyce! Hello!'

'Oh… Cleo, come here and give me a cuddle. Look at you! Why aren't you ready for school?'

'She's easing into the day,' I reply. Cleo comes over and hugs her tightly.

'Where's Maya?' Joyce asks.

'Outside, trying to persuade birds to be her friends.'

'Naturally.'

'What are you doing here?' Cleo asks curiously. My eyes seem to ask the same question.

'Visiting some of my favourite people. Do I need an excuse? Now go get changed for school. I can come on the walk and help drop you off, how does that sound?' Joyce says excitedly.

'Cool!' Cleo replies and legs it up the stairs. Joyce's gaze follows her.

'Excuse me, how big? What are you feeding her?'

I laugh and lead her through to the kitchen where she spies all the reading books and spelling lists lined up with Post-it notes and packed lunchboxes. We have a blackboard on which the week is planned out to the letter. Ham for Cleo, cheese for Maya. Not the cereal bars with the dried fruity bits because they get stuck in Cleo's teeth. Not the squeezy yoghurts as Maya can't open them without squeezing them all down her front. Joyce runs her fingers over the red school cardigans hanging off the backs of the chairs.

'Look at you. I was awful at the morning school runs – so disorganised. Did Tom ever tell you how I once made him bring a Pot Noodle to school and ask the teachers for hot water?' she says. I shake my head. 'Awful parenting but a story of legend. Apparently, he even knocked on the staff room door.'

Joyce makes her way to the kettle. She still looks the same as when I met her all those years ago, ten to be exact. She's a fan of a pair of biker boots, black leggings and a massive woollen jumper that she wears like a dress, her hair bushy and crispy on her head. *Come home and meet my mum,* Tom had said. *She's mad as a hatter.* I was cautious; it was meeting the mother, no? That's an event of status in a relationship. I also did not want to reciprocate by introducing Tom to mine because my mother also came with my four sisters who would have gone lioness-pride mode and torn him apart with questions. But as soon as we drove up to his house in North London and the door opened, the reception was exactly the same as the one moments ago. Joyce was warm and inviting and ever since Tom's passing she comes down on occasion to visit. To her, I am a daughter who replaced a lost son. To the girls she is Aunty Joyce, and she treats them like her own grandchildren. I have no doubt she's brought them candy necklaces too.

'Cleo's right, to what do we owe the pleasure?' I ask, as she reaches up to retrieve some mugs. Out of the corner of her eye, she sees a photo of Tom and me from university; one of those shots where we look completely fresh-faced, clueless and drunk out of our eyeballs. She studies it for a moment.

'I actually have a meeting later at Latymer Academy…' she tells me.

'Tom's old school?'

'One of the governors got in touch after my last marathon to say they're naming a new wing after him.'

This is what Joyce does. When Tom died, the grief hit us differently, from all angles really, but we sought out our coping mechanisms. I left. I travelled. After Tom and I graduated, we split up for a while and he did a world tour of teaching. He needed to get something out of his system. I never understood that, why he left me. Even though we stayed in contact for most of that time, I later traced his steps, filled in the gaps and found out where he'd gone, who he'd met, to find some peace on random beaches and the bottom of foreign bottles of alcohol. Joyce ran. She ran many marathons, too many to count but they doubled up as fundraising opportunities. She is good at all of that – at getting people to hand their money over and keep Tom alive. I cheered her on when I could but she always made me wear this T-shirt with his face on. I imagined Tom would have hated that, especially as she chose his LinkedIn photo so it looked like we were honouring the passing of a very cheesy-looking estate agent who could find you a good deal on a three-bed with en suite.

'That's cool. You did contribute quite a lot to that,' I reply.

'It's what he wanted.'

We pause for a moment. Tom left instructions after he died that were to the letter. No sad social media posts where people he'd not spoken to in years could leave empty words of condolence. No flowers at his funeral. No super-depressing music. That was to his mum. *Please don't honour my passing my blasting out Joni Mitchell albums and inhaling my leftover scent on my clothes. The thought of dying is hard enough without knowing how much it will hurt the ones I leave behind. Celebrate my life, give my money to charity, stick some fingers up to cancer for me.*

'The school want to do a big thing, a memorial event of sorts, in a few months' time when the building's finished. I suspect they'll want me to cut a ribbon or something. You should be there.'

'Of course I will,' I say, grabbing her hand.

'I was also thinking of inviting people. Help me with the list? I don't want it to be shit. Can you help me organise?'

'He didn't like canapés on sticks if that helps.'

'That was because when he was younger he got a skewer stuck up his nose. I always blamed his bad dancing on that. I thought it penetrated the grey matter responsible for co-ordination and rhythm.'

I laugh. 'He told me he didn't like standing there with a skewer and not knowing where to put it.' His dancing had been extraordinary – it was a series of co-ordinated jumps, such freedom with his arms, expression in every inch of his face, too. 'Of course I'll help. A whole wing. I'm not sure what he would have made of that.'

'He would have gone full ostentatious. He'd have wanted a wax model in the hallway. Maybe a portrait of him dressed as a king in oils.'

The thing is, it's true. But he'd also have had beanbags in every room and winding shelves of books of every shape, size and colour. He'd have brought back the blackboard for sure. There'd have been hand-painted quotes that he'd have attributed to himself but which would most likely have been stolen song lyrics. The wing would have beaten with his energy and enthusiasm. I imagine the colour scheme would have been awful too, lime-green walls – he'd have wanted it to be seen.

'Apparently, the school band have written a song in his honour too.'

I bite my lip, trying to hold back the giggles. 'Will you be singing it?'

'No, I've said you can. Can you imagine, he'd strike me down with lightning.'

I cackle with laughter. Now the pain has faded somewhat, this is what connects us both. All those stories, all those little Tom quotes and moments that brought us so much happiness.

'I also had an interesting letter from my editor too.'

That was the other thing Joyce did. After he passed, she wrote his biography, an outpouring of longing and her experiences as a mother who'd lost her child. *Goodnight, Major Tom* did very well. It was translated into Latvian and eight other different languages and all the proceeds went to charity. Did I read it? I did. Did I cry all the way through? Perhaps. Again, I don't think Tom would have approved of half the childhood stories she chose to mention (I didn't know he wet the bed until he was nine) but it was the ultimate love letter to her son.

'There's some production company interested in making a film about his life.'

'Oh, like a film or a documentary?' I ask.

'I wasn't quite sure. I'm meeting them next week.'

'If it's a film, make sure they cast…'

'Jason Momoa. But first check he can do accents,' she says, laughing to herself.

That was in Tom's will, the idiot. He looked nothing like him. That would take some serious prosthetics and a dramatic haircut.

'My editor also had a question for you. Given the success of the book, they were wondering if you were interested in talking to them. They were thinking about a sequel, from his widow's perspective? I know you both wrote letters to each other when he travelled.'

I pause for a moment, standing over the kitchen counter. We did. They're all under my bed in a box. I sometimes get them out and have a moment, usually accompanied by a vat of wine. Sometimes I think about doing something sensible like scanning them into a hard drive or borrowing the PTA laminator to preserve them all, but what I love is that those letters are part of our story. At times in our relationship, I felt like I shared him with so many people, but those secret letters are just about us. Do I want to share them?

'They'd raise money for charity,' Joyce adds, sensing my hesitation. 'I mean, it's just an idea. Think about it.'

'I will. Leave me a website. I'll look them up.'

Maya's head pops around the door and she runs into Joyce's arms when she sees her.

'Aunty Joyce!' she shrieks.

'Little pickle!'

'There's a bird outside! I've made friends with a bird and he's eating my toast.'

We crane our heads out the window to see the biggest effing crow I've ever seen in my life glaring at us. That thing looks like he lives in the Tower of London at the weekends.

'I'm calling him Colin!' Maya says. 'Do we have anything else we can feed him?'

*

I moved to Bristol six months after we returned to England. I thought we'd live in London nearer family and where I'd been raised, but Bristol was Tom. I needed to come back and be near him. It was where we'd met and lived before he passed away and it felt manageable when faced with the daunting task of being a mother to two little people, a place to rebuild a life with him watching over us. He'd have liked that we're back here. He'd have approved of the school I chose for the girls, with the big leafy grounds and the commitment to international links, and I'd have got a high five for choosing a house with character that was a fifteen-minute walk to the zoo. He'd have had huge respect for the fact I have a zoo membership card too.

'Stay for dinner, Aunty Joyce. We're having Macaroni Monday tonight,' Maya says, skipping along the street as we walk them to school.

'You are?'

'Yes.' Maya adds, 'Mummy puts the menu on the fridge at the weekend so we can plan ahead.'

'Well, she is your mummy. I wouldn't expect any less. It's why your coats match and you're both covered in fluorescent strips.'

I smile. The sisters also mock me for those but have we been run over yet? I rest my case.

'I will see what I can do,' Joyce replies.

As we approach the gates to The Downs, Cleo says her hasty goodbyes and runs in to greet friends but I feel the familiar grasp of Maya's fingers around mine. I chose the school for the trees. You can hardly see the building for all the greenery and, for that reason, it felt safe, it felt like a nest. I mean, I wouldn't be me if I hadn't scoured the internet for reviews and OFSTED reports, but I was a sucker for the landscape too. Today, the sounds of the morning hang in the air, excitable children being herded like naughty cats. *Now is not the time for the climbing frame. Remember to select lunch B otherwise you'll get the pizza and you don't like the pizza. Do up your coat. What do you mean, it's a school trip today? You need wellies? Where's your brother gone? What do you mean, he's on the roof?*

Joyce looks at Maya clinging to me and bends down to her level, putting a finger to her lips. 'Don't get this out at school but it's for afterwards, yes?'

She slips a candy necklace in the pocket of her red puffa coat and beams, winking at her. The tension in Maya's shoulders seems to melt away and I lead her across the threshold of the school. Has Maya settled in here? Not as much as Cleo. Cleo has more confidence, more chat, but Maya is wary of people. She has a crow for a friend, she builds worlds around her that are creative and fantastical, but she lets few people in, instead sitting in her class and observing, taking it all in, quietly.

There's a queue for the classroom today and we all know why that is. Carrie Cantello is at the front with a reading diary out, giving the teacher, Miss Loveday, a hard time about something. She raised merry hell last week when her daughter's cardigan went missing. She even made flyers for it. *Have You Seen This Cardigan?* Check your car boot and washing basket like the rest of us, Carrie.

'Every. Morning,' mutters a mum behind me. 'I have to get to work,' she says, looking at her watch. In front of me, one of Maya's classmates, the one with the fetching bowl-cut, shivers. The line snakes right to the back of the playground and I feel the tension again in Maya's grip. We are a term into their first year at school but there are residual nerves which mean hanging around, prolonging our goodbyes, doesn't help.

'Excuse me, the children are freezing. Please can we let them into the classroom?' I say. Two parents in front of me don't hesitate and push their little ones past. Carrie stands there clutching a red book bag as the children all file in, looking aggrieved at the interruption, the rudeness of not waiting our turn. She turns to glare at Miss Loveday.

'I will take this up later with Mrs Funnell. I just don't think this is an acceptable way to start the school year.'

'I'm very sorry you feel that way, Mrs Cantello,' Miss Loveday replies. *Please don't apologise to her*, I should say. She's no boss of yours or a course assessor. She's just Carrie Cantello and she gets her kicks out of picking on you because you're a new, young teacher, with youth and beauty on your side, still learning the ropes. Tom used to speak about parents like this all the time. He once had a dad who called him a young wannabe c-word because he said his son hadn't handed in homework all term. I look down at Lily Cantello now and she's licking the condensation off one of the classroom windows.

'Well, I think you're doing a great job, Miss Loveday,' I add. Standing here and letting Carrie burn this girl's self-esteem into nothing doesn't feel like the right way to start a Monday morning. Carrie glares at me.

'Grace, I didn't see you there.' She scans down to Maya, obviously trying to register all the information she learnt about me last week. It makes me want to sweep her legs from under her. I don't need to do that, though. A small firecracker of a child called Spencer, who I regularly see hurling around the playground, jousting with tree branches, misjudges his entry into the classroom and runs straight into Carrie. From the angle I'm standing at it looks like he nuts her in the crotch. Good work, that kid. Miss Loveday tries extremely hard not to laugh.

'Spencer! Brakes! Brakes! Soz, Carrie!' screams Spencer's mum.

Carrie glares at us all like it's a conspiracy. 'Well, I'm glad you think so, Grace. I have my concerns that the children are having too much fun and not learning enough.'

Spencer's mum looks confused but doesn't want to join in this conversation. She tosses a lunchbox in her son's direction.

'I like Miss Loveday,' a small voice pipes up beside me. Equally as perturbed as me, Maya looks up at Carrie and transfers her hand from mine over to her teacher's. 'She's my only friend at this school.'

Carrie looks down at Maya's scowling expression. Unfortunately, this may be true. Maya only ever talks about Miss Loveday and a lunch lady with an extremely tight perm called Pamela. She doesn't seem to have taken to any of the children but, as I look down at Lily still licking the windows, I think I understand why. That said, Lily seems to have spelt her name with her tongue which, to me, is a sign of academic progress. Miss Loveday looks vindicated, even if the support comes from a four-year-old girl. Carrie storms off in a huff and I bend down to say goodbye to my daughter.

'You can never have too much fun,' she whispers to me.

I cup her face in my hands. 'Who told you that?'

'Aunty Lucy.'

My youngest, single sister: the avatar of fun. I hand over Maya's water bottle and watch as she makes her way into the classroom.

'Thank you, Mrs Callaghan,' says Miss Loveday as I stand up. Christ, she really is young. She has that twenty-something smooth skin which you can tell means she survives on tinted moisturiser and a touch of mascara.

'It's Miss, actually. I'm not married.' I'm not a Mrs, any more. I feel too young to be Ms. Back to Miss it is.

'I'm sorry,' Miss Loveday replies, horrified. She knows the ins and out of our family situation but she seems the sort who wants to get everything right, all of the time.

'It's fine. Please don't worry.'

'Actually, with Maya. She's doing something new in class and I just wanted to bring it to your attention.'

'Oh…'

She turns me away from the melee of the classroom and the door where other parents have congregated.

'She's taken to biting people.'

My eyes widen. 'Crap. Sorry. I didn't mean to swear. Like, properly? Is she drawing blood?'

'No. And it's never direct flesh where she could leave a mark. She went for a shoulder the other day in story time.'

This is when the zoo membership is perhaps not a great thing; we do spend a lot of time looking at the jungle cats.

'Is it a reaction to something?' I ask. This is the sort of advice Aunty Lucy would also give her nieces. When in doubt, bite. Lucy was a biter. Being my youngest sister meant she needed secret fighting tools in her arsenal.

'I'm not quite sure. These first months, there is always a lot of adjustment emotionally. I can keep an eye on it. We've had a chat about it.'

'Does she bite you?' I ask.

'Well, no. I'm her only friend,' Miss Loveday says jokingly. 'I'm sorry, I should have given you this information at another time when things are less rushed…'

'It's fine. Let me process it. Go… teach, have fun. Lots of fun.'

She smiles and I weave my way out of the playground, reaching for my phone. I google *why do children bite?* Shit. Maya could be feral. Maybe it's a tooth problem, something to do with her jaw.

What if she's being bullied and biting is her way of defending herself? I should message Emma. Emma is the doctor sister. There are other sisters too: Meg and Beth are also mothers with their own broods. Have they had these problems? Beth has a son called Joe. He doesn't bite but he likes to hide and Beth regularly has coronaries in supermarkets when she thinks he's been abducted but really he's hiding on a shelf of fizzy drinks.

'Problems?' Joyce asks, studying my face as I walk back through the gate.

'Maybe.'

'Nice to see the school gate hasn't changed since Tom's days. Still the same old cliques and horror shows. There's a woman over there in actual house slippers.'

'You should be here in the summer. Sometimes the dads don't wear shirts. It's a real feast for the eyes.'

'I bet that one is trouble.' She gestures to Carrie. Carrie is standing and gesticulating to Liz and a couple of her other parent disciples. She glares over at me and Joyce. I don't need to deal with that, right now. I just pray Maya isn't biting one of her kids. If that happens, she'll start advertising it. She'd rent out actual billboards.

'The playground mafia has been around for years,' Joyce carries on. 'In my day it was Jeanie McGovern. I had her son round to play and he came to my house and crapped in a drawer. When I told her, and I was discreet about it, she told me I'd made it up and then spent years spreading rumours around about Tom.'

'What sort of rumours?' I ask, mortified at the thought of someone defecating in a drawer.

'It was such a bizarre reaction. She made him the centre of every nits outbreak for years. It ended with me slapping her in the playground.'

I grin. I can imagine that; I like the gumption.

'Choose your allies in this place. Avoid people in Barbour coats and who come to the gate with full make-up. No one has time for that shit,' she says.

'Why Barbour coats?'

'I just think they look rubbish. They remind me of fox hunting.'

Joyce links her arm in mine. I love that she's still a part of my life. She's like a security blanket, a human connection to Tom. He inherited her eyes, that smile – the Tom twinkle, she used to call it. The plan is to go off and find a tasty coffee now. It's the arse end of winter, those lost months post-Christmas when no one has any money and the misery of the cold envelops us and makes us debate the merits of hibernation. I huddle into her.

'So, the memorial thing. I think we should call it Project Major Tom.'

Joyce smiles broadly as we turn away from the school, down towards Whiteladies Road to find a warm cafe with cinnamon rolls and sofas. Bristol has plenty of these on many a street corner – there are lukewarm pastries and flat whites in its very foundations.

'I think that's lovely,' she says, the emotion clear on her face.

'I'll get out my travel journals, scan social media for contacts. Tom did so much exploring after university, all that charity work too. There's a list of people who I know would like to be there. People who didn't get to the funeral. But…'

'There's a but?' Joyce asks hesitantly.

'Let me think about the book thing. I don't mind sharing our story for good but I need to think about me. It's taken me this long to just find some sense of normality, to know how to exist without him, so I'm just worried about revisiting it all.'

'Of dredging it all up? I get it. Oh, Grace…' We stop in the street and embrace for a moment. 'You do you. Whatever you feel comfortable with. We can focus on the ceremony thing too. You're right. When he died, it was a complete shock, we were all numb and the funeral felt very rushed. This gives us some time to do things properly. I knew I'd asked the right person to help. The school have also asked if they can release balloons.'

'No. He hated balloons. He was scared of them.'

Joyce chuckles heartily. 'I said exactly the same thing. He once shat himself after one burst in his face when he was thirteen.'

'That story never made your book.'

She laughs, tears in her eyes. 'It didn't. Feel free to use that one yourself.'

Chapter Three

Dear G,

I hate writing this. I hate having to leave you, that we've fought so much over this, but this is where we are and if I don't do this now then I will regret everything. I will resent you and our relationship and I never want to do that.

The fact of the matter is I'm not done. I'm not ready to just leave university and start some suburban life with 2.4 children in some new-build house near a good school with excellent travel links to the city. I want to travel. I want to see more and do more and swim in different seas and sleep under different skies. I want a passport full of stamps. I want to have a story that starts, 'So there was this one time when I was in Mongolia being chased on a horse…' I want really bad tan lines. I want to come back and tell you all about it. Everything.

Don't hate me. I love you.
T x

*

I did hate him after that letter. I thought he was selfish and reckless, not to mention he'd be adding to his student debt. It was a Dear John letter laced with romanticism but it also mocked my sensibility. There is nothing wrong with investing in property with good travel links. Have you seen house prices? Did you want to live with your mother forever?

I also remember being very angry that he thought everywhere had a different sky too. It's the same bloody sky, you idiot. It surrounds the whole planet. And I hoped he'd fall off that horse and get the shit kicked out of him by angry Mongolians. Back then we were twenty-one and we were G&T. It was such a good joke and it meant we always got a lot of decent bottles of gin for Christmas presents, back when gin wasn't even in fashion. But he left. After university, he made me feel that I wasn't enough, that my plans for the world weren't big enough. He broke my heart.

I never told him of course, my ego wouldn't let me, but it meant for three or four years we ended up toing and froing. Some days, he'd call me from a karaoke lounge and tell me in drunk tones how he'd sung Elvis. He'd croon it for me and inform me he was standing outside a 7-Eleven with his heart bleeding into the pavement because he loved me so much. I say heart bleeding. It'd be a massive outpouring of emotion followed by him chucking up his guts and then me worrying he was going to die in Japan, alone, not knowing the language or having the appropriate medical insurance.

Other times, he'd have been pickpocketed in Kuala Lumpur and he'd ring me in a panic asking me to send him money and a screen grab of his bank details. Then I'd spot a picture of him on social media, on a beach with a girl draped over him wearing a string bikini. I'd usually see this while I was on my period or revising for an exam in trackies, with chronic acne, and my heart would fracture. Then we'd have these long, drawn-out, accusatory conversations where we'd break up all over again. He wouldn't message for weeks sometimes. He'd post things on Facebook and my fingers would hover over the keyboard in the comments. *Are you coming back? I miss you. Are you OK?* I felt he was living his best life jetting everywhere and I was the one at home building the nest egg. *Come out and see me*, he'd say. *The sea is so warm. The people are so friendly. The food tastes different.* I never did. *But you haven't had the right vaccinations for that part of the world. Be careful with your roaming charges. Hot dogs pretty much taste the same everywhere you go.*

I scan over the letter now. I kept all of them, plus the postcards, the novelty fridge magnets he sent me. He once wrote me a love letter on a beer mat. I keep that in a Ziploc bag because it went a bit mouldy. I have it all in a box under my bed and, on particularly bad days, I get the box out and I lie here in my bed with a glass of wine as big as my head and I cry about how this box is all I have. Right now though, I'm not crying for once. I have the contents out on my bed like I'm undergoing some criminal investigation. Do people want to read about these things? It would make for a very sad love story, the moral being travel is wildly overrated and people in their twenties have pretty messed-up life goals.

I can put all these letters and souvenirs in a line and retrace the steps of our whole journey right here on my bed. I did retrace them after he died. I went to some of the places he went, the hostels, apartments and schools he called home. I met all those friendly people and I swam in those seas. They are warmer but that's because of currents and tidal movements. Like the lost widow I was, I went to search out the missing parts of him to keep him with me. Was it healing? It was something. It moved me out of my grief and to somewhere else. All the anger I felt at him passing was muted by sunsets and standing on foreign train concourses trying to work out where the hell I was going.

'What are you doing, Mummy?' Cleo asks, her head craned around the door.

She sees my computer open, my notebook full of lists and the stack of invitations on my nightstand.

'Are you planning a party?' she asks. She sees Tom's face on the invite. Her mind whirrs, trying to work out what this is about. To the girls, he was never their father but he's Uncle Tom. He's like some mythical creature. He was married to their mother and without him I wouldn't have met these girls so they understand his magic.

'Kinda. It's called a memorial, to celebrate Uncle Tom's life because Aunty Joyce gave some money to his school so they want to throw a party.'

'Will there be cake?' she asks.

'I will make sure of it. I just need to work out who to send invites to. I thought I put you to bed?'

'You did. I just couldn't sleep.'

I beckon her over and get her to sit on my lap as I stroke her hair. It's always had a gorgeous sheen to it. A month ago, she took to parts of it with scissors so there are strands of fringe that don't quite line up. She puts her head against my chest and I cradle her for a moment.

'Tell me what happened again,' Cleo says.

'When?'

'After Uncle Tom died. You went on a big holiday.'

'Of sorts. I didn't do half the travelling Uncle Tom did but I went to New York, Australia, Japan, Amsterdam and, of course, I went to Vietnam.'

'That's where you picked us up.'

I laugh; she makes it sound like they were hitchhikers. 'Yes, that was where I found you.'

'I'm glad you did,' she says, stroking my hand. It is true. People come back from travels with all sorts: new language skills, a transformed sense of the world we live in, herpes. I came back a mother.

'All your aunties are going to be online soon… do you want to say hello?'

Cleo looks up animatedly at me and jumps off my lap to dance on the spot as I fire up the computer. You see, it's Thursday night so that means it's also time for the sister chat: a ritual we set up once we all moved away from each other. Meg is up North in Kendal, Emma, Beth and Lucy are in London. The chats started during that horrible 2020 when lockdown meant we couldn't see each other but they continue to be a weekly event. Sometimes us five sisters talk, sometimes we fight, sometimes we watch Lucy fall over drunk while we try and have a quiz where Emma makes the questions too hard. *I don't know what that chamber of the brain is called, stop showing off, Ems.* I log in and see faces pop up in little squares like we're about to enter into some sort of game show. Whatever the weather and despite the distances that separate us, I always feel peace to see them. I think that comes from being #4 of five; you're weaved so tightly into the fabric that you don't know how to exist in any other way.

'Greetings all,' Meg (our fearless leader) says from her kitchen. In the background, I see her husband, boiling the kettle for tea, and a moody teenage daughter on her phone. 'Piss off, both of you, it's a sister chat.' Her eldest, Tess, is now thirteen and seems to be reliving Meg's goth phase. I hope they can keep her in eyeliner.

Emma (the doctor and second in command) signs in from a pristine living room, the decor of which she's not changed for years. Beth (middle sister syndrome) is in maternity dungarees cradling a mug of tea, and Lucy (the wastrel youngest) checks in from her bed. I hope she's wearing clothes. I can see the shape of another arm in that bed that might not be hers. I hope that person is wearing clothes too.

I see Emma squinting at the scene in judgement. 'Lucy, it's a sister chat. No extras.'

'There's no one here.'

I wink at Cleo as she stays out of shot, ready to surprise them.

'Did you grow a third arm when we weren't looking?' Emma replies.

'I just bloody hope that's an arm,' mutters Beth.

We all lean into our screens. Lucy shoos someone out of her bed, but not before he flashes an arse cheek on screen. I manage to cover Cleo's eyes before she can see much else.

'LUCY!' Emma shouts in disgust.

'I saw penis,' Meg says, cackling. 'Seriously, we should all place bets on what we will see in Lucy's box each week. Lucy Zoom Bingo.'

I cup my hands over Cleo's ears.

'I see a condom wrapper. Last week, I saw half a spliff,' Beth says, holding her hand in the air.

'It's medicinal,' Lucy says, shaking out her hair.

'Guys, Cleo is right here…'

The sisters stop in their tracks as her cheesy grin comes into view.

'Sorry, Gracie…' Beth says, bending forward to study her face. Everyone waves at her, beaming. That's the thing: for all their faults, these sisters of mine have had no problems welcoming Maya and Cleo into the fold. They're ours, they're family.

'Shouldn't you be in bed, little lady?' asks Meg.

'Was that your boyfriend, Aunty Lucy?' Cleo asks.

Emma smiles knowingly.

'He sort of is. He's like a man friend.'

'Is that like a grown-up version of a boyfriend?'

'Yes,' Lucy says, like she's an authority on the matter.

'Like Mummy has with Sam?'

We all freeze. This is new information to the sisters but I am suddenly worried about what Cleo may have seen. I thought I'd been super careful when Sam had been around.

'Cleo, you must tell us about Sam immediately…' Meg replies. Beth shuffles in her bed to make herself more comfortable.

'The other day,' says Cleo, 'Sam was babysitting us and then when you said goodbye to him I saw you kiss him goodbye, on the lips.'

I sigh with relief, grateful she didn't see more. 'You were up?' I ask her.

'I went to the toilet. I was standing on the landing.'

'Sam is not my man friend. I kiss lots of people like that.'

'You don't kiss the shopping delivery man like that,' Cleo asks.

Lucy is in hysterics at this point and holds her hand up to the screen. She's not wearing a bra, is she?

'High five, little wonder.'

Cleo smiles and fake high fives her back. I shake my head at all of them grinning at me.

'Bed, little one,' I tell Cleo. 'Wave everyone off and go to sleep.'

She blows kisses into the air that are returned as I sit back on my bed to await the interrogation.

'Sam?' Meg asks.

'Sam,' I reply.

'Oh, give over, you cow. Details, now!' Beth commands.

I look at all their expectant faces. 'Don't judge me. He's a school-gate dad. He's just come out of a divorce and we are basically...' I quieten my voice in case Cleo is still lurking. 'Sex friends.'

Lucy seems to be overly excited by that revelation. Beth is laughing but Meg and Emma look a tad more concerned.

'What's that now?' Emma asks.

'Gracie's got a fuck buddy,' Lucy explains.

'Nooo. It's more grown-up than that. It's a very nice arrangement.'

'I bet,' Beth says.

'He doesn't want commitment, neither do I. It's just two adults pleasuring each other.'

Lucy is in fits of giggles now, which sets Beth off. I phrased that wrong, didn't I? It sounds like we sit together on the edge of a bed giving each other hand jobs.

'But with a school-gate dad?' Meg asks worriedly. 'That's next-level politics there. That could go very wrong if his ex-wife finds out. It's shitting where you eat.'

'If you're into the sort of thing,' Lucy adds.

Meg rolls her eyes. 'Just tread carefully. All it takes is Cleo to say something and then it'll backfire. Is he at least any good?'

Emma throws her hands up in the air, not keen on the direction the conversation is going.

'It is what it is.'

Beth looks confused. 'Glowing review there. I guess if you're happy?'

I nod, unconvincingly. I'm not sure what I'm supposed to do to display my levels of sexual satisfaction. Lucy would give us a play-by-play; I'd learn about the actual shape of his bell-end, which is not me at all. But then I also understand my arrangement with Sam. I care for him deeply, but to entertain anything beyond that isn't very wise given what he's just been through.

Lucy studies my face through the screen. 'I think it's cool. It's called sexual independence. She's getting what she wants and she understands the line. Unless you're shagging him because you feel sorry for him. He looks like he has a dad bod.'

Emma looks shocked at the thought.

I shake my head. 'How do you know what he…?'

'I've found him on social media,' Lucy announces. 'Sam Headley. He's on her friends list. His profile picture is him with a pumpkin; tell him he needs to update that. It's January.'

I see all the other sisters scramble about on their devices to stalk him. Bitches. Meg cocks her head to one side.

'He looks like a lumberjack,' Emma mumbles.

'Because he has a beard?' I ask.

'Strong 7,' Lucy adds. 'Big hands. Can I ask about the—'

'Strong 7,' I reply, knowing what she's about to say. 'Bigger than the glimpse of what I just saw on that screen.'

It's Emma's turn to laugh now.

'Piss off, he's a grower,' Lucy replies.

'Well, let us know how that goes, Gracie,' Meg says.

I sense all of their collective gazes on me. The sisters have been protective since Tom passed. They mourned with me, they worried and huddled around me, but they were wise and kind enough to never tell me I needed to move on. They let me swim in my grief and held out their hands to stop me falling adrift. They knew however I moved on would be done on my own terms but I see hope in all their faces. They want me to transition and find the next Tom. The truth is, I'm glad for the company, but the idea of love, finding real Tom love again, is not on my radar. In truth, it terrifies me.

'Any other news to report?' Meg asks.

'Maya's a biter,' I say.

'Are you feeding her enough?' Emma asks. 'Could be teething?'

'But she has all her teeth?' I say.

'They grow for years,' Meg informs me. 'Then they fall out. Then you have to put braces on them and they hate you for ruining their lives. Tess grew too many teeth. She looked like a shark.'

'She must have my teeth then. I got my braces stuck on someone's foreskin once,' Lucy tells us.

'I remember that! You had to use tweezers to set him free,' Beth says, doubling over in hysterics.

Emma and Meg look on in horror while I feel left out at not knowing that story and wondering why Beth was there.

'Probably someone in her class being a wanker and she's dealing with it,' Meg adds. 'She's a very capable little girl.'

'If I was four and a boy was being crap then I'd bite him,' Lucy adds. This doesn't surprise any of us.

'Eve has a streak. She used to give the boys a good slapping if they were out of line,' Meg tells us, referring to her second eldest.

I see the wrinkle in Emma's nose. She doesn't raise feral children but her two survived Emma's divorce so are the hardiest little girls I know.

'We are Callaghan women,' says Emma. 'It's the fire in us. Teach her to ignore the idiots. Don't overthink it.'

We *are* Callaghan women. I gave the girls my surname when I adopted them and changed mine back to match. I always feel guilty over that, removing a memory of Tom from me. But I couldn't face the explanations and the fact it would have been something to further distance myself from my little girls. And all these traits in them, I always wonder to what extent it's their genes at work, or perhaps it's being entrenched in a family full of women, full of fire and energy and in-jokes. How much have they taken in through my nurturing, through family gatherings, or when Lucy has taken them aside to teach them all her special turns of phrase?

'What's that stack of things behind you, G?' asks Beth. I hold up one of the invitation cards emblazoned with Tom's face. The mood drops a bit when they see his image there, almost like a ghost.

'Tom's mum is holding a memorial. His old school have named a wing after him so there will be a ceremony thing, do save the date. You're all invited.'

'Oh, G…' Lucy says. 'You should have said something before this. Are you all right?'

Their stares penetrate through the screen like a collective hug.

'It's a nice thing. I just told Joyce I'd help out, sort a guest list and organise people. It's what I do.'

'But lean on us, yeah?' Meg adds. 'We can help if it's too much.'

It's always too much. Bottom line, I became a widow in my twenties. That only happens in movies and the majority of the time the man in question has been at war. This was never supposed to happen. It shouldn't have happened. He should be here. But he's not. Instead we'll celebrate his life over a cocktail sausage, which he would have loved. He was fond of those, me less so.

'I mean, will there be cake?' Beth asks, echoing her niece's question from earlier.

'I'll make it happen.'

Beth smiles back, knowing instinctively when I need the focus to shift away from me. Come, have cake. Let's mourn that wonderful man all over again. Beth is the one who knows that sometimes I don't want a constant reminder of that pain or for it to be unearthed yet again.

'So, Lucy…' Beth pipes up. 'You're next… who's the bloke and why was his crotch seventy per cent pube?'

Chapter Four

Hey G. I miss you. I've got a gig teaching English in Kuala Lumpur with the British Council. It sounds more highbrow than it is but it's mainly university kids. It makes me think of university when our lives were a bit simpler. Were they simpler? I remember we ate a lot of toasties – like, a criminal amount of melted cheese. I crave toasties now. I also teach kids. Mountains of kids who don't want to learn English. We bond because I know random things about computer games and dinosaurs. This is when my Jurassic Park knowledge that you said was juvenile and pointless is useful. When in doubt, little kids go batshit crazy for dinosaur-related facts. And these tiny jellies that come in pots. They down those like shots. We used to do those too, eh? I'm thinking of New York soon, soak in some of that big city vibe. I want to see Doug, relive the Brizzle days.

T x

Is there an illegal number of times you can watch a film? For my two it's *Moana* and it's now at the point where I could enter

Mastermind on the subject. *How long has Moana been standing on the edge of the water? For as long as she can remember; it calls to her, John.* I hear the song lyrics drift through the wall and hope the last of the film will babysit the children while I try and finish up with this email to a client. There are numerous kids today as I promised the girls play dates, so in between day-job duties I've been trying to ensure one of our house guests, Isaac, has not eaten too many Hula Hoops. How many is too many? Well, it's lucky I'm an accountant really.

There will never be anything interesting to say about my job other than I work from home and I make my own tea. It used to be bigger than this. It used to be a nine-to-five in London, in an office which overlooked the Thames where I wore trainers on the commute and courted my fair share of sharp tailoring. It was precise work and it suited my personality. I liked achieving, moving forward with a career and seeing it go somewhere, so I threw my all into it. It's different now. It's work at a small desk in the corner of my bedroom and I wear a lot of leggings. That said, these clients are taking the piss. I'm not sure you can claim the dog food on expenses. A message of an incoming call pops up on my computer. Can I take this now? Hell, why not?

'Dougie Doug.'

'Gracie Grace.'

'You have ten minutes, that's how long it will take for *Moana* to finish next door.'

'You're welcome!' he sings back to me.

'How do you know *Moana*?'

'Because I am a man of culture, no?'

I grin at the screen, watching Doug against the backdrop of his super-shiny New York office, grinning because this is Doug. Tom and I shared a house with him in Bristol when we were students. He used to wash his dishes in the bath and he got drunk one night and tried to boil pasta in a kettle. It's always been so strange to see him in tailoring, in a proper job, with a fake houseplant on his mahogany shelves and a haircut that looks like he didn't do it in a mirror with a pair of blunt IKEA scissors.

'I guess you got the invite then?' I tell him.

'I did. Just booked the time off. You OK?'

'You're coming back to the motherland. I'm more than OK.'

Doug was one of Tom's most loyal friends, the sort of ride-or-die friend, the male equivalent of the person who'd hold your hair back when you were throwing up completely bladdered. During Tom's adventures in travel, New York was a huge stop. He was there for six months and tried his hand at everything from beat poetry (how I laughed) to artisan bagel making and, all that time, Doug enabled these adventures and offered him his very expensive sofa free of rent. The same sofa I slept on when I visited him after Tom died. It's a good sofa. I see Doug scanning the bedroom behind me, the same shift of the eyes you always get on these calls. I know I have a stupid amount of throw cushions. I keep them there for a reason, so I can pretend they're a person in the bed. That's not sad. A blow-up doll would be sad.

'What's going on with your beard?' I ask him, trying to distract him.

'Does the beard work? I'm trying to impress a girl with this hipster-look thing. I'm also slightly vegan.'

'Slightly?'

'I still eat bacon.'

I laugh. 'The beard makes you look like you have higher religious intentions. Like a semi-hot Jesus.'

It's his turn to laugh now. He gazes towards the giant window of his office where you can tell he's accessing memories.

'Do you remember that time we got drunk on a night out, we ended up in a real church and a vicar tried to chase us out by throwing a Bible at Tom?'

'Remember it? You sobbed because you had drugs hidden in your shoes and thought you were going to hell,' I add.

'And then I dragged you to that skanky club, Tom tried to pay with his library card and I pulled that girl... what was her name? The one with the face.'

'You've dated girls without faces?' I giggle.

'Anna. God, she was out of my league... we had some fun in ol' Brizzle, didn't we? I'm always chuffed you ended up back there,' he says, lolling back on his leather chair. It always feels nice to have Doug to walk through all those Bristol memories with. The halcyon days of the cheapest alcohol we'll ever have access to, zero responsibility and my obsession with incense sticks that drowned out the general stench of sweaty bollocks and old trainers that inhabit any house share involving men in their early twenties.

'You say that like you don't have fun any more?' I add.

'Oh, I do. Just not Tom fun, you know...'

'I think our definitions of Tom fun might be quite different...'

Doug guffaws at this point and I like hearing that sound. Tom was the sort of person who'd make everything fun. It was annoying. It was never a quiet night in. It was drunk Cluedo and listening to The Smiths at a volume you knew was disturbing the neighbours.

'You're getting out there, though, right? Still having fun, Gracie?' he asks.

I nod. I mean, after I log off this call and bid farewell to the girls' play dates, I'll probably have a glass of wine. I'll bathe the girls, wash and dry their hair and put them to a bed with a story where we've already got to page one hundred and twenty-three. Once the lights are out, I'll have another glass of wine and I'll fold the tea towels and maybe treat myself to a few squares of Galaxy and watch an episode of that new crime drama everyone's talking about, making sure I don't go on Twitter to see any spoilers. I will do this on my own. This is my fun now.

'Yeah, I go down to Blue Mountain every weekend, drop a few tabs and break it down in my old Adidas Superstars.'

'Really?'

That is also the beauty of Doug. New York hasn't chipped away at how utterly gullible he is. I remember when he went out there post-university, headhunted by a massive finance start-up. Tom and I assumed they had him mixed up with someone else. You want Doug? He owns one suit and Puma Gazelles. He believed in Father Christmas until he was fifteen.

'Who are you?' A small person suddenly emerges from behind me like an elf. I jump out of my seat. It's Isaac, Cleo's best friend at school, Helen's son, who should be next door watching *Moana*. I hope he didn't hear that bit about me dropping tabs at the weekend. He cranes his neck to study Doug's face.

'Why is it daytime there? Are you at work? Is he your husband?' he asks. I try to unpack what Isaac just said. I don't mind this kid. I like that he widens Cleo's friendship groups beyond the girls and their preoccupations with unicorns but he uses his entire right sleeve as a handkerchief. It literally flakes with how crusty it is.

'Hello. I'm Doug,' he says, waving through the screen.

'Doug, this is Isaac, one of Cleo's mates from school. Doug is in New York.'

'REALLY? Can you see the Statue of Liberty from where you are?' he asks. 'Is he a lawyer? He looks like a lawyer?'

Doug sits there trying to deal with the words per minute. In the meanwhile, Cleo skulks into my room, having realised she's let her puppy escape.

'I'm not a lawyer. Grace and I are just friends from university.'

'Hi, Uncle Doug!' Cleo says, waving through the screen.

'Hey, Cleo. So, you have a boyfriend now?' he asks.

Cleo's face drops, aghast. 'Isaac is a friend. Girls and boys can be friends, you know?' I think there was almost an eye-roll there. I chuckle under my breath, widening my eyes at Doug.

'And where is Maya?'

'Next door with *Moana*.'

'The actual Moana?'

Cleo giggles. 'No, silly. She's watching the film with her friend, Jess, from school.'

Jess. Very sweet unassuming Jess, who I'm not even sure Maya likes but it was a way to try and push Maya into being a bit more sociable with people her own age instead of chatting to the birds in our garden.

'What's it like in New York?' Isaac asks, as he and Cleo commandeer my office chair to take control of this call.

'Well, I was here when the Avengers came and saved us all from those aliens. That was scary.'

'Yeah… that never happened,' Isaac says, unimpressed.

They're a tough crowd, Doug. You'll have to try harder.

'Cleo's mum, can we change the filter on this so I look like I'm floating in space?' Isaac asks.

'I'd rather you didn't… I also said you can call me Grace if you want?'

'Grace rhymes with space, race and face. Can I call you Grace Face?'

Doug tries to stifle his giggles.

'I'd rather you didn't…' I reply.

'Are you going to have hot dogs for lunch?' he asks, returning to Doug. 'You can get good hot dogs in New York.'

'No. I was going to have a sandwich. You should ask Grace Face about hot dogs. Actually, ask Grace about New York. She had an amazing time when she visited me here.'

I shake my head at him.

'You've been to New York?' Isaac asks, like it's impossible someone as dull as me could have ever gone anywhere so cool.

'I did,' I say. 'And it's an awful, awful place.'

'How so?' Cleo asks.

Alas, New York. *You must go there Gracie, it's the best place on the planet,* Tom had said. He had hyped it up so much, even leaving me a list of things to do and places to eat. But for all its magic and familiarity, my whole trip there was a catalogue of disasters.

'Well, it started when I got my phone stolen and then I got run over by a rollerblader in Central Park.'

'Was that when you flattened that pigeon?' Doug pulls a face.

I nod. I'd thought pigeons had better reflexes than that but I was wrong. We ended up having to hide said pigeon in a bush so it wouldn't scare young children. The blood flowed out of me in rivulets, so much so I fainted.

'Anyways, I needed stitches on my leg so Uncle Doug looked after me.'

He accompanied me to an emergency room (my insurance documents in a folder, colour-coded of course) and they stitched me up and gave me some other medicine. I say some other medicine because, to this day, I still don't know what it was and am convinced I downed some tablets in a cup meant for someone else. Someone in a coma perhaps because, an hour after leaving that hospital, I was high as a fucking kite.

'That doesn't sound too bad. I got stitches after I fell off my scooter,' Isaac says, locating a knobbly scar on his chin. The problem is the story just devolves. As those drugs seemed to perk me up, I begged Doug to take me out that evening. He made some calls and, an hour later, his then girlfriend showed up with a range of dayglo fishnet rave gear and a list of places to go. Do I remember said party? Sort of. I remember music with no words, someone making me a glowstick necklace and the fishnet element being super draughty. I recall trying to snog Doug but I'm not even sure I made contact – I may have even snogged his ear, thinking it was his mouth.

I hold back these details from the children.

'Well, the day after, I then ate a hot dog but it was from an unlicensed vendor and I got very sick.'

'How bad?' Isaac asks, suddenly fascinated.

'Very bad,' I say, not really knowing if I need to tell a seven-year-old that I had to send Doug to an Old Navy to buy me all new underwear. In fact, so bad, I put a hand to my mouth and clench a little to relive the memory. I think it was recompense for all the times I'd lectured Tom as he travelled through the more tropical parts of the Southern hemisphere and refused to take his malaria medicine. And there was me in the most developed country in the world, on the floor of Doug's flat throwing up through my nose.

This is why I will always owe Doug. I was only supposed to be in New York for six weeks and I spent four of those ill. Too fearful and traumatised to leave the apartment after that, I stayed inside, we binge-watched about six different shows and Doug even sourced Marmite for me to have with some super-nice bagels. He knew that on top of all of the hell the universe had chosen to dump on me in that precise moment, there was grief swimming in my soul and I needed to have the space to just wrap myself up in a duvet and recover.

Doug beams at me through the call. You were there. You, my sir, are a gem of a mate.

The moment is felt less by Isaac, though, whose interest in my New York stories has now waned, and he proceeds to wander around my bedroom. He's one of those kids who's constantly moving, like he's dancing to a song we all can't hear, a funky song at that. 'Eccentric', I think is the word. He also has quite a bushel of hair, like something you'd see on the mane of a horse. Cleo is seemingly fascinated by him, though, and I get it. She could have invited over some real boring Betty, some kid whose most exciting news is that they once went down a slide backwards. This kind of kid is interesting to her. Someone who's full of questions, someone who's taken my tea towels to make capes. Oi, I was going to fold them later. That was my evening's fun. Doug watches them in bemusement. I hope this Isaac is like a Doug to you, Cleo. I watch as they speed around my room.

'Do you have more Hula Hoops?' Isaac asks.

'You had a lot of Hula Hoops before…'

'He is a guest, Grace Face…' Cleo adds. I give her a look.

'You'll turn into a Hula Hoop.'

'Hasn't happened yet…' Isaac says, confidently throwing a disco-pose-style lunge to the middle of the room. He's wearing sweatbands on each wrist, isn't he? He hasn't procured those from my house. It's a look. Cleo gazes over at him adoringly.

'Can you see my house from your window?' he asks, pulling at my curtains.

'Ummm, no. You live the other side of…'

'Who's he?' Isaac asks, pointing to Tom's photo. How is he moving so quickly? Did we give him Coke? Speed?

'That's Tom.'

'He was married to my mum,' Cleo adds.

'And my best mate…' Doug adds from the screen.

'He looks fun.'

'He was fun.'

'*Was* because you divorced or because he's dead? If you still have a picture of someone you divorced by your bed then you need to move on.'

Wow, this kid.

'He passed away.'

'Mum talks to that picture every night,' Cleo says.

Doug looks down like he didn't hear that bit.

'That's sad. My dog passed away last year. We buried him in the garden but don't tell anyone that or Dad thinks we might not be able to sell our house.'

'I won't,' I reply.

'Is Tom in our garden?' asks a curious Cleo.

'No. We cremated him and I left ashes in one of his favourite places.'

'I'd want my ashes sprinkled in McDonald's,' Isaac announces.

Doug laughs through his nose. I don't know how to respond to that. Which branch? You'd just be hoovered up, no? Isaac moves through the room, mercurially.

'You move like a velociraptor...' I tell him. It's no lie. He's loud like one too. He mounts beds/chairs with excellent balance and agility. He stops for a moment, seemingly impressed by the comparison.

'And what's this?' But before I can catch the little whirling dervish, he's gone in my bedside drawer and pulled out a vibrator. How? Doug's face goes crimson. Yes, after I watch my drama series, and in the absence of my regular sex friend, I am probably going to spend the evening with that. See, I can be fun. Luckily, I don't think it has much battery life in it. Except it does. As proven by Isaac when he presses a button and turns it on.

'DON'T DO THAT!' I shout. Isaac drops it and it starts buzzing around the floor like a very angry mouse. I can literally hear Doug wetting himself with laughter. You bastard.

'I'm sorry. Are you angry?' Isaac asks me. I freeze. Don't make the visiting child cry. Don't cry. 'Don't be. My mum has, like, five. CLEO, LET'S GO AND SEE IF I CAN FLY DOWN YOUR STAIRS!'

Chapter Five

'I don't think bollocks should look like that. It's starting to look a bit cauliflower-like.'

'Rudeness. All breasts don't look the same. Your right nipple points north-east while the other one points due north.'

'You should get it checked out.'

'"Hi, could you have a look at my knackers as my wife is obsessed with the fact they're not smooth like plums?" Maybe it's because you play with them too much.'

'I do not.'

'You do. You play with them to avoid having to pay attention to my knob. He notices these things, it makes him sad you love the bollocks more than me.'

'Did you just personify your penis?'

'I did.'

I sit up in bed. Do I dream about Tom? Quite a lot. If we were to put a number on it, like 'how many units of alcohol do you drink in a week,' I'd be ticking the three-times-a-week box. Sometimes the dreams are surreal and have no meaning. I once dreamt we were pro-wrestlers, some WWF super team where our major trick was to slap people across the head with chairs. There was a wonderfully exuberant theme to our leotards (naturally, we also had capes) and we were raking it in with the endorsements (we had action figures, our own breakfast cereal and a cartoon tie-in show). But other times, they play to me like flashbacks, snippets of conversations in which his humour and good nature shine through, or I'm taken back to moments where it should have gone differently.

I look over at the clock now and it's 3.13 in the morning. The thirteenth of March was Tom's birthday. Sometimes I think he does this to mock me. I wonder if all widows have insomnia like this. I've tried everything. Hot milk, teas, massage and sex with school-run dads. Sometimes they work; more often than not they don't. Usually I'm sitting here overthinking the small details of my life, staring at my ceiling and the strange patch of paint where the brushstrokes don't quite line up. Or sometimes I talk. To him.

You're haunting me. You said you'd do that.

I really feel that I need to do it properly. Film-worthy haunting where I crawl out of the television or visit you via old VHS tapes.

That wouldn't work as I haven't seen a VCR since the nineties. You'd need to upgrade to DVD or haunt me via Netflix.

Have you tried hot milk to sleep?

Doesn't work.

What about apps that play ambient noise?

No. I tried listening to a river and it made me want to pee. How did you do it? You used to fall asleep in seconds, as soon as your head hit the pillow.

You. You made me feel safe. That or I'd get you to talk accounting to me, that always worked.

Piss off.

These conversations are always filled with our repartee and in-jokes. They don't make me sad; they're a comfort blanket when I'm alone, gazing into the darkness. They're spoken in small whispers, though I am now conscious Cleo's heard them. Has she told anyone else I speak to pictures? People will question my sanity. In these chats I sometimes think of alternative realities where Tom didn't have cancer and instead we travelled to Vietnam, picked up these girls of ours and raised them together. God, they would have loved Tom. The bedtime stories would have been theatrical events. I see him sitting by a toy kitchen having tea parties with Maya and her stuffed animals; he'd have actually sung to them. He had an awful singing voice, like an extremely drunk Ed Sheeran, but he'd have sung loud and hard.

The room is swallowed in grey, the streams of light tipping in from the street lamps, and I pick up my phone and scroll through the usual suspects: social media, emails, news sites. I add a laugh emoji to a picture of a tree trunk Lucy posted that she thinks looks like a snatch. I send Beth a heart emoji in response to a gorgeous photo of Joe playing football. An advert tells me I need something in my life that is a cross between a rug, a sleeping bag and pyjamas. It's like they're mocking my inability to sleep. I read a thread on the school group where mums discuss the traffic at the school gate. The answer is simple, Jenny. Don't find a bit of kerb and stop your car. That is why people are coming out of their houses and leaving angry notes on your Qashqai. Next, I read a message from Sam.

It's not a proper message. We seem to communicate via the power of meme. It's a GIF of a cat playing a piano, wearing a T-shirt. I smile. I won't go back to sleep so I dig around on the floor to find my slippers and dressing gown. I could binge-watch something. I could have a coffee. I could iron. No, I'm not that desperate, not yet.

I head downstairs ensuring I don't wake the girls, using my phone as a torch. Sometimes when I do this, I tiptoe through the house pretending I'm an explorer in an Egyptian pyramid. This sounds sadder than it is. In the kitchen, I put the kettle on and get a mug out of the cupboard. Tom used to joke about my mugs. I like mugs that match, I am fussy over well-sized handles and I don't like see-through ones. There's nothing attractive about the colour of tea or coffee. My phone suddenly glows on the counter, illuminating the gloom.

What on earth are you doing awake? You're not looking after yourself.

I smile to see the message and the recipient.

How did you know I was awake?

You checked your WhatsApp. It said 'last seen three minutes ago.'

Stop stalking me ☺ How are you? What is the weather like in Vietnam?

Beautiful. I'm having your favourite dragonfruit for breakfast too.

The message is accompanied by a picture of said fruit and her delicate hand next to it. Linh.

When Tom died, his will was detailed to the letter and there was a proviso in there that we make a contribution to a school and orphanage that he used to work at in Vietnam. I was given explicit instructions. *Get to Saigon. Get a taxi and go to this place.* I remember that taxi ride well, a foreign pop song playing on full volume, air conditioning that gave me goose bumps. My car stuck in sweltering dusty streets, surrounded by rickety food stalls with Perspex windows and rows of tangerine plastic stools, swarms of mopeds surrounding us, almost carrying us to our destination. I couldn't take it all in; every corner had life, detail, noise. And then the car turned into the courtyard of a low-rise building, the window frames and doors painted yellow, the wonderful buzz of children chattering, playing. I felt strangely nervous stepping out into the heat. I was greeted by a dog. He had one ear. Of course, I immediately thought about rabies but patted him on the head, hoping my kindliness would save me. Inside, I got swallowed by the cool of the shade, the patterned tiles on the floor. A lady emerged with a walking stick. *Hello? Can I help you?* And then she took pause to study my face. *You're Grace.* I nodded. *I'm Linh.* My eyes teared up. By her side were two young children. Their names were Cleo and Maya.

The story of these little girls is a sad one as well. Cleo and Maya's mother was British Vietnamese, a wonderful, kind girl called Cam who was married to a French teacher called Olivier. Tom had got to know both of them in Vietnam where they volunteered in a school and lived in the same house. After Tom left, they started their own family, and Tom kept in touch with them on the socials. Then one night, they both were killed in a car accident.

It was the most tragic of news and I remember being there. I remember Tom getting that call and falling to his knees in our then kitchen, the telephone bouncing across the tiles. He went out for the funerals, to help, to say his goodbyes. He came back from that trip tired. More tired than usual. He blamed jet lag and his infinite levels of sadness to have lost two dear friends. To see two little girls without parents, one who was practically months old. He didn't think it could be anything else. He really didn't but it turned out he was very ill, very ill indeed.

Cam and Olivier's girls stayed in Vietnam with their grandmother Linh after their parents' death and I met them on my travels, staying with them for a few months. Those months were transformative. All four of us seemed to be bonded by our grief, our shared experience of losing loved ones before their time. Linh was in her late sixties but serene, so incredibly kind and funny. She had moved to the UK as an immigrant in the 1970s and had trained and worked as a nurse. The day we met, she embraced me so hard. She grabbed me by both shoulders and loved me from that first moment.

I got your invitation to Tom's memorial.

Good. You are coming, yes? Come down for an extended stay and see the girls?

Grace, I've already booked tickets. How are my girlies?

Wonderful. They've drawn you some pictures, I'll send them over. Maya is biting people.

She might get that from her mother. Tell her to aim for the soft bits.

I may phrase it differently.

Don't you dare.

How are you? How's your heart?

I'm on a new medication. It makes my ankles swell up.

Good excuse to put them up?

I'll do that if you promise to sleep more.

Agreed.

Has it really been three years? It feels like a lifetime without them, doesn't it?

I take pause to rewind all those years in my mind. It's often felt like that. Like a different life. After Linh lost her daughter, she took on her grandchildren but, by the time I visited her, it was clear looking after these young girls had become a struggle. She was suffering with acute angina, arthritis threatening her mobility. For all the ways she loved them, her health was failing her and she was consumed by worry of what would happen if she wasn't around. I'll always remember her words to me. *I want a different life for them. Their mother wanted them to live in Europe and have the same education she had. I want them to be safe if I am not here. Please help me look after these girls.*

Doesn't it?

When I come down this time, please can you take me to Brighton?

Of course we can go down there. Do you like rock?

What like Bon Jovi? I prefer jazz myself.

Haha, it's rock you eat. Not actual rock either. I'll get you some rock. We miss you, Linh.

I sit down and rest my head on the kitchen table.

Not as much as I miss you. Give those girls big hugs from me.

I'm glad you're coming over. Tom would love to have you there. Thank you for coming.

Never thank me. Please look after yourself, darling girl x

Linh was the reason I started to see things differently after Tom's death. I sensed that she understood I was sinking. Up to that point, I'd lost myself in the novelty of the travel. I escaped everyone's sadness, all the memories and all those people who'd been writing me cards. I got so many cards with single flowers on the front, all well-meaning with lovely recollections of Tom, ones that made me ache with how much he was missed. So I went against my better judgement. I boarded planes and boats and trains and I went looking for him in all these places he'd been. I kept moving because the emotions were still so fresh, so raw. If I stopped then I worried I'd fall into a black hole of nothing.

Saigon was where muddy waters cleared slightly. My travel suddenly had purpose in this orphanage surrounded by little people in matching cotton T-shirts and shorts. Linh got me to volunteer there. I did everything I was asked to do; I swept floors, I made beds and learnt the right and only way to cook rice. I took the money Tom had donated to them and shopped locally to keep them in nappies and supplies. I would have hours sitting there under the whirring of the ceiling fans reading to kids or singing them songs. Like, badly. I don't think I was remembered there for my sense of tune.

The work gave me focus, reason, the children made me realise the real lottery life can give us and, despite everything, I laughed. There were moments when a child would want a hug or want to brush my hair or play a game and suddenly these moments shifted me to a happier place. Linh watched over me the whole time and let me stay in her house. She had wonderful stories about her own life but also about Tom, and I'd curl up on her rattan sofa and take them all in. She fed me the most amazing broths full of herbs and fresh chilli that made my tongue itch. But she also knew grief. She understood my grief. And then at the moment when she thought I was ready, she pushed two little girls in my direction.

'Mummy?' A voice suddenly pierces the gloom of the kitchen.

I jump up in a fright. Cleo likes to wear my T-shirts to sleep. They creep all the way down to her toes but, with her tired look and black unkempt hair, she looks a little like a gremlin.

'Why are you in the dark?' she asks. I go to turn on a light, and we both adjust our eyes as the brightness hits us.

'I couldn't sleep.'

'You never sleep.' She comes and sits on the bench next to me. Realising how cold it is, I put a side of my dressing gown over her like a protective wing.

'I'm chatting to Ba Linh. She's coming over soon.'

'That's so good. I miss her.'

That is something that haunts me. That I took these girls away from their home, their culture, their family. However, Linh was so sure. Olivier had no existing family so that left her as the last surviving relative of the girls and she always said she knew what her daughter would have wanted for them. She signed the forms, looked me in the eyes and told me it was the easiest thing she'd ever done. Now we stay in touch, she is always present and involved and has extended visits every year.

Linh told me all about Cam and Olivier and, even though I never met them, I always feel their essence is in Maya and Cleo. Like, through these children, I'm encountering all these different people. They will always be theirs. I don't think kids ever belong to anyone but I feel blessed to have them here. *You and your sister saved me.* They gave me purpose, a reason to keep going. Linh gave me the greatest gift. I'll never say these things out loud because I don't want to scare the girls, to feel that weight on their tiny shoulders.

'Do you want a drink?' I ask Cleo as she curls her feet up onto the bench.

'Can I have a Sprite?'

'Like, no?'

'Isaac's mum lets him have Monster energy drinks.'

'This explains so much, Cleo. The options are milk or water.'

'Hot chocolate?'

'OK,' I say reluctantly, knowing it will require more energy than I can easily muster at this hour.

'With marshmallows?'

'Don't push your luck.'

She smiles back. It's the cheekiest smile I know. It's one that peeks over the line, every time, looking for trouble. She has such bravery, such wonder in life. But confidence too – who is that all from? She'll chat to anyone and go up on any stage at a Christmas play and sing as loudly as her little lungs let her. She'll walk up to people in supermarkets and tell them she likes their jumpers.

'Then do you want to watch some YouTube with me?' she asks. 'We could snuggle on the sofa and get the big blankets.'

'Is it those videos of the people playing with toys?' I ask. 'I don't get those videos.'

'Oh no, it's a dance tutorial for a song. Isaac and I are learning it.'

'You like Isaac, don't you?' I ask as I go to heat some milk up in the microwave.

'He's not my boyfriend. But I think he's very interesting. He's very smart.'

I sigh to hear her choosing someone for the strength of their character rather than their looks.

'Do you like him?' she asks.

'He's very… entertaining,' I say, taking the polite route.

'People like him and me need to stick together,' she adds.

'What do you mean?' I ask.

'I mean, we're different. I'm adopted, for example. I don't have a dad. We don't look the same,' she says, very matter-of-factly, her finger pointing between the two of us.

Her last three statements seem to penetrate a part of me that leaves me staring at our microwave longer than I need to. She senses my upset and wraps her arms around me.

'It's not a bad thing, Mummy. Different isn't bad. Aunty Lucy tells us that all the time.'

I smile, heaping spoonfuls of hot chocolate powder into the warm milk, but there's worry there. There's the worry that we don't match, that this little unit that we call family is flawed in some ways because it's not conventional. I can't work out if it's a good or bad thing. Cleo climbs on a chair to remind me about her marshmallows.

'Have I upset you?' she asks, dipping her fingers into the bag, topping her hot drink with at least five mini marshmallows too many.

'I just worry. I worry that we're not like other families, that people will be mean. Sometimes people will chat about other people, especially people who are different.'

'That's called gossip. People gossip when their own lives are so boring they have nothing left to talk about.'

I laugh as she props her elbows up on the kitchen counter.

'Let me guess, Aunty Lucy?'

'That was Aunty Meg, and we don't need a dad. I think we're good, just the three of us for now. The Three Amigos, The Three Musketeers. There's not a good one for four if we adopted anyone else.'

I think what I'd do if I adopted a man. Please can I have one at about the six-foot mark, maybe someone who knows to wipe down the splashbacks of a kitchen and can pee in a straight line?

'We'll just stick at three for now then.'

'Deal.' She links her little finger into mine to seal that promise. 'YouTube?'

'Do I have to?' I ask, pained.

'Yes. And you must dance too. You need to dance more. Dancing is life. Isaac told me that.'

'He is smart, eh?'

'The smartest.'

Chapter Six

Tom, where are you? Do let me know, I haven't heard from you in a while and I can have all the cups of tea with your mum but she will always worry and I will be the person she always calls so go easy on her and drop her a line or two. I can't keep track of where you are any more. We should have just put a tracker on you like a pigeon.

I'm attaching some links below because, even though you jest, it's important to keep abreast of what vaccinations you need for different countries. And just remember that everywhere you go isn't a party. Malaysia is a Muslim country so don't booze your way around Kuala Lumpur. And when you talk about random new-wave-style music and all your super-cool vibes, you do sound a bit like a muso-wanker. That's free advice.

I don't know if you want to hear about me. Emma had another gorgeous little girl called Violet but she's still married to her wanker. Lucy is dating a tattoo-covered dwarf called Tony. Mum's started hot yoga. I want to say I miss you but I don't know where you are so technically I don't know what to feel.

Please look at those links.

Grace x

*

- White wash (to include PE kits)
- Semi-skimmed milk
- Pay C's school trip
- Check wellies still fit, re-label wellies
- Look at desserts menu for memorial
- Call Mum
- Profits spreadsheet for Carrie Cantello

I'm crouched next to the washing machine sorting dirty clothes. I have a thing for socks. They're all the same colour in this house and tiny odd socks make me sad. I think about socks out there on their own without a partner so I'm religious at making sure they stick together. I do a white wash on a Thursday. I drop the girls to school, go for a half-hour swim. Then I come home, have a long shower, check my emails and break at eleven o'clock for a coffee and two biscuits. I mean, I'm not completely sad – the biscuits have chocolate on them.

My phone buzzes on the kitchen counter and I look at it, briefly. Carrie Cantello has posted something on the class WhatsApp group.

Just checking, how many times has Miss Loveday read with your children in the past week?

I stare at my phone while a couple of replies pop up.

Oh, Carrie. Give over. I volunteer at the school on Tuesday afternoons to read with some of the kids and the job gets done. I think about whether to reply. *Go and bloody poof up your Ravenclaw pillows.* But the doorbell suddenly rings to stop me from getting involved in that fight. I head into the hallway tentatively. At this hour, it's either the dodgy men going door-to-door trying to sell new fascias or some delivery man asking me to hold a parcel for the neighbours, who seem to shop exclusively at Amazon.

'*Hola*, bitchface,' says the person behind it.

'Meg?' I answer. I step over the threshold and throw my arms around my sister. 'Seriously? You're here?'

'I'm here.' She has a rucksack on her back, a wheelie bag by her feet and suddenly my brain goes into overdrive.

'What's happened? Have you left Danny?' I mutter, shocked. Danny is her husband and she broke all our hearts when she moved to the Lake District with him and their family.

'Errr, no. Why would I leave Danny and come here?'

'Because if you went back to London, there's Mum.'

'True. But no, I came here to see you actually. Danny's taken charge of the girls and I thought I'd come and spend some time with my little sister.'

I eye her up suspiciously as she enters the house. Meg used to be ultra-London trendy, and there are elements of that still there, but the Lakes also make her value the benefits of a proper outdoor coat. She takes off her beanie and sits on the steps to take off her boots.

'You drove?' I continue.

'I trained it. What exactly are you wearing by the way?'

I wasn't expecting visitors so I'm in my work leisurewear of choice. It's fleece leggings with woollen socks, fingerless gloves, slippers and, well, I was wooed over by that ad I saw on Instagram the other day so I'm also wearing a jumper that doubles as a blanket. It means I don't have to turn on the heating in the day so it saves money, even though I look like I'm surviving an apocalyptic winter.

'It's a Huggly.'

'It's a style statement.'

'It's work-from-home chic. I don't wear this for meetings, obviously.'

'No, but there seems to be a pocket on it specifically for your phone.'

'Or remote control. Tea?'

'Stupid question.' Meg shakes out her matted hat hair and stands up to hug me again.

'Why are you here?' I ask.

'Is it really obvious?' she asks.

I nod.

'The sisters, we all had a chat, and after you told us about that memorial thing for Tom, we thought one of us should come down for a while. I was the only one with a gap in my schedule. And I thought it'd be nice. You and I don't spend nearly enough time together.'

I laugh and shake my head. 'So it's a conspiracy?'

'In part. I've also been told to meet this Sam you're shagging and check you're looking after yourself. But I also need to prepare you…'

'Prepare me? For what?'

'Mum got her invite and she's gone next level. She and Dad have rented a house for the week of the memorial. Some giant gaff and we're all going to be staying there, together. Like a big family cult meeting.'

Meg looks thrilled at the prospect but I understand why I needed to be warned. Those logistics will either be amazing or a disaster and I'm hedging my bets on the latter. Meg helps herself to the two biscuits on the plate on the kitchen counter and opens the cabinets searching for more. She stands back from the cupboard with an expression that I can't quite read as either confusion or admiration.

'G, why are your cupboards labelled?'

'For organisation. I got myself a DYMO label maker for Christmas.'

She doesn't look as excited as I do by that reveal.

'So if I did this…' She puts a hand inside the cupboard and moves three tins of chopped tomatoes on the right of the shelf to the left marked *Baking,* '…would the world implode?'

'Yes, and kids would starve. Do not knock the system.'

She fakes a smile. 'It's why we love you, babe. You better have more than two biscuits, though. Why so many vitamins?'

'It's recommended. I read an article. Yours don't take vitamins?'

'They eat fruit; I assume they're all in there.' She looks at the jars curiously.

'How long are you staying?' I enquire, wondering exactly how many more packets of biscuits I need to get in.

'You have me for two weeks then I'll come back for the big day,' she replies, putting her hand in mine. 'Let me just help. Whether it's with the girls or with this memorial. Don't take it all on yourself.'

The sisters worry about me like this. They worry the grief has the capacity to crush me and it's their job to stop that, to distract me, to offer assistance by eating all my biscuits. Meg scans my kitchen and the list on my counter, laughing at the detail in my organisation. I do this everywhere. Lists are the way I sort stuff in my head, how I make sense of madness.

'What are the desserts options for the memorial?' she asks.

'Brownies, fruit tarts or profiteroles.'

'Profiteroles, every day of the week – see how useful I am?' she says, laughing. She pulls up a chair and puts her feet up on another. 'And who is Carrie Cantello?'

'Bitch mum from school, head of the PTA.'

'You joined the PTA?' she asks.

'Emma told me it would be a good way to make friends.'

'Never listen to Emma. Her girls are in a private school where everyone wears padded gilets and eats pheasant. Their PTA raffles off cars. Mine raffles off dusty bottles of cherry brandy. I won a bottle once that was half-drunk.'

'Carrie Cantello has a Harry-Potter-themed living room.'

'And this is someone you want to be friends with?'

I smile and grab a mug to make another cup of tea. Meg takes a lot of sugar in hers, making us worry about the state of her teeth, but they all still seem to be there. I take out a teaspoon from my drawer, which is also labelled. This time she says nothing but I think I can physically hear her bite her tongue.

'When you moved up North, how did you do it? Make friends and that?' I ask her, trying to distract her from mocking my organisational skills.

'Are you telling me you have no friends?' she asks jokingly.

'I just… I feel too old to be doing the rounds again, trying to prove myself and work out who I like. I'm not at university any more. New city, new people.'

'It's part of the adventure. Just don't force it. I have a handful of people up North that I really like. Everyone else is just an acquaintance. Think of it as an office: you don't have to like everyone but you display the civility needed to survive the everyday.'

Meg is such an oracle. Maybe it's because she was the first daughter, the one who tread the path down life and motherhood before us.

'Tell me more about this Carrie Cantello. I bet she drives a Renault Scenic and wears midwash jeans.'

'How did you…?' I scan through social media and show Meg a picture of her. She scowls. 'Oooh, and she also has just started this debate on the class WhatsApp group. She's being pretty harsh on our new teacher.'

Meg navigates through my phone to read the conversation. Her face winces as she scrolls down.

'There's always one. Who is Liz?'

'Her bezzie mate.'

She reads aloud from my phone. '*It's important that the children read with the teacher so they can work out if the children need help with specific phonic issues*. Bullshit. What a way to show up a teacher just doing her job. This stuff makes my piss boil.'

This is classic Meg, who remains, unbeknownst to her, our kingpin, our pioneer. None of us would have had the courage to leave London were it not for her. I remember when she left her comfort zone and started a life elsewhere. Would I have travelled the world if she'd not persuaded me it were possible? Probably not. I've always loved that bravery in her, that steel she seems to find from inside; it's what all older sisters should be made of.

As I watch her, though, I see her fingers deftly move over the screen and a mischievous smile spread across her face. I launch myself at her.

'What the hell, Meggers?'

She leans back on her chair and nearly falls off as I retrieve my phone and see what she's written.

Just checking, how many times have your children lost their cardigans/eaten chicken nuggets/wiped their own arses/played Minecraft until they've gone cross-eyed in the last week?

'What have you done?' I gasp.

'You fight bitchy with sarcasm. Have we, as sisters, taught you nothing?'

My face blanches as I think what Carrie will do now. Christ. Will she throw me out of the PTA? I mean, that would be no bad thing but she'll create drama at the gate. Worse, she'll spread gossip and I'll have to put up defences to protect me, the girls. We both look down at the screen as laughing and clapping emojis appear from Helen and another telephone number that I don't recognise. Yikes. Carrie's going to rear-end me at pick-up, isn't she?

Are you being serious, Grace? I expect better. Lily may have serious learning difficulties and I don't take kindly to you mocking my attempts to ensure she has the best possible start in life.

Meg snarls to see it. She grabs the phone back, her fingers moving like lightning.

They're five. Take your issues up directly with the school. You don't put a comment like that on a group chat and create a feeling of mistrust in a teacher. We all expect better.

That's also the problem with Meg. She has a tendency to poke the beehive. She's not as impulsive as Lucy but she likes questioning authority and calling people out on things. Ask my mother about this. She puts the phone down on the kitchen table and folds her arms.

A message suddenly pops up on my phone.

Feeling brave to take on the Cantello?

Meg leans over to see it and notices the avatar.

'Ooooh, that's the school-gate dad? Give!'

Again, we engage in a war of reflexes to see who'll get to my phone first. This level of snatching is something I've not seen since the nineties when we'd do the same over heated tongs and magazines. However, being stronger, and sneakier, she succeeds, her eyes bulging at a particular picture that Sam sent to me a couple of days ago: a photo of him lying in bed with his appendage in his hand.

'Bleeding monkeys! Is that his cock?' she says, laughing hysterically.

'No?' I say, trying quite terribly to convince her otherwise. That's not his cock. He's lying naked in bed holding a Toblerone against his naked crotch. I'm not sure if that's worse.

'You told us a strong 7. You never mentioned that he had girth.'

'He has girth. Seriously, put the phone down. Unless you want to see my…'

The phone drops onto the kitchen table, luckily protected by my high-grade silicone cover. Meg narrows her eyes at me.

'That's not just shagging then. That's conversation and dick pics.'

'It's porn. But with someone I know so it's safer and more convenient and I don't have to worry about firewalls.'

Meg studies my face for a moment. I can't quite tell if she thinks I'm a genius or is disappointed for me.

'Do you have sex on set days? Do you make lists for that too? Blow Job Monday, Toys on Tuesday?'

I smile wryly to show her that, when provoked properly, I can do sarcasm as well as the next Callaghan without even opening my mouth.

'What do you send him?' she asks.

'Boobs. Boomerangs.'

'You refer to your minge as a boomerang?' she asks.

'It's a short video clip. It's a shame you got so old.'

'Cowbag.'

Meg won't judge. She never does. She's been with the same man now for nearly fifteen years and I don't want to know about her sex life, but I assume she's not too much of a prude to know how modern sex has evolved.

'I send Danny boob pics sometimes.'

'Good to know.'

'I mean, I put a filter on them these days so as not to scare the bastard, but I get it. Does this Sam… does he make you happy?'

I pause for a moment. I don't know whether to give her the truth or the answer she wants. Because she wants me to say yes, he makes me very happy. She wants to see the beginnings of a relationship, that

I might be moving away from my grief, my loneliness, my Tom. She doesn't want to think this is dry, mechanical sex without meaning.

'He's a good distraction.'

'From?'

'A boring life where I sit at home in the evenings, listen to podcasts and label my cupboards.'

'In your big blanket dress thing… do you both fit under that?'

She's joking but I see her fold her arms trying to keep in the warmth. She claims she's half Northern now and can cope with the colder climes but really she will always have Southern blood running through her.

'Can I say something?' Meg asks.

'You're asking permission to speak?'

'Do you remember the day you left on your travels?'

I do. Meg was the one sister who came with me to the airport to see me off, to say goodbye, to laugh at the fact I had traveller's cheques. She likened me to Dora the Explorer. I had my passport in a Ziploc bag in case the plane crashed and I needed proof that I was on that plane so they could tell my family. I told Meg this as she embraced me hard. We both sobbed. *Go*, she told me. *Be bold, be all those things Tom was.*

'When you went away, I thought Tom's passing ignited something in you. My wonderfully ordered and sensible Gracie was going out into the world to experience all this chaos and adventure and I thought you'd bring a bit of that back…'

I am silent as I take that in. I'm not sure how travel is supposed to completely change your personality. You read about it all the time. *She went to India, found yoga and suddenly came back dressed in linen and addicted to lentils, she went to Greece and found a fit waiter and discovered the workings of her clitoris.* I went out Grace. I came back Grace.

'Instead you brought us back nieces,' Meg continues. 'And it was gorgeous and wonderful, but suddenly you became a mother, you threw everything into it, and I adore you for it. But...'

'But?'

'Your life revolves around this. You work from home, you don't go out, you became a martyr to the cause.'

Deep down I know why I do all of this. It's all distraction. What else is there to do? Start a relationship with someone like Sam? But what if I lost him? I wouldn't be able to deal with that so instead I invest what I have elsewhere. I have daughters; I want to give them everything while I can and do it right.

'When was the last time you went out?' she asks.

'I swim. I went to soft play last week.'

'Exercise and child-based endeavours don't count.'

'They do very good coffee at soft play with the Biscoff biscuits in the wrapper and it's very reasonably priced.'

Meg glares at me from across the kitchen table.

'I did some research. There's a posh lido with a very nice restaurant we can go to. Let me treat you.' She puts a hand in mine.

'Can I wear this?'

'No. Wear that out of this house and I'll disown you.'

Reaching over, she takes a large sip of tea and then eats three chocolate digestives like a sandwich. She looks over at another one of my lists.

'You know someone called Delphine?' she says, spying a name at the bottom.

'Oh, that's Joyce Kennedy's editor. As Joyce's book did so well, she was thinking I might want to write something similar. My widow's tale.'

Meg pauses. She's a part-time journalist by trade who would probably be able to advise me best in all of this but she gets that to pour my heart out on a piece of paper is not my bag. To put all those words down into sentences and have them make sense to anyone else seems an unfathomable task.

'That's quite an emotional thing to do. Really think it through. It's either cathartic or it can dredge up a lot of pain.' She snuggles into me. 'I could help you, if you wanted to do that.'

'You would?'

'Yeah, out of all the sisters I have the best spelling for a start.' She smiles broadly at me.

I'm glad you're here. You're mildly sensible and you give good advice. I'm relieved they didn't send Lucy.

'Now, tell me who's invited to this memorial thing,' she asks me.

'All the usual London lot. Family, mates. Doug. Linh's coming down. Amsterdam mates. There's a whole contingent of teachers Tom knew from Japan who are using it as a chance for a reunion. Oh… and Ellie flies in at the end of the week from Australia.'

'The one who made you get your shit tattoo, Ellie?'

'Yeah, did I tell you she had a baby? A little girl. She called it Kennedy.'

'She gave her baby Tom's last name?'

'Right? I've told her I'll meet her for dinner. Look, at me… I'll be going out.'

'We'll have to make you look hotter than her, though, yes? I'll lend you a good bra.'

'You have those?'

'You know… I'm not so old that I can't hit you, properly.'

She doesn't hit me. She hasn't done that properly since I was eight, she sixteen and I read her diary, but she edges a little closer to me and I sense her snuggling into my Huggly. *I told you it was warm.*

Chapter Seven

G,

Are you still talking to me? I hope so. I'm in Australia now and fuck me, it's hot here. Like that dry heat you hate because you say it's like standing in the middle of a hairdryer. It feels like home here except the dress code is more casual and I'm going to have to work out how to wear flip-flops. Except here they call them thongs so that's confusing.

I've met some really cool peeps down here, surfer chicks and dudes. They're so laid-back they're verging on horizontal. I'm enclosing some Tim Tams with this letter as requested but I should tell you that I think you can pick these biscuits up on Amazon now. Just saying.

How are your exams going? Please reply to this. I'm getting that full feeling of Callaghan hatred coming at me. I half-expect to turn a corner and see Lucy coming at me with a knife. That's scarier than the thought of any of the wildlife down here. Talk to me?

T x

*

Tom went travelling for three years and we fully broke up for one of those years. It was around the time he went to Australia. During that time I went out with an accountant called Ben, who wore tartan boxer shorts and didn't understand the need for foreplay. He, however, understood the importance of being financially solvent so I liked that he had a pension scheme. It was grown-up dating. It wasn't this emotional tug-of-war drenched in drama that Tom and I had lived through. It was sensible dates in restaurants where we'd discuss wine lists and have lively political debates over the merits of stamp duty. I used to sit there in those restaurants and revel in how mature it was compared to what Tom called dating: afternoons drinking in parks where we'd eat picnic selection packs and he'd ask me what three superpowers I would have (invisibility, X-ray vision and the ability to fly, obviously).

Tom being on the other side of the world just put too much distance between us. It was starting to be painful, these failed attempts at keeping in touch, the time difference, the realisation that his attention was elsewhere. In Australia, he lived the surfers' dream in Sydney and dotted his way up to the Gold Coast. He got a tan which made him look permanently dirty and he met a girl called Ellie. Ellie wasn't me, not by a long shot. She had a big uncontrollable nest of hair and looked like she spent at least eighty per cent of her time in board shorts and swimwear. Together, the two of them travelled around in a camper van called Cyril and documented all their sun-kissed adventures via social media. Did it break me? Yes. But I had sensible Ben, who used to take me away on weekends to the Cotswolds. We'd go on walks. And drink tea. And have very uncomfortable sex because, well, foreplay is necessary.

But all that time, I thought that was how life was supposed to be. Tom had found someone who was obviously far more suited to his sense of adventure and need for freedom. They could dine out on sunsets and undiscovered beaches in their assorted Billabong wear and he'd be that boy I once knew at university. I'd found my person who I could settle with, who could wrap me up in all the security I could ever wish for, even if he did have a Supercuts haircut and wore white sports socks with everything. But then the posts of Tom and Ellie stopped (I wasn't stalking them, really…). And before I knew it, he'd posted a new picture of himself in New Zealand. Ellie wasn't there. They broke up? Why? How? But he was single again. Ben and I lasted two more weeks after that. I dumped him in a Pizza Express in Wimbledon. He didn't even cry. He shook my hand. *Is what it is, thank you for your time.* But please don't worry about him. He went on to marry a mortgage advisor called Jane. You could measure levels on the straightness of her fringe and she plays the cello at the weekends.

*

'I got wine. Australian wine. Will she think I'm taking the piss? I could get some cocktails in?'

I shake my head. Wine, wherever it comes from, is good. Can I just drink this straight from the bottle? Are there straws? This might be the best or worst idea I've ever had in my life. Ellie is in town for the memorial and we're having a reunion dinner of sorts. I'm in a dress, I've straightened my hair and buying the first round of wine is Sam. I didn't want to do this alone. I didn't want to show up to meet her new husband and be sitting here looking like a saddo so I asked Sam for the moral support. My sister's borrowed bra allows for the other type of support. Sam's made an effort tonight. He wears a fisherman's jumper and it appears like he's put some sort of product in his beard. He can tell I'm nervous and slips a hand into mine as I scan the windows of this waterfront restaurant looking for them. I picked a trendy eatery out on the docks for this meeting to make myself seem more interesting than I really am.

'I went to Australia on my honeymoon,' Sam says. 'Orlagh and I did Melbourne. We went to that street where they filmed *Neighbours*. I also nearly got eaten by a shark. But I fought him off with skills I'd learnt from *Baywatch*.'

'What was that?' I ask. He laughs and studies my face. '*Baywatch*?'

'Relax. When was the last time you saw her?'

'Two years ago. I went on a trip after my husband passed. Australia was part of it and she showed me round, we reminisced.'

It was a bizarre meeting of wounded hearts. To both of us, Tom was a lost love for different reasons but it was clear that we were also rivals in some way. *You stole him from me for that year. He left you because he still loved me.* For this, we were cautious about each other. We were glued together in grief but I'm not sure we completely liked each other. I am not sure how to describe this dynamic to Sam but he senses my unease. He fills our glasses with wine and pushes one in my direction.

'Is she nice?' Sam asks.

'She's different to me, shall we say. She's bouncy.'

'You're bouncy.'

As soon as the words leave Sam's mouth, he realises there are sexual connotations there and pulls a face. Luckily it makes me laugh. That was the distraction I needed. I do like you, Sam. I like how you turn up your jeans like a trendy dad and top up my glass generously, right to the top.

'Thank you for doing this,' I tell him, leaning over to give him a peck on the cheek.

It takes him aback and he blushes. 'Is this a date? I can't quite tell. I wasn't sure if I was supposed to bring flowers.'

'Oh, god no. I think we're past the stage of courting. We're almost dating in reverse, eh?'

'True. Can I go on record and say what we have, our arrangement… I like it. I like that there's no pressure. That you don't care that I randomly say my wife's name when you have me in your hand or leave my socks on.'

He makes it sound like I shag him out of pity and I'm not at that stage. Yet.

'We sleep together because I enjoy it. I'm attracted to you. You're definitely in the top five of school dads at that school.'

'Really? Who's number one on that list?'

'The plumber dad. The one in the boots with the dirty white van.'

'Greg? With the buzz cut? You really don't have standards.'

I laugh, taking a big sip of my wine. 'He has shapely calves.'

'Well, ditto. I am also attracted to you. Very much so. And also top five.'

'Your number one being…?'

'I can't say Orlagh, can I?'

I look over at him, cocking my head to the side, knowing where his heart still belongs. Oh, Sam. I wonder if this has legs. I don't think it does. All his heartache is still so fresh. I've seen the way he sometimes tears up when he's having sex. He always says it's because he's not used to the physical exertion but I know it's because he misses her. As awful as it sounds, sometimes I close my eyes and pretend he's Tom. I don't tell him that obviously, but I have a feeling he knows.

'And the deal still stands, yes? If we meet new people then we move on, we shake hands and call it a day?' he asks.

'I'd at least hug you for your service.'

'I'd hug you back. And we'd still be friends, yes?'

'Of course.'

He puts a hand in mine again. He may very well be one of my few school-gate mates so I can hold onto that at least. We can most certainly be friends.

'OH MY GOD, GRACIE!!!'

My head turns sharply as shrill Aussie tones ring through the air, and Sam's eyes open widely. In fact most of the bar turns around to the source. Ellie. She really has not changed. She's supposed to have had a baby but she's still stick thin, the hair a wonder of curls and frizz. The clothes are typically her: she's cool with her vintage jeans, surfer-label fleece and headscarf with big statement earrings and a stud in her nose. She comes over and hugs me tightly. She was always a big hugger.

'You look gorge! This place is gorge! Look at you!'

Look at me. Ellie and I are polar opposites. She is ethereally beautiful, effortlessly so, whereas for me just getting out of the house meant thirty minutes of struggling with eye make-up because liquid eyeliner is evil.

'And who are you?' she asks, glancing over to my right.

'This is Sam. Sam, this is Ellie.'

She throws her arms around him and Sam takes a step back to steady himself.

'Love, you're dating? This is epic! You're cute. I'm bowled over to meet ya. And this is Ryan!'

A figure emerges from behind her. He's wearing shorts in a British winter with Vans trainers but I stop for a minute to see his face. Tom? I can't breathe. He's exactly the same height, build and hair colour. No. I'd seen random pics of him but I hadn't seen a close-up. Sam senses my shock and goes over to shake his hand.

'Mate, I'm Sam – good to meet you.'

Ellie grabs him by the shoulders. 'I know, right, Gracie. Isn't Ry the spit of our Tom?'

'It's uncanny,' I mutter awkwardly. 'I'm Grace.'

'*The* Grace,' he says.

'You make me sound like a boat.'

This makes Ellie howl with laughter. She really did this, didn't she? She married someone who's a physical clone of Tom. I can't stop staring at Ryan's face. I want to grab it and feel it to see if it's real or not. Ellie, this is weird.

'How about we all start with some drinks? I'll get some glasses – this wine is decent if you want to share?' Sam continues.

'Now you're talking, Sam. I'm also famished. Food please, veggo menu if they have it.'

Ellie links arms with Sam and they head to the bar, leaving me standing there with Tom 2.0.

'I'm sorry. You just took me aback. You really do look like him. Apart from the accent of course. It's lovely to meet you. And congrats with the wedding and the baby and everything.'

'Cheers. It's good to be here.'

We hear Ellie at the bar as she leans into Sam, who studies her partly in shock, partly in wonder. Ellie will do that; she's a bit of a force of nature.

Ryan turns to me. 'Can I ask you a question? How much do I look like him? Really?'

I study his face. 'I'd be doing some genetic testing to find out if you're a relation.'

He laughs. 'Well, that doesn't make me paranoid.'

'What do you do, Ryan? For work?'

'I'm a teacher.'

'Seriously?'

'Nah, pranked ya. I'm a roofer.' He smiles broadly. I let out a huge sigh of relief. *You're not Tom. The laugh is different. You don't have that twinkle.* Tom was also mildly scared of heights. But full marks for effort.

*

'So she stayed with me in Sydney,' says Ellie, recalling our time together, 'and we had this mad night out where we got absolutely shitfaced and we got these tattoos off one of my mates, Ripper, and it was hysterical…'

It turns out Ellie and Ryan are vegetarian so all their stories tonight are being accompanied by halloumi, dip and chips. I really hope they have the nutritional requirements needed to soak up all the wine in our systems as I count three bottles on the table. Ellie and Ryan are also the type of drunks who get exponentially louder the more they drink. It's like they are competing with the background music. It was all Ellie and I did in Australia. Drank. From the moment she picked me up at the airport in the camper van that she still had, we boozed our way around beaches and bars. They have drive-in off-licences out there which made things super easy and we drank a lot of beer. Cases of the amber nectar and occasionally lovely bottles of Tasmanian Riesling that we necked straight from the bottle.

As we drank, we had strange drunken discussions over whether Marmite or Vegemite was better. I think I rugby-tackled her on a beach when she suggested the latter. But then she'd also tell me all her Tom stories against expanses of sky reflected in the sea like a mirror, on untouched wild beaches, and we'd cry and toast him and go for a swim in his honour. Naturally, she always did this better than me. She'd been around the sea her whole life so would emerge looking like a mermaid. I was raised completely landlocked so would swim out and worry about the marine life eating me, do a manic front crawl back to the beach and emerge like I'd been shipwrecked. I always imagined Tom got a huge kick looking down on that.

'She had no idea what tattoo she wanted,' Ellie carries on, 'so I chose her a shark and, oh my god, you have to get it out. Have you seen it, Sam?'

Sam has seen the shark because he's seen me naked. It's on my shoulder so it means I can't wear vest tops any more without some sense of paranoia.

'I have. It didn't look like a shark to me,' Sam says.

I roll down the top of my dress over my shoulder. Ellie sits there open-mouthed.

'That's because I got one of Lucy's friends to cover it up for me. It's now a rose. The shark looked evil. Something had to be done.'

Ellie removes her fleece and does the same. She got a dove tattoo that was both classy and well done to the point where, after, I wondered if she paid her mate to do a botch job on me. However, below the dove I notice something that wasn't there before. It's Tom's date of birth. Wow. Is this some sort of competition over who can mourn him better, who loved him more? *Look at me, I scoured Sydney for someone who looks just like him, I've named my daughter after him and etched his details onto my skin.* The grief almost feels comparative.

'So, Ry and I are going to get up to London, have a proper honeymoon, and then we'll be down for the memorial. I spoke to Joyce too and she said I could recite some of my poetry. I've written something about Tom.'

'You have?' I ask. 'I guess that would be OK.' Seriously? Tom hated poetry. He hated the fact it was cryptic. He only had time for things that rhymed. Is her poem going to rhyme? I can think of lots of words that rhyme with Ellie: smelly, welly, telly. This is when I need Cleo's mate, Isaac.

'I mean, it was such an honour to be invited,' Ellie says, reaching out to grab my hand.

That was all Joyce. *We need to invite the loud Aussie girl, don't we? The one who keeps posting pics of him on Facebook with song lyrics?* I was hesitant because of the strange nature of our relationship but it was also the right thing to do, to have everyone there who had been part of his life.

'Oh, you are kidding me?' Sam suddenly says. He shields his face with his hand and looks in the opposite direction. Ellie and Ryan shift their eyes from side to side.

'Something I said?' Ellie mutters.

I glance over at the bar and suddenly get it. Orlagh and her new man friend are standing there, perusing a drinks menu. Orlagh is one of those mums who's very dedicated to the upkeep. I've never seen her without her fake lashes and she's wearing a stylish leather jacket today. It gives her a polished look but I wonder if she's getting any warmth from that layer at all. I don't think it's lined and so this is where she and I differ greatly. All I need to say about the new boyfriend, Jordan, is that he's wearing spray-on jeans, so skinny I can see the outline of his keys. Even to the casual observer, the age difference is immediately apparent. Next to me, Sam goes completely beetroot and the hand in mine grows clammy and warm. I grip tightly.

'That's Sam's ex-wife,' I say. Ellie and Ryan do very unsubtle detective work and check them both out immediately. Orlagh notices and then her eyes scan to me. Yeah, she didn't know this was a thing. This is awks, as the young people, like the one standing next to her, would say. She whispers to Jordan and they walk over to the table. I'm glad I borrowed Meg's good bra.

'Sam?'

Pull it together, man. Don't cry.

'Orlagh. Hey…' he replies, his voice squeaking a little.

'You're Grace, from school,' she says to me.

'I am.' I really don't know what to do here. Sam doesn't want to let on that this is a date and, to be fair, I don't want this to be fodder for the school gate either. But then how will this appear to Ellie and Ryan?

'These are my friends, Ellie and Ryan. I was just making some introductions because they're starting up their own business and needed some IT support. I've been doing their accounts,' I reply.

Ellie glances over at me. Play ball, hun.

'Yes, we have opened a restaurant,' she says, in strange mock British tones like she's married into royalty. 'It's plant-based.' It's either the alcohol or her terrible acting skills. Ryan nods in agreement. Jordan waves at everyone.

'So a business meeting?' Orlagh asks suspiciously, looking at all the bottles lined up on the table.

'Of sorts,' Sam says.

'We're just on a night out,' Orlagh says, folding her body into Jordan's.

I sense Sam examining every movement between the two of them, the way they're conjoined at the hip, how she's casual in where she places her hands. Do I do the same? I can just grab him by the crotch to make her feel the same level of distress he obviously feels. What I really want to do is hug him.

'Well, enjoy. It's good to see you out for once, Sam. You were always such a homebody.'

Oh, Orlagh. Don't. You're halfway to saying he was boring and he's not. I don't know what to do to remedy this.

'Sam? Are we talking about the same Sam?' Ellie suddenly says, seeming to forget her put-on accent and falling back into her broad Australian tones.

Sam looks over at her strangely.

'He's a fucking riot. How many times have we met up now? Each time, we end up at a club. A casino. Remember that time you took us for burlesque? I thought I could hold my alcohol... but this man? This man is a legend.'

Sam looks over at Orlagh curiously. Club, maybe. Casino and burlesque make him sound like he's traded in his Honda Accord for an Aston Martin and a new playboy agenda complete with bunnies and a burgundy robe.

'Can't think of anyone else I'd rather have look after our business. What do you do, Jordy?' asks Ellie.

Jordan realises that's his cue to speak. 'I work at a cinema.' God, he even sounds young. I'm not sure if his voice has fully broken yet.

'But he's going for a supervisor role, aren't you babe?' Orlagh interrupts him.

'Well, we need to talk about those spreadsheets, Sam, so I think we should get back on it. Also chat about taking my brand global. Another bottle of wine, maybe?' Ellie adds. 'So lovely to meet you, Jordy and Olly. What is that? Is that a name?'

I look down and smile. The girl does have her uses and, for a moment, I get that Tom would have been highly amused and drawn to that candour, that confidence.

'It's Orlagh.'

'Oh. Yeah. Have a good evening. I recommend the Shiraz. It's Aussie too.'

Orlagh pulls at Jordan's arm and strides away while I literally hear Sam deflate with relief. He looks unsure whether he wants to laugh or cry.

'I've literally got bras older than him,' Ellie says. I try not to laugh. Not because it was funny but her volume is still set to max. The whole bar heard that, didn't they?

*

We order another bottle at the bar and Ellie uses it as an opportunity to be a bit louder and play into our charade. She actually goes over and sits in Sam's lap at one point and also dances to the toilets. It looks choreographed, like it's a well-used routine. Had it just been me and Sam he'd have sat there getting drunker and more embarrassed by the situation. And drunker. I wouldn't have had the nerve to stand up to Orlagh. With Ellie, he finally had the arsenal to fight back.

We've now left and are milling around the Millennium Square area of the waterfront, gazing into the fountains and walking Ellie and Ryan back to their hotel. She weaves her arm through mine and huddles in close. She always afforded me such intimacy, even when we first met. I remember going to her flat and she told me we'd be sharing a bed together because her sofa had been invaded by moths. OK then. I used to find her spooned into me in the mornings, literally in just her pants and a vest top.

'So basically, he's just giving you a root to get over the ex-wife?' Ellie asks candidly.

'We root each other, it's a mutual rooting.'

Ellie cackles to hear me talk like this.

'He's cute. But I get it. He's like a fresh scab, he needs to heal over.'

Not an image I want to associate with our coupling but it's pretty true.

'It's just functional. We get what we need out of things. He's kind. I know the history, he knows mine.'

She pulls a face. 'It's very clinical. Is he the only person you've banged since…?'

'Yeah.'

She doesn't quite know how to reply to that. She seems sad for me.

'Thanks for covering back there,' I tell her, trying to change the subject.

'Oh no, that was super fun. She had bitch vibes anyway. I wasn't digging her general aura.'

That's the other thing that separates us out, the ideas we share about Tom's passing. As I'd seen all of the ugly end, the way chemo and steroids ravaged him, the rampant physical demise of his body, I perceived everything so vividly but also organically. He was gone. Ellie speaks of auras and spirits and feeling him in the air, like a celestial being. As proven now as she gazes up into the stars.

'Do you think he's looking down on us?' she mutters.

I glance up. 'I hope he is. But he was atheist. So probably no.'

She punches me in the arm. 'I miss his energy, that presence he had. God, I miss him, Gracie.'

'You don't say?' I say, glancing over at Ryan chatting to Sam as they walk ahead. 'I thought I was the sad widow but you've gone the full hog with the doppelganger husband, you even stole his name for your daughter.'

I'm lucky she finds this amusing. 'It's a good name, it's solid. What do you think of Ry?' she asks.

'He seems like a good guy.'

'He is. He's a little too Aussie in that he's never left Australia before this but he's got a decent heart. What he wants out of life is pretty simple and I like that. After Tom, I just realised I didn't want someone who'd…'

'Leave?'

We smile at each other. Whether it was through travel or death, Tom liked to make a grand exit and break some hearts on the way out.

'Remember, he came back to you, though. It was always you, Gracie Callaghan.'

'And then what did he do? He pissed off again.'

'He's still here,' she says, putting her hand to my heart.

If you want to know the one overused condolence that people use when someone you love dies, it's that. They tell you he's in you, that your heart will remember him. I wish it were that simple. The fact is I sometimes feel possessed by him. He inhabits my thoughts, my brain, my movement, my every breath.

'And well, my Kennedy is a little ladybug. You'd like her. It's a shame I couldn't bring her down this time. I can't wait to meet your girls too.'

'We'll make it happen,' I reply.

'Do you like me, Gracie?' Ellie asks. 'I can never quite tell.'

I scan her face. In death, Tom left me a legacy of relationships that have now become mine. We will forever be linked by that man.

It means that, despite everything, I care about her, I will look out for her. I know she'll do the same for me.

'I do. I think I just have trouble recollecting our time together in Australia. We used to start drinking at midday. There was that time we got drunk at the beach and I tanned to the colour of a frigging flamingo.'

I'm not sure why this is funny to her. I couldn't wear a bra for two weeks.

'They were fun times, though. I was such a good host. I took you to the Opera House.'

'You see… all I remember there are the loos because I was busy puking in them. That's literally all I remember: the beetroot on the burgers, Paul Hogan on the telly and the monster hangovers.'

She shows me a scar on her elbow.

'And I hope you remember that time you beat me up for saying Vegemite was far superior to Marmite.'

'I did that?' I say, poking at said scar. 'God, that's awful…'

'On Bondi Beach, that's when the lifeguards chased us off thinking we were a bunch of smashed yobbos. That was when I knew I liked you. I liked the spark.'

I vaguely remember that incident. I'd turned back to said lifeguards and said I'd seen them on the television and that they weren't a patch on Hasselhoff.

'So you didn't think I was a drongo after that?' I say, in a terrible Aussie accent. Her laugh seems to part the clouds. I don't mind that sound so much any more.

'See, you can't have been that drunk because you remember your Aussie.'

'I remember you calling me a flaming galah every time I fell over drunk.'

But I remember her helping me up again afterwards. I mean, she'd be laughing her tits off but her arm was always there. Just like it is now.

'I thought you were a proper smashing bird...' she says in British tones.

'All right there, Mary Poppins?'

That laugh again.

'Mates?' she asks.

'Mates,' I say, my accent returning for one last time.

Chapter Eight

Tom, I am enclosing all the things you asked for in the package. I have not made a note of any of the customs details for Romania but I will assume that there is nothing here that will see you seized to the ground by Romanians. Apart from that ounce of cocaine, of course. I hope that made you laugh. If a customs officer is reading this, this is a joke as I've never taken drugs in my life.

Can you really not find teaching supplies out there? Seriously? Or was this a ploy for me to make contact with you? Highlighters? You could have just written a note and asked me how I am? Or asked your mum? Amazon? Anyway, I've also included some chocolate in here because I am pretty sure you won't be able to get Wispas in Bucharest. I know you also like to teach via flash card so I included some blank ones and also some good-quality whiteboard pens because they were on offer. Yes, I'm still supremely sensible in case you thought I'd changed.

G x

*

Tom loved teaching. I know why he liked it. He liked the showman-ship of standing in front of a classroom and making people laugh. There was something in his heart that was so determined to create change. I mocked it openly. It was the cynic in me that felt the world was too big, too broken to be mended just by one person teaching passive verbs via the power of role play. Through teaching, Tom bonded with my older sister, Beth and my parents, all teachers, and later on, when we lived together and married, I saw him turn his hand to secondary education where he became fun Mr Kennedy. He'd have me around our kitchen table with scissors and wine on a school night cutting out shapes for his recommended reading charts. He made stars out of kitchen foil. We got his large Sharpie collection out for that too. He loved his Sharpies, sometimes, I joked, more than he loved me. He never disputed that.

When I see Miss Loveday now, she brings me back to Tom. She has all that brightness and enthusiasm in her eyes; she just wants to make a difference. She has all her qualifications and pedagogy that her degrees gave her and now she's been set on the world. Except where was the unit on having to deal with mums who don't understand their kids are not the only kids in the world? The one that teaches you that kids are also unpredictable and occasionally ridiculous? Those are important units.

The problem with pick-up at The Downs Primary School is that as we all stand around the playground waiting for our little ones, we have a view into the classrooms to see how the day is winding down. Maya's looks like a hurricane has just hit it, as if every stray bit of paper and rubbish has been swallowed up by a storm and spat out again. Miss Loveday is attempting to read a story to the class and I spy two kids full-on wrestling on the carpet space and another at the back staring into space, tucking into the contents of their nostrils. Ever since Meg decided to act on my behalf on the class WhatsApp group, I've been doing pick-up like a ninja – which sounds stealthy but means I'm currently trying to crouch next to a gazebo, half-hidden in a rowan bush.

'I just think it's a disgrace that our children are basically being used as practice for her teaching. What if they fall behind? It's not fair on them.'

In the middle of the playground, Carrie preaches to those too socially confused by school politics to know any better. I wish I had something to throw at her.

'She's inexperienced and she's also far too young.'

A voice joins in from the group. 'The children seem happy enough.'

There is no discernible reply to that so I assume Carrie answers with her eyes.

'Look at the state of that classroom.'

I can feel the bile rise in me. Thank god she never saw Tom's classrooms. He did papier mâché once and they had to call in specialist cleaners as he put too much flour into the mix and it set into the carpet like concrete. He was messy. But fun. Children will remember fun, he said. Not sitting in quiet lines learning things by rote. I always think about what he would have been like as a parent. Christ, the mess he would have made, all in the name of fun.

'Hiding, are we?' It's Helen, Isaac's mum.

'That was all my sister, she hijacked my phone.'

Helen puts an arm around me. 'Don't apologise to me, love. You know someone screen grabbed it and sent it around the school? You're a bloody hero, you are…'

You forget about the cascading effect of social media in these playground battles. One moment you tell a group that your son has a rash and the next he's a social pariah with possible leprosy.

'I mean,' she carries on, 'I like giving the woman what for but I love how you went for the sucker punch. It's also got people signed up for the PTA. Nothing like real-life beef to add some flavour to people's lives.'

Oh, Jesus. Thanks, Meg. Have I created a turf war situation here? The doors of the classroom fly open and children are suddenly released to parents. Maya does what she does, which is linger and help tidy up things, returning pencils to pots and chairs to standing. I have no idea where she gets that from. I stand by the bush watching her as she shakes her head at boys who still continue to wrestle and use their school sweatshirts as whips to attack each other. Helen's little one comes over and hands her a piece of paper, which she quickly scans.

'Seriously? Oh no, what a shame.'

She shows me the note, on official school letterhead paper telling us Miss Loveday will start a new job in another school after Easter. I look up at Carrie Cantello and some of her esteemed cronies, murmurs of nods and satisfaction coming from them.

'This is all them,' Helen says. 'I wouldn't be surprised if they forced that poor girl out.' She shakes her head. 'I've got to run but carry on the good work, Grace. I look forward to hearing your next rant.'

I survey the rest of the parents. Some take the letter and stuff it into book bags while others read it in confusion, or concern that their children will lose a teacher for the last term of their first year at school. Through the glass, I spy Miss Loveday, who can hardly bear to look up at anyone. She stares down at tables, filing books away. I head over to the door.

'Come on, slowcoach,' I tell Maya.

Her face lights up to see me but there's also concern in her face. 'Mummy, Miss Loveday is leaving.'

I bend down to sweep the hair from her face. We experimented with clips this morning but the sheen of her hair sees them displaced at random parts of her head. I unclip them and put them in her book bag, which is filled with leaves, twigs and random pieces of paper with drawings on them.

'I know. I just heard. Are you OK, Miss Loveday?' I ask her.

Miss Loveday's look always devolves over the course of the day. She starts like Miss Honey but ends looking like Miss Hannigan, where strong alcohol served out of a bath tub might be the answer. She looks up at me.

'I'm so sorry. I feel awful for the children, they deserve better. I wish I could stay out the year.'

'Don't apologise. You've done an awesome job.' She seems surprised by my statement and I am sad that I never expressed enough gratitude. I wish I'd bought her a better Christmas present as opposed to a random bottle of wine that I thought could smooth over the cracks, like it regularly does for me. 'Where are you moving on to?' I enquire.

'I found somewhere back home looking for maternity cover for the summer term and they've said they'll pick up my assessments.'

'Where's home?'

'London. I moved here last summer. It was probably the wrong thing to do. I took on too much, too soon. I don't have support down here.' Her eyes glaze over and I instinctively move her round so no one can spy too much through the window.

'Maya. Could you go outside for a moment? Just have a play.'

Maya comes and throws her arms around Miss Loveday's waist before she does so.

'Bye, Miss Loveday. I'll see you tomorrow!'

She scampers off and I watch her throw her book bag to the damp ground and mount a wooden train in the playground, scaling its roof. I turn back to Miss Loveday.

'We're not supposed to have favourites but she is so receptive,' she says.

'Thank you. She loves you. You can tell. She draws a lot of pictures of you.'

'I love that.'

A tear catches on her eyelashes and she tries to blink rapidly to stop it from falling.

'Seriously, are you OK, Miss Loveday?' I ask.

'I just didn't expect it to be like this. Some of those parents are beyond savage.'

'Mrs Cantello?'

'It would be unprofessional to say who…' she mumbles.

'Don't worry, we all know what she's like. I am sorry she's put you in such a difficult position. The other teachers, the head here – I hope they've been supporting you?'

'I've just not gelled with anyone. I get the sense that I'm supposed to suck it up. It's part of our profession now. And it's not just one parent, there are a few. They seem to be totally obsessed with their kids, they call me to task on everything. I thought it'd be a kinder atmosphere. They're not all like you. You write in your reading record in a rainbow-coloured Biro.'

'Maya demands it. I'm from a family of teachers – my parents, my sister… my husband. So I try to be respectful and let you get on with your job.'

She pauses for a moment to hear me bring up Tom, wondering whether to delve further.

'They all teach secondary, so different to you, but I get the chaos and the stress. Tom used to have tales too of parents and kids who made his life hell. He had a dad try and beat him up outside a school gate once.'

'Really?'

Really. Tom was a charmer and this man's wife used to flirt with him through her daughter's homework diary with winky faces and show up at school events in low-cut tops. All Tom's problem, of course. He was offered a stand-off in the playground, which Tom refused. The man called him a prickless wonder then tripped over a basketball hoop and fell on his face. Tom got his revenge when his deputy head had to stop his bleeding nose by sticking a tampon up his nostrils.

'Some of these mums are pussycats in comparison,' I say. That might be the wrong comparison. Carrie Cantello is one of those grumpy cats with a perma-frown who scratches your sofa and pretends it had nothing to do with her.

'Do you think I'm giving up? Running away when it gets tough?'

'Do you think that?'

'I think I'm trying to preserve my mental health. Trying to get out before the stress turns me away from education for good.' That stress is etched in her face, in the frizz of her hair and the sadness and redness of her eyes. She thought things would end up differently; illusions have been shattered. I can empathise with that feeling.

'Who do you live with here?' I enquire. 'Are you doing this all on your own?'

'I rent a room from a couple. It's cosy, maybe not ideal.'

I suddenly think of a person who did the same, who relocated to this part of the world two years ago with two little girls. I knew exactly zero people as most of my university acquaintances had moved away. The girls buoyed me, I distracted myself, I had a career so didn't need to find one. But I did cry. I cried because I missed people, because I wondered if I was doing the right thing. I think of Miss Loveday crying in a rented room, clutching the bad wine I gave her for Christmas and not knowing where her life is headed. I grab a coloured pencil from a pot and a scrap of paper.

'Look, I know this is not the done thing but this is my mobile number. If you're stressed and worried then you shouldn't be alone. Call me if you need me.'

She looks at the number tentatively but smiles and puts it on her desk.

'Thank you.'

'You know, you are liked. The kids love you, that's all that should matter.'

'Thank you, Miss Callaghan. It's appreciated.'

'This classroom, this stress, won't be the worst thing you go through. Stick with this because it'll make you better and stronger. Prove them wrong.' I don't know where those words come from and I am not sure if I've overstepped but I hope they are of worth.

She nods but her expression drops for a moment. 'Ummm, where is Maya?' she suddenly asks.

I scan the playground outside and my heart plummets. Maya? Crap. We run out of the classroom and I look for hints of movement in the bushes and toys. Shit. Where are you? You've never been a runner. Where are you, little one? The tumult of a million and one emotions and possibilities rush through my entire body. Call the police. Road blocks, helicopters. However, I pop my head out of the gate and instead find her merrily swinging on the fence with her sister. Fuck fuck fuck. My heart. I go over and bundle her into my arms, trying not to let the panic show in my face.

'You. Little cheeky chicken. Were told to wait. You didn't wait.'

Miss Loveday exhales with relief while Cleo and Maya stand there looking worried by my breathlessness. My heart races, out of sheer panic but partly due to the fact that my sense of guardianship and responsibility always feels more important as it's been bequeathed to me. There are too many people watching.

'I'm sorry. I wanted to show Cleo a rock I found,' Maya says matter-of-factly.

I cup her face and hold the girls close to me.

'She let her run off into the road, seriously? No wonder the school are letting her go.' The voice wafts in like a bad smell. *Don't.*

'Seriously, Carrie. Piss. Off.' My stress forces the words out of my mouth.

Cleo holds her hands up to her mouth to giggle. Miss Loveday's eyes are like saucers, not quite knowing where to look, where to go. A few mums in the vicinity stop talking, trying to hush their children so they can hear better.

'Excuse me, Grace? Are we seriously using language like that around the children?'

'It was my fault. I kept my eye off my daughter for a minute so if you want to start your witch-hunt then blame me.'

'It was my fault. I ran off when I wasn't supposed to,' Maya remarks, mortified to be the source of this fight. I look down at her. I can see the fire in her eyes.

'I don't know why you're blaming Miss Loveday. You're not a nice person, are you?' Maya says firmly.

Oh dear. Never mind me confronting this grown woman, my daughter's going to do that for me. Carrie stands there glaring at Maya. Don't give her that sort of look. I think your older son is in a bush over there having an actual whizz.

'That's not a kind thing to say. You should apologise to me,' she tells Maya.

'No, she shouldn't. Don't talk to my daughter like that.'

'Well, she's not really your daughter, is she?'

And for a moment, the world shuts itself down. I see red, like a bull, like real raw anger. I want to launch myself at her. I seriously want to beat her and I've not done that in my life, like, ever. Not even when my husband died or someone stole my phone in New

York or when Lucy used to lock our bedroom door and not let me in while she was trying on all my clothes. But I don't need to express that rage. Not at all. No no no no no no. Not when my own daughter charges at her teeth first like a crazed warthog. I see incisors sink into Carrie's hand. Oh. Mother of Crap.

'Owwww…' Carrie screams. I pull her back immediately.

'Maya, nooooo. You can't do that,' I say.

'Well, she did. Control that child.'

'Carrie, I think she's drawn blood,' says Liz, standing by her side, her eyes stern and unforgiving. Another mum rushes to grab tissues from her pocket muttering about jabs. Christ, she's not a dog. I'm just glad she's only got baby teeth. I grab Maya and she hides her face in my jacket.

'Maya… say sorry,' I say.

'No,' she mumbles into me, her voice muted and emotional. I get it completely. The way she's clamped onto me so tightly. The way her sister also stands there seething with anger. What Carrie said was awful. Maya's actions were done out of defence, ownership, honour. Don't ask me to double down.

'Well, I can see you're doing an excellent job raising them, Grace.'

Do you want to sink that knife in any deeper, Carrie? At present it feels like a sword slicing through my back, ripping down my spine. The collective glances of other parents are pinned to me.

'Stop now, Mrs Cantello,' Miss Loveday says, her voice warbling.

'I'm actually glad you're here to witness this, Miss Loveday, before I tell the head.'

'I didn't see anything actually?' the teacher says.

'Maya Callaghan bit her. That is assault,' Liz says.

'I saw a child defend herself.'

'Excuse me?' Carrie pretends to cradle her hand with a look like she might be deemed incapacitated for life. I mean, I can amputate that now for you if you want.

'What I will say is that I saw a parent provoke a child with verbal and discriminatory language. Someone who should know better as the chair of the PTA.'

And then just like that, laughter. The pleasing peals ring around the pavement mixed with the sound of one mum who stands there clapping. Clap away, love. Someone call the burns unit because this lady just got roasted by someone who I think just found her fire. Carrie and Liz stand there with their mouths agape, before storming off, ushering their children away. Oh, the WhatsApp group will be super angry now. Maya's face is still hidden but I can't quite tell if the shudders of her body are laughs or cries.

'Are you OK, Miss Callaghan?' Miss Loveday says. 'I'd better go and document this with the head now.'

Her face reads shock but you can also see there's relief there, that something has energised her. I nod and see her run off to the main school building. Carrie's words still sit in my heart like a thick, splintery stake. I bend to my knees and try to unwrap Maya from my torso as Cleo grips my arm, tightly.

'I'm sorry, Mummy. I'm so sorry. She can't say those sorts of things, she can't,' she says, her face damp and ruddy with tears. I wipe them away with my thumb.

'Will Mrs Cantello have to get a jab? Will Maya go to prison?' Cleo asks curiously. 'I saw this thing on the television once where a man ran someone over and they put him in prison and he got beaten up and had to poo in the same room as someone else in a metal toilet.'

Maya flings her hands around my neck. 'Cleo, no.' I widen my eyes at her. 'We might get told off, that's all. Don't worry. I'll fight anyone who tries to take you away from me.'

The girls huddle into me but there's a sense of disbelief that I'd be able to take anyone on in a fight. It's true. My arms are very spindly.

'You're a good mummy,' Maya whispers. 'What she said was complete bullshit.'

I pause for a second, grateful if a little shocked to hear that term.

'Can we use another word there? Maybe?'

'Crap?' she asks.

'No.' I can't deal with being a human lexicon now so simply hold them both tight. 'Let's just go home,' I say, thinking of the security of our four walls, away from the eyes of a thousand mothers piercing the back of my head.

'Is Aunty Meg at home?' Maya asks.

'Yeah,' I say, in whispers. Thank god for that. I may need someone to catch me and pour me a stiff drink after this.

'Good. She said we could make pizzas and I'm starving.'

I study her tiny face for a moment. 'Is that why you bit Mrs Cantello?' I ask.

'I bit her because she's a poo.'

'Again, we need a different word there. And we don't bite people. At least if you're going to bite something, it should be tasty. Not nasty and bitter,' I whisper.

A big grin radiates across her face. It's all I need to see. Is this parenting? I don't know. But she bit someone. For me, for us. If that isn't love, I don't know what is. *Come on you, let's go home and find Aunty Meg. Let's get you something proper to sink your teeth into.*

Chapter Nine

Dear Gracie,

I'm still in Vietnam and it's still frigging amazing. I wish you were here to see everything and meet all these people. Today, we went up to some smaller villages and Linh and Cam introduced me to a group of people building schools out here. It feels like really good work to be building something from the bricks up. The kids are so receptive, like sponges. One of them calls me David Beckham but Olivier jokes that's also the kid who's been treated for cataracts. It's just a simpler life. I wake up, I walk to the markets and I'm wooed by all these people selling fruit on fold-out tables. I have no idea what anything is so I buy one of everything and Linh gives me a masterclass when I go home. I want to show you rambutans. They're hairy like bollocks.

Olivier and Cam are getting married in the next month or so. Olivier has asked me to be best man. I've taken him under my wing like a brother as he seems to be short on family. He's so French. He smokes like a fucking chimney and we have arguments over football and queue etiquette. He's not good at queuing. I'll have to write a speech but I also think they're making me wear some sort of pastel linen shirt which is less good. I'll send photos.

Is it terrible that sometimes I see them together and I think of you? I know we're not quite together but I miss you. Did I mention you're in my lessons now? I've made flash cards with your face on. This is your friend, Grace. Grace is lost. She needs directions to the post office and she'd like you to help her buy stamps to send a parcel to Canada. All my kids and students adore you now. I adore you. That's one step up from love, I've decided. Write me back. Please. I need to hear your words and for you to scold me and tell me to wear insect repellent.

Good luck in all your exams.

T xx

I am pretty sure when Linh Nguyen was placed on a boat by her father, pregnant and on her own, he had hoped that she would go on to do amazing things in her life. She'd find a country that would look after her and keep her safe, give her an education and embrace her tightly. I'm not sure he would have imagined that forty years later she'd be sitting in the Membury service station looking up at a coffee menu and wondering why there are five different types of milk.

'You can milk oats?' she asks me.

'I guess.'

'But they don't have nipples.' She cackles at her own joke as the man behind the counters looks at her strangely. She has a point. 'I guess... a black coffee?' she adds. 'I've been told no sugar. Make it strong. Your coffees in this country lack kick.'

I laugh, taken back to a time when Linh first took me for a Vietnamese coffee served in a glass cup laced with condensed milk. It grew hairs on my chest, I swear I could feel them busting through my skin.

'Latte for me, hun,' Meg says and she ushers Linh over to a table in this dull if overlit services where the fragrance of floor cleaner and old burgers hangs sweet in the air. Meg accompanied me on the airport run and we've made the brief stop to refresh and caffeinate. She's never met Linh before and I think she probably had preconceptions of who we were picking up: some frail older lady in floral pyjamas who doesn't speak English and was raised on a rice paddy, but that stereotype couldn't be further from the truth. It means Meg hangs on her every word, intrigued by this woman who's shown up in a velour tracksuit and bum bag, her salt and pepper hair in a neat bob, the one her granddaughters still share.

That's not to say Linh isn't fascinated by Meg too. She's always loved tales of my own huge family. When she left Vietnam, she found herself seeking refuge in London. She lost contact with her parents, her siblings and, soon, the only family she had was a daughter, born in Queen Charlotte's Hospital. She called her Cam and they lived in West London's Shepherd's Bush, which was a mystery to her as there were no sheep. No bush either.

'Coffees all round,' I say, joining them at the table. Linh grins broadly, all her teeth on show to have the steaming mug handed over. She does what Linh does; she takes out a tissue and wipes down the spoon and the table space in front of her. The ex-nurse in her values cleanliness.

'This will do for now,' Linh says, grabbing onto my hand as Meg watches. She knows what this lady did for me, how she saved me, how she cared for me in a way the sisters couldn't, so the look reads gratitude, awe. It's a good hand, always impeccably moisturised, but Linh always clasps it and shakes it around like we're doing a dance.

'I was drinking my coffee on the flight. That sort of weak fluid that feels like it's been brewed with soil and the man next to me suddenly gets nail clippers out and starts cutting his own toenails, right next to me. They flicked everywhere.'

Meg erupts with laughter.

'He did what?' I ask. 'Did you ask him to stop?'

'My darling, I didn't want a fuss. I had to sit next to him for another four hours. So I kept the clippings that fell my way and put them in his tea on the next drinks service.'

Meg continues to giggle in disbelief. Linh is like this – she has a wonderfully mischievous streak and an energy and kindness in her eyes which make her impossible not to love.

'So Grace tells me you want to go down to Brighton on this trip?' Meg asks.

'Yes, I have a friend who lives there now and owns a cafe. I'd like to see her and the pier. Maybe we can take the girls.'

'That can be arranged,' I say.

'You still have friends here?' Meg asks her, her elbows on the table to take in the detail like a bedtime tale. There is a wonderful sense of storytelling with Linh and this draws me back to nights around her kitchen table, sitting on a lime-green plastic stool as she fed me beer and stories well into the late hours of the balmy nights I spent in Vietnam.

'A few dotted around. I went to nursing college in London, I still have friends who work in your NHS. I was here for nearly twenty years.'

'Wow. And so what made you return to Vietnam?'

'Cam. She was wildly introspective about who she was and where she came from. She wanted to track down her father's family but she was also a teacher, a nurturer, and she wanted to do that in a place she could connect with. I came along for the ride. Her willingness to help people was infectious.'

'She sounds like a wonderful girl,' Meg says.

'She was. She reconnected me to a home I thought I'd lost. I was so lucky to have her help me find my roots again. I was lucky to have her, full stop.'

This is what always gets me. To have lost a husband is heart-breaking but to have lost a child, to have not seen her full potential unleashed on the world, even more so. But Linh deals with it all with such serenity and dignity, and the grief she feels is warming, never sad or despairing. The emotion hits Meg hard and she looks away for a moment. Linh senses this and turns to her.

'So you are the eldest?' Linh asks her.

'I am.'

'Meg, is it short for another? Like Megan? Margaret?'

I choke a little on my cappuccino. I think Meg may have murdered our mother as a toddler if she'd named her Margaret.

'No, I think my mum had literary aspirations. I'm told I was named after Meg March from *Little Women*, so was Beth. Lucy was Narnia and Emma was Austen.'

Linh looks to me, confused. 'Grace was different,' Meg continues. 'She bucked the trend. She was premature and we weren't sure if she was going to survive so she became our amazing grace.'

Linh seems happy with that. I always thought it a little corny, especially when Lucy sings it to me. Drunk. On the Tube. Like a deer caught in a trap.

'I've seen your husband,' Linh says to Meg. 'He doesn't have a lot of hair.'

That's another thing you get with Linh, a brave sense of honesty.

'It's going that way,' Meg says, slightly embarrassed.

'Baldness is a sign of virility. I like a bald head on a man. You can rub it for luck like Buddha.'

Meg flares her nostrils to hear her Danny compared to a bald, overweight deity. 'I'll try that.'

'So Emma is the doctor with the bastard husband who now has the Indian boyfriend with the nice skin.'

'Yes,' I confirm.

'And I've met Beth and your parents.'

It was lunch at my parents' house. Mum didn't know what to cook. I told her chicken. She served it with boil in the bag rice. The crux of the meeting was to welcome Linh into our family in the same way Joyce is an honorary aunt but I also knew Mum was curious to meet the woman who gave up two granddaughters. In her mind, she didn't believe it was possible, to let two girls go, but after that meal she understood the sacrifice, the security Linh wanted to give those girls for the future. This floored our mother completely. Linh didn't want to abandon her daughter's work in Vietnam but she didn't want these girls to be alone if she wasn't there. Linh loved meeting everyone but the rice was a huge disappointment, so much so she made me drive her to a large oriental hypermarket in Wembley and buy my mother a rice cooker.

'I just have to meet this Lucy girl now.'

'She's not met Lucy?' asks Meg.

'No. There needs to be the right time to release Lucy upon people.'

Meg nods in agreement. Linh looks over at me and studies my face. She does this a lot, searching for signs of my good health, but it's always like she's scanning my edges, as if she can see something I can't.

'Your face looks different. Are you having sex?' she asks.

'Linh!' I say. We're in a service station. There's a man in a hi-vis jacket next to us tucking into a full English breakfast with an unhealthy amount of baked beans on his plate. I'm glad I won't be in an enclosed space with him later on.

'Your skin looks good,' she mentions.

'Maybe I've changed moisturiser?'

Meg can't seem to hide her delight. 'She is. She's having sex with a man called Sam. He's a dad at the school gate.'

I shake my head at my sister. This is not meant to be public information. This is also my daughters' grandmother. I don't want her to think badly of me or that I'm promiscuous or having sex to fill a gap, which is exactly what it is. I need to think how to reword that properly.

'And how is Sam?' she asks.

'He's well?' I reply, knowing full well she's curious because this man may be a future father figure to her grandchildren.

'No, you dingbat. Like, how is he?' she says, giggling.

'I don't want to talk about—'

'Strong 7,' Meg interrupts.

Linh looks disappointed for me.

'Meg, I—'

'But in other ways. How is he? Is he a nice man? Is he nice to you?' Linh asks.

'He's…' I don't know what to say. 'Nice' is such a horrific way to describe someone. 'Nice' is a word to describe an attractive garden or a pleasant cup of tea. 'Nice' makes him sound smarmy or average.

'He works in IT, he's recently divorced with two kids of his own and he drives a Honda Accord,' Meg reels off, excitedly.

I shift a look to my sister in disbelief. I know some of that information will have been procured from her and the sisters' deep social media analyses.

'Is he bald?' asks Linh.

'He has hair. He's just—'

Before I have a chance to speak, Meg gets out her phone and shows Linh a picture. I hope it's a decent one where there's at least good lighting. Linh reaches into her bum bag to retrieve her reading glasses.

'He has a good neck,' she says. I guess a good neck is better than a bad neck or no neck at all, which would mean he'd just be chin and shoulders.

'He's a great guy. He's just—'

'Not Tom,' Linh finishes my sentence and grasps my hand that much tighter. She still gets it.

'He's very nice to me. But he's not ready, neither am I. The girls and I are happy as a threesome. It works.'

Linh for a moment seems baffled. 'But it's not the three of you, really?'

Meg nods, shrugging. The older lady has a point.

'I mean… I just don't want to replace Tom.'

Linh studies my eyes for a moment, calmly. It's a look which always prefaces a moment of wisdom.

'Gracie,' she says, softly. 'We lost Cam, her dear Olivier and our wonderful Tom. We will never replace them. That light has gone out. We shouldn't replace them. But never think people can't come in, that we've lost some capacity to love. We're still alive, it does our loved ones no justice to be sitting here in darkness.'

And there it is. This is why I welcomed Linh into my world. Beautiful turns of phrase like that soothed my tired and confused soul; they still do. And she's right. We lost three amazing people but, through their loss, our lives all became entwined. Our girls are certainly propped up by a whole network of individuals who love them and hold them tight. It's why Linh doesn't worry about them. Meg sits there speechless. I never speak so openly of my grief, or at least not in such eloquent terms.

'Sam's just divorced his wife. I don't think he's in a particularly good head space, which is why I'm reluctant to get too involved with him.'

'That makes more sense,' Linh adds. 'But you're at least enjoying him?'

'Thank you for putting it in politer terms than my sisters.'

Meg shifts me a look. *Don't say cock in front of your nieces'
grandmother*, I silently communicate to her.

'Well, let's see where it goes. Maybe he'll discover all your charms
and wonder and it may be the start of something wonderful.'

'Perhaps,' I say hesitantly.

'Can I meet him?'

'Maybe.'

She grins cheekily at my hesitance. She and Meg will find a way
to make this work.

'I was also told this memorial was a celebration so I expect good
things on this trip too. I want to meet more of your people. And
I love you, Gracie, but we always go to the same park with the
swings and I've seen that park many times now. Somewhere new,
please. I'm on holiday.'

Meg laughs. She knows I have my comfort zone, and she
applauds anyone who wants to drag me out of it.

'I take you to good places,' I tell Linh.

She looks around the barren, uninspiring surrounds of the
Membury services. Linh, there's a condiments counter over there
and a small Waitrose.

'You take me to Tesco. Not that I'm grumbling, I love shopping
in there. I have a list too. I want to buy Cup a Soup.'

'Really?' Meg asks.

'Yes. It's both convenient and tasty. I researched places this time
round. What is the Clifton Sausage?'

'It's a restaurant.'

'Yeah, take me there. I like sausage.'

'Careful how you phrase that, Linh,' I warn her.

Meg laughs, glancing over at me. *You never told me about this one, Gracie.*

'Come, we'd better make a move. The girls are dying to see you.'

Linh's face lights up and she knocks back the rest of her coffee.

'Yes. Oh, and before I left, Maya was telling me a story about a woman at school. She bit her? Is this true?'

Meg's face sours. She knows I only like to report the good bits to Linh. To have been given custodianship over these girls always feels like I should keep all the bad news to myself.

'It is. I'm sorry. It's a bit of a thing at school. The lady that Maya bit caused a fuss. She's since informed that I should resign from the PTA. Another mum was cruel and said she needed a jab. The inference being Maya is rabid but she's not, obviously.'

My face rises to a blush. Carrie has not been kind and I've not dealt with it well. Words were said and they've stuck to me like thick gluey mud. I await Linh's judgement on the matter.

'Maya told me the woman said you were a bad mother?'

Meg flares her nostrils. It was all I could do to stop her stalking Carrie on social media, going to her house and crapping on her doorstep. I don't reply.

'Then, in my opinion, Maya should have bit harder.'

My sister actually claps in the middle of the services. A person restacking the forks turns to look at us. Yeah, that wasn't for you but stellar job you're doing there.

'That's an insult to me, completely. I didn't just choose anyone to mother those girls. I chose the best person. Am I allowed to come to the gate and meet this woman?' Linh asks.

I shake my head. She responds by sticking her tongue out at me. I always love her being here. I love how she wears white lace-up plimsolls with her tracksuit and the delicate crepe-like skin stretched across her knuckles. I especially love how she's so plugged in to the world; the way she wants a throwdown now with Carrie Cantello, how she grimaces at the man troughing down breakfast next to us but also has her ear tuned into the conversation of the couple on the next table. She's been through the very worst and best of life and she's still standing, still fighting; she's always trying to find some level of human connection and exist meaningfully. And if it wasn't for Tom, we wouldn't be here – together, a fixture in each other's lives.

'Is that a WHSmith?' she asks me.

'It is,' Meg says.

'I remember that place. I'm going to the bathroom. Could you be a dear and buy me some Dairy Milk?' she asks my sister.

'Of course,' Meg replies. 'With fruit, nuts?'

'All of them, my dear. I'm on holiday remember. Also an *OK!* magazine and salt and vinegar crisps if they have them,' she says. 'And another coffee please, Grace. I need something as strong as… what's that phrase you sisters use? I like it.'

'Strong as tits?'

Meg erupts with laughter.

'Strong as tits and this time with milk. Something that's come out of a cow please.'

Chapter Ten

Dear Tom,

I hate it when you write letters like that to me. You make it sound boring, like I've stayed behind to do exams and use insect repellent because I'm dull. Don't wear insect repellent then. Get malaria or dengue fever. You'll need the good drugs for both. I asked Emma, one of them is haemorrhagic, and that to me just conjures up images of your eyeballs bleeding. I know for a fact that your travel insurance won't cover that. Make sure you wash all your fruit too, well, and be careful when you drink water. I had a friend who went to Manila and drank a drink from a roadside vendor and she got cholera. You think these things don't exist but they do. They even called a priest to her bedside because she vomited with such velocity they thought she was possessed.

Also, what pictures of me are you using for your flash cards? You're using bad ones, aren't you? Where I'm gurning or drunk or not wearing a bra. I never know what to write in these letters, Tom, as I feel like some sensible conscience the other side of the world telling you to look after yourself. You put so much into the world but I sometimes think you fail to take care of yourself. I

worry you imbue too much trust in others and make sure you
also trim your toenails because you were never good at that and
now, given that all you wear are flip-flops, I sense your nails
will start to gnarl over.

Life ticks along here. I rewatched The West Wing *the other*
day. I also passed all my exams. I miss you. Send Olivier and
Cam my love. She's so beautiful. Don't just make it a best man
speech full of jokes that you've copied off the internet and don't
be lazy and write something which is actually lyrics of a Snow
Patrol song. You are better than that.

G xx

The memorial is in a month's time and people are starting to filter
in and out of my life. Lines are blurring and my once ordered
existence is now filled to the brim with decorations and me signing
off chair configurations and menus and having to listen to brass
band versions of a song known as 'Tom's Theme'. It's very heavy
on the flute, which I think Tom would have liked because he could
have made multiple jokes about 'that time in band camp'. Linh
is still battling jet lag so is fast asleep. Having her here has made
the girls' year and I particularly love the culinary treats that come
with her, the fragrant noodle dishes, the ways she can transform a
chicken breast without drying it out, the fearlessness with which
she can cook seafood. A head pops round the door.

'Girls are asleep.' Meg scampers in and puts her hands on my
shoulders, kissing the top of my head.

'Thanks for sitting in on this. Do I look all right? Maybe I should wear all black?'

'So you look more widow-y? No. You look great. You make this sound like an interview, it really isn't. If anything, you should be quizzing her. You could wear your Huggly,' she says, rearranging my hair. I didn't realise that was an option.

Tonight, I'm having a Zoom meeting with Delphine Le Marre. If that name sounds posh, well, she is. She's a literary agent based in London and after several emails from both her and Joyce about this book they're hoping I write, I agreed to at least hear them talk about it. Their excitement is rooted in the fact there definitely will be a film made about Joyce's book. Rights have been optioned, meetings have been had. I need to ask if they've got Jason Momoa. Tom will be upset if you get anyone else. What about me? If I get a say, I'm going to tell them to go down the Meryl route. Meryl would give me some proper gravitas. That would have Oscar written all over it.

However, they also hang onto the idea of my story being weaved through the narrative. The problem is I've read through all our letters and postcards and, while our story is no doubt imbued with sadness, it doesn't cast either of us in the best light. Early Tom letters treated my heart and person badly. They were selfish and cast me aside. My later letters were dull. There's one when I took two paragraphs to speak to him about mortgage rates and my relief that I'd managed to save a deposit by putting my savings into a high-yield interest account. If you were reading that book, later Tom would become the hero, playing football with kids in the dirt and building them schools while I sat like queen geek at home trying to bag myself the best gas and electricity deals. To know how this would be of interest to anyone is confusing to me.

'Gracie!' Joyce's face is the first to appear on the screen. She sits in her front room, which is a wild menagerie of ornaments and books piled high. Meg dodges out of view. 'Lovely, how are you? I'm so glad you agreed to do this.'

'I'm good.'

Joyce's internet connection is scrappy so she jolts in and out of view. 'So memorial stuff, I've done what I can from here. I'm sorry that a lot of that got given to you. Did you get the new T-shirts?'

She got more tees printed with Tom's face on. If this event is anything to go by then at least we won't forget what he looked like.

'I did. And don't worry. Linh is here, Meg's been staying with me too, so we're sorted. All hands on deck.'

Delphine's face suddenly appears and splits the screen into three. I had an image of what an agent might look like and I was right – she's willowy with pronounced cheekbones, a streak of white in her dark hair like a badger. That was the wrong animal to imagine. Now all I can think about are badgers. Her accessories are bright and primary-coloured.

'JOYCE! LOVE!' You get the sense that if she could double air kiss the screen then she would.

'Delphine, good to see you. Can I introduce my wonderful daughter-in-law to you? This is Grace Callaghan.'

I hold my hand up in the air. Yep, that's me. Delphine studies the screen like she's giving me the once-over.

'Why, hello! Well, I'm sure Joyce has told you about me. I am Delphine. A pleasure.'

'Indeed,' I reply, trying to act posher than I am.

'So, I guess I should try and sell myself. I run a very small agency in London but I'm good at what I do. I've just sold Joyce's rights in Italy, which is super exciting, and, seriously, I am entranced by your story, what happened to you, to Tom. I think people would want to hear that story.'

I smile. They would? I guess we all like hearing about a bit of tragedy to make our own lives seem better in comparison.

'And god, you're young. Of course you're young. And a beauty! Joyce, you didn't tell me she was beautiful.'

Joyce smiles.

'Umm, thank you?'

Off screen, Meg stands beside my computer screen and puts her thumb up in the air. She told me to put on powder and that obviously has had an effect. I look at the screen and realise I should have gone for another view behind me, though. All Delphine can see is my bed and I am suddenly obsessed by the dust bunnies I can see under it, the bedsheet not quite pulled over the mattress.

'My love, I am so glad we got a chance to talk to you.'

'No, thank you. And for all the emails outlining everything. You've obviously gone to some lengths to think about Tom's story and how we could raise some more money for charity. He'd love this.'

'Of course, I mean after the runaway success of Joyce's book, it was a no-brainer. And Joyce has told me all the ins and outs of your love story. Will they? Won't they? Years of heartache and distance. It just has so much potential. That's got epic romcom written all over it.'

I smile but the words fly over my head. Being a work-from-homer, I am queen of the Zoom call and, naturally, these sorts of meetings become a necessity, though I like the joy in not having to exert too much energy in them. You don't have to be too conscious about maintaining eye contact and I can wear my yoga pants and not worry. It's also means I've become preoccupied with people's living spaces. Those are some bookshelf goals, Delphine. Those are not MDF. There is also a bronze sculpture of some pendulous, wonky boobs that I bet are hers. The nipples stare at me like eyes.

'Joyce said you wrote letters to each other?'

I mentally come back into my own room and re-engage in the conversation.

'Well, yes. We corresponded, whether it was by letter or email.' She claps like a seal.

'Then I love this. It's what's missing from the romance market: these relationships of real substance. It's a modern yet old-fashioned romance for our times. I'm sick of reading treatments of romcoms where people meet in coffee shops and on Tinder.'

I am not sure how to reply. If we were to scan through all our emails, there's one where I swear at Tom in all the colours of the rainbow. That was the one where he was mid-Aussie adventure and dumped me in one line:

I think it's best we go our separate ways.

Well, off you fuck, you selfish, selfish wanker.

That has *Wuthering Heights* angst written all over it.

'I'm just unsure how honest you want me to be in all of this,' I say. 'When Tom was travelling, it wasn't always pretty. We broke up many times and the letters aren't very well written.'

'Oh, we can embellish. Leave that to me. I loved how you wrote letters too, that's so old school.'

'It was mainly because he was without a phone. He wanted a technological detox so he'd write letters, and emails if he could find internet cafes. He once Skyped me from an internet cafe in Fukuoka, Japan, and then realised it was a sex cafe and all the other occupants were watching porn.'

Delphine throws her head back in laughter. Joyce is shaking her head, as that's the sort of trouble that Tom was renowned for.

'So tell me, after all those years of ups and downs, how did you two finally get together? Really...'

Joyce smiles in the corner of my screen. She knows the story all too well. However, Meg senses my unease and crouches down next to me to grip my knee.

'We met in Amsterdam. We were visiting mates.'

I pause. I've always blamed all those picturesque bridges that frame the setting, Rembrandt, the bicycles. Bicycles really do heighten the romance of a situation. We were there out of sheer coincidence visiting mutual friends. It was after an epic night out and we had all the alcohol in our systems so Tom and I walked around the city. I trotted around those cobbled streets in two-inch heels and I didn't care because I was with him. He told me stories and six hours felt like ten minutes in his company. We even walked past windows of naked women masturbating on bar stools and he didn't flinch once.

'That was when you realised you belonged together?' Delphine asks me.

I nod. She probably thinks the night ended with us slow-dancing in the middle of the street while a man offered us bunches of tulips. In fact there was a man. He tried to sell us weed. Tom bought some and we shared a spliff on some steps outside a church-like building. We kissed after three long years apart. A look was all that was needed to let me know how much he loved me. We had sex in our friends' house, in the toilet for privacy, and it wasn't particularly pretty but how we laughed when his arse turned on the cold water tap. Why was their downstairs bathroom the size of an airplane cubicle? After that, we were inseparable. And that feeling re-emerges of how intolerable it is that the universe would choose to separate us. Meg grasps my knee that little bit tighter.

'And after that we came back to the UK, we got married and lived in Bristol.'

The call is quiet for a moment.

'You know… our story is quite a personal one. It wasn't straightforward. I was thinking a better story may be about his work he did. He travelled extensively, always volunteering and teaching. It was all steeped in something very genuine.'

Joyce puts a hand to her chest. I'm not sure if it's because she knows that was true of her boy or because she knows I just can't talk about him like that, like a fairy tale, like a story, because it, us, him – it all happened. It was all very true. There was no happy ending.

'Possibly. I just like your angle. I like all of that pieced together. I also liked how you travelled the world after he died. It's so *Eat Pray Love* but younger, trendier.'

'With less meditation perhaps, more wine.'

She laughs heartily. 'And just like that, you've come up with a tag line. But I think people will really connect with your grand finale. You came back with your daughters that you met because of him.

People will adore the kismet, how you were bonded by your grief, like a guardian angel.'

To emphasise that point, she does swooping arms like I indeed did fly in. However, she makes Cleo and Maya sound like souvenirs I picked up on the way back.

'I'd rather they were left out of this. We saved each other. This is Tom's story.'

'Oh, it is – definitely. Did you remarry?'

Meg glares at the screen now from her lowered position. Joyce, I can tell, sits in her corner of the screen blushing.

'I didn't.'

'Then people will love that more. You're still bonded in love, even after death.'

I hold my hand up to the screen.

'I just… my girls are the priority now. I'm a mum. It's not that I… I just…'

'I've even thought of a title, *Tell My Grace I Love Her Very Much*. Like from the song, "Space Oddity". A real tearjerker. I think this would sell in the millions.'

Joyce sits there and studies my face. I can read the apology, the fact I've been cornered and told to confess snippets of a story so personal yet painful to me. I don't care for millions. It would be a lovely nod to charity but I'd run five hundred marathons and swim ten thousand lengths if it meant I didn't have to bring up how sad our story makes me feel. If I read that book, all I'd be thinking about is those years when we should have been together. I'd be throwing that book at the wall and writing it a shit Amazon review.

'Well, I'll certainly think about it. Thank you, Delphine.'

Delphine looks a bit shocked that she hasn't been able to seal the deal in a single conversation. Look at all these books I own. I am books. I could give you the world. You could be a film. Name someone to play you, anyone. I have them on speed dial. Do you have Meryl?

'Is there anything I can do to persuade you? Have you pitched this to other agents?'

Joyce intervenes. 'Oh no, it's not like that at all, but Grace and I are very different. How we've chosen to respect Tom's story, how we've grieved. Whatever Grace decides is very much up to her. I'd like us to respect that.'

'Oh, of course. I didn't mean to tread. Please promise me you'll think about it. Like I say, people seek out stories like this. Real love stories. We've all fallen in love with Tom after Joyce's book so we'd like to know every side of him.'

'I will think about it.'

She nods slowly. 'Joyce, I have another call but always a pleasure, and Grace, it really was lovely to meet you.'

'You too, Delphine.'

'Bye, bye, bye,' she says, waving with two hands.

Her screen goes blank. Joyce and I sit here in silence for a moment as Meg comes in to hug me. The sisters – well, everyone I know – hears about my love story with Tom in snippets, like puzzle pieces that I expect them to slot together for the full picture.

'Meg, I am so glad you're there,' says Joyce. 'Hug that girl hard please. I'm so sorry, Gracie. She is so full-on. I should have thought that she might not have much tact.'

I put a hand up. 'Please don't apologise. There were far worse moments she could have asked me about.'

Joyce and I stare at each other. We were both at the hospice when Tom passed. Joyce wrote about it beautifully, a moment of resignation when she felt his soul leave his physical body. I would never be able to write about that because, at the core of everything, I felt anger. I think I still do. Fucking cancer.

'It's just an idea for now. She wanted to pitch it and she's done that now but I'll totally get it if it's not for you.'

'And if Grace chooses not to write it?' asks Meg.

'Delphine wants to milk the success of my book. Very likely she'll find another story. She asked about Ellie?'

Meg's face curls into a sneer. 'The Australian girlfriend?'

'Or we were thinking of writing a book about my marathon running. *One Step at a Time*. She's obsessed with her titles.'

'So basically, she just wants to profiteer off a man's death?' my sister says.

'Meg, don't – it also does good, the profits go to charity,' I intervene. 'Joyce, please – no harm done at all here but understand if I need to do things differently. Are you OK?'

It's not my intention for her to feel bad. There is no wrong or right way to grieve Tom and she did what gave her peace. I get that completely.

'You know I am. Meg, look after our girl. I'll catch up with you in the week and let you know when I'll be down, yes?'

I smile and nod as she logs off. I turn to Meg. Her big sister protective shield is on full beam.

I grip her shoulders tightly. 'That wasn't her fault,' I tell her.

'I'm just trying to put things plainly for both of you,' Meg says. 'I know how these sorts of publishing deals work. Agents and the like, it's all pretty cut-throat and not always particularly pleasant.'

'You do? How?'

She gets up to pace the room, sitting on the edge of my bed to search for her reply. 'Through all my magazine work… I know people who've published books. I know some people who've even tried to do it anonymously and you still get entrenched in that circus. Contracts and rights and agents. I'll respect your wishes, whatever you want to do with this, but I just want to be a good big sister here. I don't want you to go through anything that will hurt you.'

I go over to the bed and extend my arms around her. Meg. The best of eggs. *I'll respect your wishes, whatever you want.* I said those exact words to Tom once. When I was up all night, emailing people in California trying to research experimental drug trials and crying at how completely useless I felt, he was so calm. *I don't want to put my body through that. I don't want to waste what time I have left jetting to California. Unless we can go to Universal Studios, climb the Hollywood sign and meet Arnold Schwarzenegger. We're not doing that, Tom. Yeah, we are. I'm the one dying. I get to call the shots. You're kind of contracted to respect my wishes. It's a marriage thing.*

'Tom wanted me to travel, to move on. It's why I went in the first place after he died. Every day I move away from him, these little tiny steps. It's like they want me to retrace them. I don't want to, Meg.'

'Then we don't. Thanks but no thanks. It's your shout.'

'The charity thing, though?'

'You can raise money in a multitude of ways. Remember when we were little? We did a skipathon once. Dad gave us a tenner for our efforts,' she says.

We all had matching legwarmers and home-cut fringes. I could cope with that. I lie down, putting my head on Meg's lap, trying to level out my very extremes of emotion. I did this a lot with Meg when we were younger. Our own mother had a tiger fire in her that burned so strong that Meg was the second maternal figure we all latched onto at times. I never knew if she wanted that mantle but it means there's a sense of safety around her; she's the hug I'll always need. She leaves tomorrow evening to return to her brood but will be back soon. That won't be soon enough, though. To have had this time, alone and to be together, has been everything.

'Delphine is a silly name, anyway. It's the name you'd give a posh dolphin.'

'What name would you give a common dolphin then?'

'Dave. They could get married and have dolphin babies all with names beginning with D. Derek, Des, Diana.'

I laugh as Meg puts an arm around me, stroking my hair. I sense she picks something out of there that I hope isn't a nit.

'Now that's a book I'd read.'

Chapter Eleven

Tom, I got a job today. A real proper job with the financial branch of an international law firm based in Southwark, I literally just got the call. They're a huge outfit and the perks of the job are amazing: gym, medical, even free bloody breakfasts. Is it strange that you were one of the first people I needed to tell? I haven't even told my mum, none of the sisters. Maybe it was just to prove to you that there was a reason I stayed behind to study and work, a reason we broke up. I now have a chance to build something in London that's very real and secure and it's exciting. I know that won't excite you as much but I needed to tell you. I think sometimes you think I'm just swimming along here, doing nothing exciting or real, but it all leads to something, somewhere.

Gx

There is some semblance of a routine that I like to keep in my life and that is my morning swim. I like the routine, the clarity of the water, I enjoy pushing off from the sides and pretending I'm taking part in a hundred-metre breaststroke dash for a Commonwealth

Gold. It's not a fancy endeavour, it's a simple pay-as-you-go affair at the local university. I swim next to students and older lecturers, and, in the pool next to us, mothers dunk their babies in and out, singing songs about ducks. We all shower together afterwards and I never fail to marvel at that one woman who strips completely naked and has the time to condition her hair separately.

Today is slightly different, though. Meg leaves tonight so has booked me into the lido instead as a farewell treat. I love this lido though have never been posh enough to be a patron. It reminds me of the ones in London with the small wooden huts for changing, a throwback to a time when people would swim in striped bathers and wear boater hats. The outdoors element takes bravery in the winter but on an early spring day like this, the sunlight dancing on the turquoise water has its appeal. Plus, we get robes, which to me is the height of luxury. Anyway, while I swim, Meg and Linh will descend on the poolside restaurant for a spot of posh brunch and to hold my towel. I see them now at a table and they give me a wave as I approach a hut to get ready. They have mimosas, don't they? Jammy cows. I push at a door and realise someone is in there.

'Oh, I'm sorry.' The person turns swiftly and eyeballs me as the door seems to have hit them in the arse. Oh. Seriously? It's Orlagh. Sam's Orlagh. This is not pleasant. Do I say something? I'm shagging your ex-husband? Given you saw us out together then you might have an inkling that's happening anyway. She looks me up and down. She's wearing full make-up to swim, isn't she? Her swimsuit is designer with navy and white nautical stripes; mine is Speedo. Our priorities are just in different boxes.

'I didn't know you swam here?' she says.

The comment has territorial tones. 'I'm just here for the day.'

'Oh. Well, I swim here most days.'

'Great. Enjoy.'

I'm not really sure what she expects. I'll stay out of her lane. She knows, doesn't she? And I get the feeling she's not particularly happy about it. This is frosty, which makes me glad for the heated pool. I slink into a vacant cubicle and pull my phone out of my rucksack.

How's breakfast? Look out into the pool, can you see a woman in a stripey swimsuit? I text Meg.

Linh is not sure avocado is a breakfast food but it's all good. Tres posh. Aye to the lady in the swimsuit, do we know her?

I'm sleeping with her ex-husband.

Oh.

Is this weird?

No. Just keep out of her way. If she tries to drown you then I'll throw you a life ring.

Nice.

I put my phone away and retrieve my hat from my bag, stretching it out over my head and tucking the errant hairs away. Maybe I should text Sam? But why? Just because we've slept with the same man, it doesn't mean we can't swim in the same pool. I sneak my head out the door. Orlagh's doing a very elegant backstroke arm. Her eyes give me a quick glance and she carries on. I go to the other end of the pool and creep my body in slowly. Twenty laps and I can go have a fancy coffee.

It's a very quiet morning at the pool except for another man with tight trunks and a furry chest. I push off the edge, doing my classic breaststroke, head bobbing in and out of the water, but suddenly notice Orlagh's presence next to me. Where did she come from? She's appeared out of nowhere like a seal. Why does she keep looking over? Oh. She wants to race? Really? I pick up the pace reluctantly. I'm not sure how this must look but it's basically two mums racing, neither of them professional swimmers so it must be like tracking a couple of polar bears treading water. I very well might give myself a stitch from the overexertion. Then suddenly, a leg out of nowhere kicks me on the hip. I go under the water for a second, not realising how close she'd been to me. I gather myself and grab at the side in front of me where she stands. Whatever gets you through the day, Orlagh.

'Sorry, did we make contact?' she says. I note the condescension in her tone.

'Yeah, we did.'

'After you?' she offers, putting out her hand to tell me to keep swimming.

So you can kick me again? 'I'm all right.' I sidestep to create some distance between us but she shifts closer to me.

'There's three of us in the pool. Maybe if you could move further to your right?' I suggest.

'But then I'll get in the way of Bob,' she says, nodding over to furry chest. I like how they're on a first-name basis.

'I don't seem to have your pace. If you swim, I'm pretty sure I won't be able to catch up with you.'

It pays to let her win this contest rather than this strange swimming gala situation where I'm going to have to increase my work rate and possibly bust a lung. She puts her goggles on and side-eyes me before setting off, spraying my face with water. I look over at Meg, who makes a gesture that I should slap her.

'I've not seen you here before?' a voice suddenly pipes in.

Oh, it's Bob. I don't come here to talk. I come to swim.

'I'm just here for the day. It's very nice here.'

'It's lovely. But I just come here for the view really,' he says, winking at me.

Christ, Bob. No. There are laws against that. Keep your eyes to yourself. I am now debating which is the lesser of two evils here, swimming away from lecherous Bob or closer to Orlagh. I smile politely and set off, doing a slow breaststroke to the other side. Orlagh's standing there waiting. Bob is in pursuit, possibly checking out my arse. Sod swimming. I long for the embrace of my overly chlorinated usual pool where the lifeguards look about twelve and the most drama I have is seeing a plaster float past me. When I get to the other side, I feel Orlagh's arm graze against mine. I stand up immediately.

'A sorry wouldn't go amiss,' she says, huffing.

'You were right there, you could see me coming. Why didn't you move?' I reply.

Orlagh immediately looks quite miffed. 'I don't know what pool you usually swim at but there's an etiquette?'

'Etiquette? Why, do you own the pool?'

You don't own the pool, not any more. Legally, you handed over all those rights.

'No, but there's a consideration one should take when coming to swim in someone else's pool,' she says, pointedly.

'So it's all right for you to swim in other pools but not other people? I think that's called double standards. I'm not doing anything wrong.'

I realise I've stretched the analogy now. She stands there quietly fuming. I hear a chair slowly scraping across the floor by the restaurant and assume it's Meg. The thing is, I'm not doing anything wrong. Sam is a free agent. This pool also allows for non-members so you keep in your lane, I'll keep in mine and we will keep swimming. Bob has caught up with us now and stands in between us. By the way she twitches, I have a feeling he brushes up against Orlagh as he does so.

'Oh, sorry there, Orlagh. I've just met your friend. Are you two girls friends?' he asks.

Orlagh shakes her head. 'She's not a member, Bob. Just a visitor.'

'I don't know. It is lovely here, maybe I'll sign up on a more permanent basis,' I say. I won't. I can't afford this.

'Well, the more the merrier. I'm not averse to seeing more lovely girls like yourself at the pool.' Bob may be another reason why I won't sign up.

'She won't be if she knows what's good for her,' Orlagh blurts out.

'Girlies…'

'I am sorry, Bob. I know we've just met but I stopped being a girly at about ten years of age. My name is Grace.'

He doesn't know whether to glide away or stay and watch this fight. Meg has got Linh involved now and both have turned in my direction and are supping at their glasses.

'You left him. You were the one who ended your marriage. However Sam chooses to move on is completely up to him. You know that, right?'

'He could have hooked up with anyone in Bristol. It's a city of thousands of people and he chooses someone at the school gate.'

'You left him for someone ten years younger than yourself. Did you ever think how much that embarrassed or hurt him?'

'That is none of your business. Sam is the father of my children… I have every right to know who's in my children's lives.'

'Your children don't know. My children don't even know.'

'Is this what you do? Just go round stealing other people's families because you can't have your own children?' she asks.

My mouth is wide open like a cod, which is fitting as I'm currently in water. 'You think I'm trying to steal your kids? What makes you think I can't have my own children?'

'Then why adopt?'

'How is that any of your business?'

'All my business if you're trying to steal my ex-husband to father your children too.'

I don't know what I'm supposed to do next. Does she want me to get tampons out of my bag to prove that I can menstruate, that I'm a woman with reproductive potential, that adoption was a choice? Does she want to know the story of my amazing little girls?

'Face it, you're just his dirty little secret. The only person he can get with at the moment is some dried-up widow.'

At this point, Bob makes a face in shock. 'Seriously, Orlagh, I don't think this is the time or place?' he says.

'Oh, piss off, Bob!' she yells.

I don't know what my default setting is at the moment. There are many retorts in my locker. I want to pull out your extensions and stick your head under the water. Dried-up widow? Not so when I've been riding your ex-husband. How lucky Sam was to get rid of you; he's certainly safer in my hands. But I am silent and just smile. I radiate some inner calm because I don't have to compete with you at all, on any level.

'The sad thing is Sam would still be married to you if you hadn't left him. He adored you and you tossed that all away. So don't blame me for what you did. He deserves better than you.'

Bob can hardly move for the drama. The colour drains from Orlagh's face and she reaches over, takes my goggles and throws them into the middle of the pool. That's all she has? I am sleeping with your husband so you're going to chuck my basic five-pound Amazon goggles over there? Even Bob looks disappointed. You can tell he wanted something akin to mud-wrestling so he could see a bit of nipple.

'Umm, Grace…' I turn to the poolside to see Meg standing over us. 'We need to leave, Linh doesn't feel too well.'

Bob and Orlagh shift their gazes to the table, where Linh is sitting with her head in her hands.

'Is she OK? Is it her heart?' I ask, concerned. Or maybe she's had too many mimosas. I look over as she rests her elbows on the table.

'I just think it's best we scoot. Get yourself dried up and throw some clothes on.' Meg stands over Orlagh like she's very close to pushing her underwater, but she resists the urge and kills her with a murderous stare instead.

I nod and turn to Orlagh. This isn't over because, now the secret is out, she'll spread all sorts of slander about me at the school gate. I can only hope that one day Maya will choose to sink her teeth into her too. I wade over to the ladder to take my leave from this awful situation. I'd like to say it's a graceful exit but it's the bedraggled sort you have when water drains out of your gusset. Meg offers me a towel.

'Quickly dry and put your clothes on over the swimsuit. You can change in the car. I'll take Linh out first.'

I grab her arm. 'You're worrying me, Meg.'

'Trust me.'

I go to my cubicle and throw my T-shirt and joggers over what I'm wearing, leaving unsightly wet patches in the wrong places, trying to dry the ends of my hair. Lordy, we may need a hospital. The Bristol Royal Infirmary is the closest. I can send Meg back to get all Linh's insurance documents, and her bags of pills too. Did Linh forget to take a pill today? She has one of those days-of-the-week containers. I didn't check. Shit. I slip my trainers on without socks and run to the entrance with my belongings to see Meg waiting and Linh perfectly upright and functioning.

'Hello?'

Linh comes and takes my hand, urging me to walk quicker.

'What is going on? Are you OK? You had me worried sick! What is going on?'

Linh and Meg giggle in unison. It's not a good sound; it's a sound filled with mischief. They usher me away from the premises in a strange marching fashion.

'Meg said that's the ex-wife of the man you are having relations with?' Linh asks.

'Yes, for want of a better term. Why? Meg, you paid good money for me to swim there and use the facilities. I feel bad wasting that.'

My sister shakes her head. 'Gracie, what I got was worth the fee alone.'

I glance between the two of them.

'No one should speak to you like that, Grace. Not ever. In any case, she has a very weak chin. Very pointed. She quite deliberately swam into you too,' mentions Linh.

'I'm glad I didn't imagine it. Didn't she go in there with some sort of agenda? I felt like she was out to get me.'

Meg nods in agreement. 'She kept glaring at you. Remind us, she left Sam first, yes? She's just doing the whole wronged woman act because…'

'She's a bitch?' Linh says, filling in the gaps. 'You're so much better than her, Gracie. And prettier too.'

'I… thank you but why did we have to leave so quickly?' I say, my steps becoming smaller to mend the discomfort at still having my soggy swimsuit on. Meg and Linh shuttle looks between each other.

'I may have gone in her cubicle and sandwiched some avocado in her towel. I think a piece of bacon slipped in there too,' Linh says, shrugging.

I cup my hands to my mouth. They didn't. I will still have to see this woman every day for as long as my children are at that school.

'But… she will know. She could sue me!'

'And they could fingerprint you and you'd be never found out. CCTV will see an old Asian lady going in the cubicle and I'll just say I was ill and confused and leave the country if I have to,' Linh says, laughing with glee.

Meg stops for a moment as we take cover by some trees. 'Grace, do you know how hard it is to watch someone you love be ganged up on by a complete and utter crapbag like that? It hurt us very much. We refused to just sit back and watch.'

'So this was your answer?' I'd like to say they look contrite but they don't. 'You didn't think to use something like baked beans? Ketchup? Something that would stain?' I say, rolling my eyes. I can't hate them. I see it in the joy in their faces, their pride that they got to do that, for me. 'I expect this crap from Lucy, not you,' I tell Meg.

'Everything we do is to look after you, Grace. To give your story a happier ending. I hope you realise that.'

I look at both of them intently. That's why all these people do anything. It's out of something I guess we can call love. A crowd of mums with pushchairs suddenly turn the corner and we realise we are supposed to be absconding from the scene of a crime so we turn and keep walking. Maybe a bit faster than we normally would. I hope Linh's heart can take it.

Chapter Twelve

Fucking hell, Grace. I'm in Japan. Like Japan Japan. It is mental. There's a shop down the road from me where everything is a hundred yen. It's a pound shop. They have pound shops in Japan but they're the best pound shops I've ever seen. You can buy outfits for your cats. I might buy a cat just so I can dress it up. And I'm spoiled for food. Sushi anywhere else is now ruined for me. And I don't understand anything at all. People talk to me and I look at all these menus and I just smile and take it all in and point to something that looks like katsu curry hoping I haven't offended them. We passed through Osaka on the way here and it was everything I dreamt of, drenched in neon. I really wish you were here to see it all. I really do. T x

Tom's post-university world tour, as he put it, was legendary. It involved moments of work but also stuff like jumping on a train and ending up in Bangkok on the back of a party invitation. One of the more structured elements of his travel was when he went to Japan for six months to teach English. It was at the very start of his travels and he ended up in a small town to the west of Japan, near

Hiroshima, called Shunan. Was it the Japanese experience that Tom had sought out? Possibly not. I think he envisioned big neon urban landscapes that were super futuristic, and Ghibli-inspired wonder but, instead, the company he worked for placed him in an industrial town where the most exciting thing was a McDonald's. *The McDonald's is different here, Gracie. You can have a Filet-O-Fish for breakfast!* Of course, Tom was so determined to prove he was enjoying himself that he explored every inch of this new land. He loved an onsen, which was mainly an excuse to post pictures of himself in steaming pools of water, with tiny square towels over his bits, and he befriended all the teachers who had come from elsewhere such as Canada, the United States and Australia.

By the time I arrived there, all those teachers had since moved on to other places in Japan or simply gone home, so it was a bizarre stop, and one Tom should have thought through in more detail. In fact the only person who remembered Tom was Naoko.

'Are you part of that group or…?' says the receptionist at a youth hostel on the Bristol docks.

'I arranged the booking but I'm not staying. There should be ten people altogether from lots of different places…'

'Oh, yes. They've all arrived except…'

'Me.'

I turn around and Naoko is standing there, a rucksack on her shoulders and a suitcase by her feet. I squeal at seeing her and bundle her into my arms.

'You made it. I'm so glad.'

She pulls out the instruction sheet I gave to everyone. I even provided map co-ordinates, which Meg said was overkill but I thought added an extra layer of accuracy so no one could blame me if they got lost.

'These are perfect. I get the coach from the airport and I am here.' Naoko's English is slightly Americanised and broken but the girl is always full of charm. I remember standing at Shunan station the first night I arrived. I'd sat on a bullet train and was just continually bowing back to people while I tried to decipher the code-like nature of their language. *What am I doing here? This is a mistake. I don't know what I'm doing. I should have worn in these brand new-boots. I shouldn't be alone.* But as soon as Naoko saw me, she welcomed me into her home like I was a sister. She and her father cooked for me every day and showed me the sights of their small town, including the street corners where Tom had rung his girlfriend back home and told her how much he loved her. And in those first nights when jet lag played with my mind and looked to smother me, she'd sit up with me and we would watch Japanese television and game shows that boggled the mind with their premise and the volume of their excitement. It seems people falling into water wearing dayglo unitards is funny in any language.

'Everyone, apparently, is here so just check in and I'll come in with you.'

She nods excitedly. This is her first trip outside of Japan and I am sad I can't show her more than a youth hostel by the docks, but the excitement simmers off her. I'm reminded of myself when I first left the UK as a teenager. It was a European exchange trip during which I snogged an actual German boy called Matthias who wore a neckerchief.

'NAOKO!' An American voice suddenly booms through reception and I turn to see a gentleman dressed in what looks like a shell suit. He has a shaved head and walks with what I think the young people call 'swag'. 'No way, come here, honey!' He embraces her tightly.

I know the man; he's called Pablo and worked and lived with Tom back in Shunan. *You liked to sing Guns N' Roses at karaoke and would annoy everyone by washing your pants in the kitchen sink.* In fact the group standing behind them are all people I know through photos and Tom's regaling of his many stories. There are ten of them from every corner of the globe, students and teachers, like a mini United Nations except with a bit more personal drama. There were love triangles, rumoured rifts and huge drunken endeavours, but they were all bonded by the experience. Poor Naoko was tasked as their co-ordinator, their woman on the ground who welcomed them in. They loved and adored her for it. I allow her a brief moment to reunite with everyone before she steps aside.

'This is Grace.'

I've never met the majority of the people here. When Tom died, their messages of condolence poured in from around the world in letters, cards and charity donations, but, until this day, they just lived as characters in a story. They all stand there for a moment watching me, giving themselves a moment to know what to say. I think that girl is crying. Pablo is the first to break the silence and comes over to embrace me.

'It's so good to finally meet you, Grace.'

'You too, Pablo. I've heard a lot about you.'

'All good?' Not really. Tom mocked his penchant for tube socks and the need to get his rocks off at any given moment (I think he's shagged two of the other teachers here) but he went home to San Francisco and is now father to three boys, one of whom carries Tom as his middle name in tribute.

'I feel like I know all of you, this is too weird,' I say, laughing.

'You think that's weird,' one teacher interrupts. 'Tom used to keep a picture of you on our fridge.'

'He did?'

'Yeah, you were the fridge lady. We used to blame you if we'd run out of milk,' jokes another. He comes over to introduce himself.

'Well... welcome, everyone. I can't believe you're all here.'

'More of us should have come for the funeral,' a girl at the back of the group adds. 'I'm Robyn.' She approaches to give me half a hug. All I know about you is that you have five brothers whose names all begin with R. That's all I have, these little factoids and big group pictures of them singing karaoke or outside an izakaya getting drunk and eating five hundred sticks of yakitori.

'You're all here now. Happy for it to be a reunion of sorts as well,' I announce.

'Thank you for sorting it all. How are you coping?' Robyn continues.

'With the memorial?'

'With Tom's death.'

Wow, Robyn. Talk about rendering the room dead quiet. Sometimes I cry myself into a bottomless void and talk to him. Other times I tick along and go about my day. There's no happy medium. They all look at me with pained expressions, with sympathy but also like they're waiting for me to collapse to the floor with grief.

'I'm OK. I'm just glad you all could come. You all meant a lot to Tom.' The girl at the back of the group is definitely crying. I need to change the subject. 'And as a treat from me, I've organised the evening for you.'

I have more handouts. Is this too much? Tom would say this is too much because I printed them in booklet style but they're all foreign to the area and I don't want to deal with lost sheep.

'So I have maps and a table booked for six p.m. at a Japanese restaurant not far from here. And then into a karaoke bar across the way.'

Pablo and another teacher high five. It has a touch of *Top Gun* about it.

'You did that for us?' asks Robyn.

'Tom loved you all very much. You became surrogate friends. It felt important to treat you for coming all this way.'

That girl at the back is really sobbing. I feel Naoko's arm fall to my shoulder.

'We loved him too.'

Oh, Tom. Your influence stretched far and wide. What terrible advice and wisdoms did you share with this lot? You were the fun one, I bet. You started the parties and poured all the shots. Did you teach them how to cook that pasta with the Doritos topping? Expose them to the supposed genius of every Adam Sandler film? I see them itching to tell me their tales, pour out their memories. People do this to me all the time. They tell me a story that will warm the cockles but then be like a punch to the guts. There's sadness that I wasn't there to witness peak Tom in his prime, at his liveliest. Afterwards, they will give me that look. It's a muted sad look of tender resignation. It says, *I'm sorry. That's all I have. Hold me?* It will be a night of that, won't it? A night of hugging.

'But first, how about a drink?' I say.

Lots of drink.

*

Wow. Karaoke. I experienced karaoke when I went to Japan. It was my second night and Naoko took me to some building that looked like a bingo hall with its lights and open foyer and I sweated cobs to think I was going to be performing 'Take Me Home, Country Roads' in front of an auditorium of Japanese people who I hoped were both tone-deaf yet would be appreciative of my bravado in trying to entertain them for the evening. Instead she led me inside a small room where there were neon lights, sofas and tambourines and huge tome-like bibles of songs to choose, like a phone book of all the songs, ever.

Naoko had brought me along with local friends and a range of different teachers from the school. I observed at first. I watched as alcohol got wheeled into the room, whisky that was strong enough to embalm your bodily organs, and I noticed that the singing wasn't meant for show, for an audience. It was a release. It was belting out a tune as loud and as hard as you could to let go of something within the very depths of your soul, the sheer meaning of catharsis.

I watched as a young lad sang a song by Queen. He channelled his best Mercury and, boy, he went for it. He even lunged. And so when it was my turn, I did the same. It would have felt like an insult to do otherwise. I went safe with Elvis because it had meaning and I think he's an artist where one can achieve an acceptable tone, safer than Adele, for example. I sang, I danced, everyone joined in. The joy was unfathomable. I remembered a moment bent over in laughter trying to curl my lip and for one moment I did but didn't think about Tom. Naoko got it completely. We sang until 1 a.m. that night and, the next day, she got her elderly father to take me there again and we sang the whole Beatles back catalogue together over cups of green tea.

'What are you doing?' I ask Naoko now, straining to hear her as a group hammer out 'I Want It That Way'. That's not harmony, lads, but you crack on. This room is not that room in Shunan – it's a strange, digitalised version in Bristol that's dark with suspiciously sticky floors. There are also no tambourines, but the fact this gang are back together seems to be carrying the evening. Naoko is scrolling through her phone.

'I am very drunk,' she tells me. 'I have sent many selfies to my fiancé back home.'

'It's five a.m. back there.'

Naoko covers her face playfully. I've seen her down whisky back in Japan so a couple of jugs of watered-down cocktails should be nothing to her, but there's a sense of drunken wonder in her eyes. Soon, she will be married to a man called Hiroshi so I suppose this final fling with travel acts as some sort of hen do, too. The biggest of adventures. She liked those. *Come, Miss Grace, let's go somewhere today*, she used to say to me. We had these tiny folding bikes and we'd cycle down these narrow urban Japanese streets, punctuated with the smallest of houses and cobwebs of telephone wires that linked into reaching tower blocks. And then we would turn a corner to a vista, a shrine. It was so silent and green and we would sit there to take it in, to reflect, to pause. With two coffees, piping hot in their tins from a vending machine, and bento, wrapped in cloth like newborn babies, all prepared by her father. I ate it all. I didn't question why there seemed to be a fascination with mayonnaise.

To me, Japan was full of these quiet corners. It jumped from moments of complete density and action to corners of peace where I was allowed to contemplate what had just happened in my life. I will always adore Naoko for letting me find those corners. She grabs me in for a selfie and I oblige, teeth gritted slightly. Peace signs. We have to do peace signs in every picture. Everyone's been doing them tonight. Her body is still swaying. To the music? Or the alcohol?

'It's the cider,' Naoko tells me. 'In America, cider is like apple juice. It's not alcoholic so when you bring us to the Coronation Tap? Yah, we thought you took us to a juice bar.'

I look around the room at the merriment in people's faces. Pablo's complexion is the colour of raw salmon. That girl who was sobbing before is asleep on a corner of the sofa, snoring like a bear.

'They sell that cider in half-pints because it's so strong. How many did everyone have?'

'Well, I had four. They were super sweet so the girls had more…'

'I WANT TO SING ENRIQUE! FOR TOM!' Robyn shrieks into the air.

Naoko shifts me a look. 'Tom used to sing this a lot. He'd put on an accent. It was very entertaining.'

Robyn starts to sing. Unfortunately, her accent is less entertaining but she looks like she's having fun. Tom never sang me this song. I'm glad he didn't. Had he done, I most likely would have smothered him with a pillow.

A group of them stand up to form a chorus line. Naoko is now on her phone babbling away in Japanese, one finger in her ear. *Aishiteru.* Tom said this to me on the phone once. I thought it was rude. It means 'I love you' in Japanese. I hope she's got her roaming on or using the Wi-Fi in this place, or that could be hella expensive.

'Is that Hiroshi?' I ask her as she hangs up.

She nods. I met him briefly when I was in Japan. Their relationship was new and budding, but I like the way he makes her glow. Unless that really is from the cider.

'It is morning in Japan and he's heading to work.'

It's a wonder to me that the world keeps turning outside of this little room. A love on the other side of the world. I remember that once.

'Are you having fun, Grace?' she asks, sensing I've gone a little quiet.

I nod. 'It's been quite the evening. Everyone's so lovely but there's been a lot of stories. Pablo apparently used to watch porn with Tom, which is nice of him to have shared.'

Naoko giggles. There are a million stories here. He went to Hiroshima with that student, climbed Fuji with another, and sought cover in a 7-Eleven with that teacher after a typhoon hit and they nearly got killed by an escaped pig. (That may have been a cider-induced memory but who knows?) But the sense I also get is that Tom didn't hide away from these people after he left Japan. He stayed connected online; he was aware that even if you grow and thrive in another place, you try and keep the roots connected, knowing that at one time that friendship meant something. Tom was good at that, growing friends.

'He was a good man, Gracie. A very good man.'

Naoko downs the rest of her drink and stands me up, handing me a fully charged microphone.

'God, I hate this song,' I say.

'Sing. We must sing.'

I mean, we may not be able to sing over Robyn but let's give it a try, open up those passages and sing the hell out of this nineties shite balladry. I hope you're hearing this, Tom. I really hope you are.

*

'Christ, Susan. What the hell? Maybe if you take the legs and I take the arms?' says a teacher, as they try and carry their former colleague out of the karaoke lounge. This may not be the best idea. Susan is the crier who slumbers so deep I fear she may be in a coma. The group is absolutely wasted. I feel responsible but if Tom is looking on I think he'd be proud. *Not a good night until someone is throwing up in a bush*, he used to tell me. I hate that these may be the words a lot of people remember him by.

As I walk among them, down the long steep pavements of Park Street, I hear murmurs of kebabs and one group member waxing lyrical about the joys of extra chilli sauce. I'm glad I won't be sharing a hostel room with him later. Don't kiss that bus stop either. I don't think that's hygienic. Naoko skips arm in arm with another down the road. I like that I've given her some freedom tonight, that Tom led her here to me, to this foreign place. An arm suddenly drapes itself around me.

'Oh my god, this night was so awesome. Thank you so much for arranging it.'

Robyn. I've not interacted much with Robyn today as she seems to have taken it on herself to be the group leader, the attention-seeker, the flirt. When she left Japan, she went on to marry a brain surgeon, divorce a brain surgeon and now works as an estate agent. You can imagine her shiny hair and teeth standing at an angle, arms crossed on a sign on someone's lawn.

'It's been nice to meet you all in person, to be fair. Before you just existed as names and stories.'

'Did Tom have stories about me?' she asks.

That you slept with Pablo and you ate tuna out of a tin like a cat?

'He did.'

She holds her hand to her chest, her eyes glazing over.

'I say a little prayer for him every night.'

'Like Aretha Franklin?' I reply.

She keels over like that might be the best joke she's ever heard.

'The time we had together,' she says, 'I will always hold that close. I think about it all the time.'

This always feels the hardest part of my grief: that it's not mine alone, I'll always have to share Tom. He was someone's friend, son, nephew, colleague or neighbour. We all knew different parts of him, in different moments in time. It is sometimes difficult to comprehend this; sometimes I feel we exist solely as him and me, Grace and Tom. Just us.

'I just can't believe that someone I slept with is actually dead.'

The words fall out of her so easily. I halt for a moment. *You know who I am, right?*

'Are you OK, honey?' she asks, as she notices the blood draining from my face.

'You slept with him? In Japan?'

My tone gives the game away and she stops walking, the mixture of that revelation and the late-night air sobering her up quite quickly. Naoko, who is in earshot, comes over to intervene, putting a hand to my back.

'Grace, Robyn – let's go back to the hostel.'

'But thousands of miles away in reality. We didn't sleep together for a long time, it was a fling. It lasted weeks.'

Naoko looks to her feet and the only thing I can think is that she knew this information too. I think that's the problem with Tom dying. He can get away with shit like this and I can't hunt him down and hit him around the head with a large stick. He hid that well from me. All the time he was in Japan, we weren't 'together' as such but he used to make these grand gestures of love, he used to write me long notes and phone me at strange hours for chats. He left out the sleeping-with-other-people bit. Robyn still has enough alcohol in her system for the guilt to suddenly stake at her but another of her colleagues comes over to console her. Naoko can see it's hit me for six.

'Grace?'

'Did everyone here know?' I ask her.

She nods, guiltily. I suddenly feel stupidly embarrassed. I know, I'll organise dinner and entertainment for your fuck buddy and a group of people I don't really know. We can sit and pretend we're bonded in our grief, in our experience of knowing you and your penis.

'But he loved you,' Naoko whispers, taking my hand. 'She was nothing to him. All the teachers, they come to me, they get drunk and do stupid things. I see it all the time. All the while, he never stopped loving you. Your picture always stayed on their fridge.'

I lean over to embrace her but still feel the emotion deep in my shoulders.

'I need to go, Naoko. You guys know where the hostel is, yes? Just down this road and you'll see the waterfront. I'm sorry. I just…'

She looks into my eyes and down at the group of people scattered and staggering down the street. Someone is throwing up next to a line of bicycles.

'I had a good night, Grace. I'll see you soon, yes?'

I nod.

'Just make sure they don't drop Susan or she'll roll.'

*

It takes longer than it should for me to walk home. I stroll through the Bristol streets thinking about Tom with Robyn and how stupidly angry that makes me. After his death, these little things pop up from time to time. I once got a letter from the library telling me he had six overdue library books and his fines ran into hundreds of pounds. I found those books, stormed to the library to give them back and settle the bill. The librarian told me off and I apologised. I apologised for a dead person. I didn't say anything else. He did this at times. He could be reckless and immature, especially during those years when the status of our relationship was so fuzzy.

It wasn't cheating, Grace. We weren't even together at that point.

You used to call me and sing to me down the phone. What was that? You sent out all these mixed messages about what I meant to you. I stayed single thinking you still loved me. I had my sex with a vibrator.

What am I doing? I'm having an imaginary fight with a man who isn't even here. Outside the Everyman Cinema. I storm up the street, imagining all the other indiscretions he probably hid from me. How many other Robyns are out there who think that they shared a moment with my husband? No. They can piss off. He was my husband. He was mine.

By the time I get home, all the anger has simmered off me and any glow I felt from being drunk has been extinguished. I now crave cheesy chips and tea. I also want to punch something. As I put the key in the front door, I notice the kitchen light is on and Linh is sitting there on her phone. I creep into the kitchen to see her in my dressing gown, her reading glasses perched on her forehead.

'Linh, what are you doing? It's so late. Are you unwell?' I say. I look down at the phone and she's playing a word game, a cup of Ovaltine on the table.

'I don't sleep much any more. How was it? How were the Japanese contingent?' she asks.

I stand with my back to her and turn on the kettle. I am too sad, too ashamed to say any more.

'It was good. They're a large crowd, lively.'

She pauses to hear my tone, possibly disappointed that some of that liveliness didn't rub off on me. I think she expected me to crawl home, drunk and full of joy. Instead, I'm ruddy-faced, my brow furrowed, and I have blisters the size of fifty-pence coins from having marched all the way home. The energy I feel is nervous; I sense it in my fingertips, through every vessel in my heart. I go over to my freezer and take out a bag of oven chips, rustling through the fridge for some cheddar.

'I think I'm going to make some chips,' I say.

'Now?'

Oven tray and grater, that's all I'll need. I turn the oven on and move through the kitchen quietly, obtaining the right utensils and ingredients. I open the cheese and grate it with more aggression than necessary. Linh comes over to the counter and puts a hand to mine. Tears roll down my cheek, dripping off the curve of my chin, and I try to wipe them off with my shoulder.

'What happened?' she asks.

I cut open the packet of chips and arrange them on the tray.

'Do you want chips?'

'No. I don't. What happened, Grace?'

I grab at the edges of the kitchen counter.

'I met a girl today who Tom slept with in Japan. I don't know what it all meant between them but…'

'But you never knew?'

I shake my head.

'Was she pretty?'

I laugh. 'I guess. She sells houses for a living.'

She urges me to sit down to calm myself.

'And this made you angry?'

'I'm angry because I feel like a fool. I am so careful and dedicated with my grief. I ache with how much I miss him, I think about him constantly. So when I get information like this, I feel like a prize idiot. Because he didn't do right by me. He slept with other people, he didn't look after himself. He's not here, Linh, and it's his fault.'

Linh cups my chin and tries to wipe the tears from my face, encouraging the emotion to flow out of me.

'He was such a twat,' I say.

'You use this word a lot, twat.'

'It means idiot.'

'Actually, it means vagina.'

'It does?' I say through my tears.

'You used it so much, I thought I'd check what it meant.'

I laugh-cry, putting my head to her shoulder.

'All these people deifying Tom. I get it. He was great. But he was so human, so annoyingly imperfect too.'

She smiles wryly. She does this smile when she knows I'm coming to my own conclusions in my head about life and all its intricacies.

'And you loved him despite of this. My Cam had her moments. She was stubborn, she was argumentative. There were times she didn't make good choices, but who does? Who isn't perfectly flawed? Whose life follows some straight and narrow path the whole way?'

'Mother Teresa?'

'I bet she had her vices. I bet she drank like a sailor.'

I exhale loudly, not really knowing where my emotion is taking me. Grief does this sometimes; it has me in a chokehold in which the tangle of thoughts are too knotted to unravel.

'I just… I still feel it, Linh. I thought it would be gone by now. That feeling of grief, of missing him so intently. I was told something today that made me so angry, that should make me want to throw him off a bridge, but instead it makes me realise how much I love him.'

She gets up to make me a cup of tea, her back turned to me.

'You know, I'm at that age now where loss is part and parcel of my life. I've lost my parents, siblings, friends and now a daughter and son-in-law.'

I am a sobbing mess now as she remains perfectly calm.

'One moment those people are there and, the next, they're not. Sometimes you get time to prepare for this, sometimes you don't. It doesn't get any easier, I don't think it's supposed to. But to feel their loss means those people meant something to you. You loved them. They loved you.'

She stirs my tea, thoughtfully.

'Tom won't be the first person you lose. I hate to say that out loud.'

'Then this is what life is? Investing all my love in people only for them to go away?'

She turns to look at me, sadly.

'Then what? Live on your own? Never get close to anyone so you can spare yourself the pain of potentially losing them? That is not the Grace I know.' Her tone is raised, almost scolding me. 'The Grace I first came to love used to send parcels to a man in Vietnam. These impeccably wrapped gifts of Marmite and Hobnob biscuits and she used to cut out newspaper articles of interest and write beautiful notes.'

'How did you…?' I ask her.

'Because he would show me. *No one has ever loved me like Grace.*'

The tears roll down my face uncontrollably now, racing in tracks down my cheeks. She comes over to put the cup of tea next to me and embrace me tightly. When she releases me, I sit here and try and catch my breath.

I take a sip of tea, still not able to find the right words.

'I never know why you English drink tea at night. This is why you don't sleep.' I try and summon up some laughter. 'And cheese with chips? This is also very confusing to me.'

'It's a reason to live,' I tell her, rubbing my blotchy eyes, trying to lighten the mood. 'Did Tom have girlfriends in Vietnam? Did he sleep with anyone while he lived out there with you?'

'He didn't sleep with me, if that's what you're asking?' she says mockingly.

I snort with disbelief.

'I can't say, Gracie. I don't think he did. Well, he never told me about it. He once got a rash on his crotch but I suspect that was heat rash. He wore his shorts far too tight.'

'He showed you his crotch?'

'No,' she says, giggling. 'He used to scratch it around me though and I told him that was uncouth.'

That made sense. We used to wait for the bus and he'd rearrange his tackle in front of people. I rest my head on the kitchen table and she puts a hand to my face.

'I shouldn't have put chips in. I'll be here all night waiting for them to cook.'

'We can sit here for as long as you want.'

'I love you, Linh.'

'Love you too, girl.'

Chapter Thirteen

G, Congrats about the job. I know how hard you've worked for that. Did you celebrate with a tin of Dr Pepper and then sort your knicker drawer? I bet you did. I jest but you worked hard for that so do celebrate, take a sister out or something. One thing, you have friends, right? You never talk about them. Work mates, school mates, uni mates? All you talk about is work and how you sit there worrying about me. You shouldn't. I'm in Phuket and it's pretty insane. Beaches and beers and soups that will scorch the gums out of your mouth. I love it. I have tan lines. I know there were pictures on social media but try not to read too much into those because everyone does go around in swimwear all the time so there are a lot of breasts in the vicinity.

T x

'And then we take our pipe cleaners and we put them through the tube and then we have a flower!' Miss Loveday announces from the front of the classroom. I look down. There's no easy way of saying this. It doesn't look like a flower. It is a tissue-paper vulva in red and pink and the pipe cleaner looks like something is crawling out of said vulva, like a furry worm. That would need strong antibiotics. I look over at Helen on my table and she holds hers up, the flowerhead dropping off immediately.

'Shit…' she mumbles.

'Mummy, we're at school. You can't say the s-word here,' says her son, William, Isaac's younger brother, disgusted.

'Yeah, you can… the only words you can't say are the f-, c- and b-words.'

I run through my alphabetical swear word thesaurus quickly.

'But there are lots of b-words,' I whisper.

She glances over at Carrie and I know exactly what word she means. 'See also the w-word.'

'That rhymes with the b-word?'

'God, no. You can say "witch" out loud. It's the one that rhymes with "tanker".'

I laugh and put a thumb up in the air. Today all the parents have been invited into the classrooms for a Craft & Create event the school likes to put on occasionally so we can bond, nose around the classrooms and mutter under our breath how we've taken a half day off work for this shite. When I came in today, the atmosphere was frosty, shall we say, close to Arctic. Near the sink, I had Carrie, who seemed to adopt a protective stance when I first walked in just in case my rabid daughter went on the attack again. And in the reading nook sat Orlagh, who glared at me intently. I've done very well at evading her at the school gate since avocado/lido gate and I hope and pray she won't shame me for it here. So, all in all, the only solace I take from the morning is that I had the good sense to put Linh in the other classroom with Cleo so she couldn't fight them all.

I've attached myself to Helen today, mainly because she's good value but also because I know it'll be handy to have her onside if any fight ensues. I like how hardy Helen is; nothing is for show. She's wearing leggings, a sequinned sweatshirt and Ugg boots, and you know she's the sort of parent who drinks and understands the need to sometimes switch on the television and let it parent your children for an evening.

It's the embellishment part of our flower project now so we let our kids loose with the sequins and the glitter. Better you fulfil these craft needs in a place that isn't our own homes. Naturally, we're all teetering over child-sized chairs so Helen pulls hers closer to mine.

'So I heard from a little bird that you and Sam Headley are doing the do?' she asks me.

'Where did you hear that from?' I enquire.

She smiles. 'You know how it is in a place like this. You only have to tell one of the childminder lot and the rumours spread quicker than Orlagh's legs for twenty-year-old lads.'

I try to hold back my laughter.

'She's not happy about that, not one little bit. I also heard some rumour that you tried to stalk her at her local pool and shat in her handbag.'

My face reads horror this time. Mainly at how badly Orlagh twisted that fact but also because my sources told me avocado and bacon in a towel. I really hope they didn't squat over a handbag.

'We bumped into each other. There were words but there was no faeces in her Michael Kors.'

Helen chuckles. 'Of course there wasn't. She's just a bitter old wench. I hear it's not going well with the young lad anyway, someone told me he got crabs and then Orlagh got the crabs so that's made things very interesting.'

We look over at Carrie and Orlagh, who are now sitting at the colouring-in table, talking in whispers. Helen senses my discomfort and nudges me with her elbow.

'Hun, they're not worth your salt. I have three more kids next to this one. You've met Isaac. Love him but god, he finds trouble. I've got into all sorts of scraps, endured all sorts of mums' nights out, and seen all sorts of characters. That one with the red curly hair…?'

I nod. She's always dressed in fitness gear, whatever the weather. You get a sense that all that's going through her head is how many steps she's getting in.

'Went to a fondue night with her once and she cried after her first glass of Chablis because she had an argument with her husband over a Hoover. We spent the whole night patting her back. Her mate next to her with the big earrings? Husband left her a year ago, just walked out because he couldn't bear to be married to her any more. She went on Tinder and ended up being conned out of a grand by a handsome Frenchman who had a twelve-inch wang.'

If the school newsletter gave us this sort of information, instead of news about the school gardening club and the height of their tomato plants, then I'd be more tempted to read it.

'All of us have all sorts of drama going on in our lives. More often than not, it just becomes gossip fodder. Whatever them bitches are saying about you, no will remember in a month's time…'

Carrie seems to have cracked a joke and Orlagh cackles, waving an orange colouring pencil around. If Carrie is funny then maybe something has changed in her DNA. Perhaps Maya biting her had an effect.

'It doesn't look like a flower, Mama?' Maya says, holding our creation up in the air. That's mainly because it's been weighed down by a heck load of glittery disco pollen. Well, at least it doesn't look like a vulva any more.

'It looks incredible. Are you having fun?' I ask.

'Yup, I like it when you come and see my classroom. Do you want to see where I hang my coat?' she asks me.

'Always.' She takes my hand and I salute Helen as I leave, watching as she tries to rake glitter out of her son's hair.

Maya's hand in mine is always a treat. She interlocks our fingers and drags me along. 'So this is it. That's my name and, every morning, I put my stuff here and then I put my water bottle here,' she tells me. 'And I hang my coat properly like you told me, not by the hood.'

I smile. Small wisdoms, I guess. A person hovering interrupts us. 'Miss Callaghan, hi.'

Miss Loveday. Ever since we had our chat and she confronted Carrie at the school gate, there is a different feel to her. She seems stronger, she's going with the flow a bit more.

'Are you showing Mum your peg, Maya?'

She nods, proudly.

'When you're done, there's the poem corner over there. Why don't you find a sheet and a pencil?'

Maya scurries off.

'She really is bright as a button, that one. I also wanted to say, I've been chatting to the head here. She's had trouble finding someone to cover me for the one term so I've agreed to stay on until the summer and finish off the year. It's not official yet but I just wanted you to know.'

I smile broadly. 'That is excellent news.'

'Thank you,' she says. Did I do that? Or was it my daughter biting your nemesis that was the game-changer? However Miss Loveday's managed to level out that crisis, I'm thrilled for Maya at least. I nod and she continues to move around the classroom. I find Maya, her pencil poised and her tongue sticking into her cheek as she concentrates really hard. I squat next to her to see what she's doing.

'What's this then?' I ask her.

'They are called acrostic poems. It says the word FAMILY and you have to pick a word for each letter to describe your family.'

I glance over what she's tried to write.

Funy
Amazeing
Maya
I love my famalee
Laff
Y

Looks like the phonics are working their magic then. I remind myself to read more with her. I am glad she at least got her own name right. I kiss her on the forehead.

'Those are some good letters.'

'I know. I just can't think of something for Y,' Maya says, confused.

That is a tricky one. Youthful? Yummy? I pull a face trying to think of something when suddenly she has a lightbulb moment.

You, Me and Cleo.

I smile as she writes it. It's kind of perfect. So perfect it makes me want to tear up, but I won't put her through that embarrassment. We have six years left in this school at least. She puts her hand in mine and squeezes it hard.

'That might be my favouritest poem that I've ever read,' I tell her.

'I'm going to show Miss Loveday,' she says, grabbing the paper and running off.

'Hello hello,' a voice suddenly says beside me. It's Sam. 'I'm so late. I had a meeting. What have I missed?'

With everything that's been going on recently, I haven't seen Sam as much, though the beauty of our arrangement means he's not been offended. If anything he's revealed himself to be a lovely friend, offering to help with lifts, shopping and the like. I don't have the time to question if I've missed him or not though because, as I look around the classroom, it's clear the other parents' interests have been piqued by Sam's appearance and the fact he's gravitated towards me. Helen looks over and waves animatedly. Orlagh and Carrie's expressions could turn things into stone.

'Hello. You're late. You missed the story. We read *The Day the Crayons Left.*'

'Read it,' he says, smiling. 'It's good to see you in the flesh for once. I feel like I only get flashes of you at the gate at the moment.'

'That sounds like I flash you at the gate.'

'Now that would cause a scene.'

I want to continue this line of repartee but I am still wary that people have shifted their attentions away from the craft for a small moment to spy on us.

'So, you know I said that Orlagh knew about us. Did you know *everyone* knows about us?'

'Oh…' He glances up as everyone pretends to look away. 'Ohhhh… should we not sit together? I don't know what to do.'

'Well, maybe don't go full snog, right now…'

He laughs. Orlagh's face turns a funny shade of plum.

'She's also been spreading some rumour that I'm stalking her and pooed in her handbag,' I tell him.

He scrunches his face up. He's already familiar with what happened after I sent him a series of frantic texts. 'Really?'

I don't know if he says that from disbelief that his ex would lie or because he thinks I'm capable of such a thing.

'You know,' he says, 'she's not said anything about the swimming-pool incident to me. Almost like she's trying to hide it or…'

'She doesn't want to let on that she's upset by all of this. Look, go to her… Today's about the kids. Don't mind me.'

I can't quite read his expression – is it disappointment or confusion? Either way, he slinks away to join Orlagh and when he goes over she greets him in a very loud and animated fashion. Is that a kiss on the cheek? Even Sam looks confused but he glances back at me and smiles faintly.

'Fanny, Arse, Minge, Idiot, Lube, Yackface… Done,' Helen says as she sits down next to me, looking at the poem sheet.

'That's a winning poem. What is a Yackface?' I ask.

'Yack means vomit in my house but if we're talking about the other sort of yak then you probably don't want to look like that either. Your boyfriend in the house then?' she says cheekily.

Orlagh currently has her legs entwined with her ex-husband's, eyeballing me narkily with her super-pointy chin. Sam appears like a very scared meerkat, wrapped in a python.

'Block it out. Let's write another poem… I can think of other words beginning with f, if you want?' Helen says, brandishing a crayon.

'I'm just a bit sad. He's not quite over her. I'm angry that she's going to take advantage and worm her way back into his life.'

Orlagh has an arm around him now. That's the problem. I don't love him in *that* way but I care enough as a friend to want his heart to remain intact.

'Then that's his mistake to make. A fool can see that she's all over him now because she believes there's some great competition between the both of you. And I'd shag you over her any day of the week.'

'Why thank you. I am flattered.'

'You free next Tuesday?'

'I can find a gap after I've had my washing machine fixed. Bring biscuits.'

She cackles loudly and some of the parents turn to us.

'Even with Carrie, you can see that she's jealous of you, right?'

I give Helen a strange look. There are parts of my life so far that I wouldn't wish on anyone. Like the whole widow thing, for starters.

'You're bloody interesting, that's why,' she carries on. 'I'd rather be friends with someone like you who's seen the world, who has a lovely diverse family, rather than her and her Harry Potter hoodie.'

'She's wearing a Harry Potter hoodie?'

She nods slowly. In amongst all of that, though, what's nice to hear is that Helen considers me a friend. It's a weird thing with school-gate mums. I'll see Helen every day now for an eternity and it strikes me that when our kids go their separate ways our friendship will fade away. It feels comforting to know I'm at least likeable enough for her to get to know me, to be an ally.

'You're not vegan or one of them strange types who don't drink coffee, are you?' she asks me.

'No.'

'Then we can definitely be mates.'

We're interrupted by her William, who jumps in her lap and my attention turns back to Sam, who is trying to catch my eye. If you go back to that woman, you won't move on. She'll win you back but the victory would be completely hollow for you; she'll just use and abuse you until the next twenty-something comes along. She may also give you crabs. He smiles at me and Orlagh clocks it immediately, whispering something into his ear.

'Miss Loveday! Miss Loveday! We're trying to make these clay coil pots but the instructions are very poor. It would help if they were clearer.'

The whole classroom stops to hear Carrie interrupt the proceedings. Miss Loveday shuttles over to appease her and the rest of the parents take a deep collective sigh.

'It'd help if she didn't have claws for fingers,' Helen mumbles.

'What did you say, Mummy?' asks William. 'Are you talking about Carrie Potter?'

Poor William doesn't have the quietest of voices so it travels and I see people sniggering under their breath.

'I've heard that the class next door are doing some real-life acrylic painting, not bargain-basement crafts. I really don't get the point in all of this,' says Carrie.

'It's all just for fun, Mrs Cantello. Some of these activities are great for their gross motor skills.'

'Really?' Carrie replies condescendingly.

I'd watch before you criticise, Carrie. I think your daughter is trimming her own fringe with the craft scissors.

'Yes. Here's a range of pots that some of the other children and parents have made… from my poor instructions.'

You go, Miss Loveday. Carrie stares daggers at her but she knows how to deal with all of that now. I look at the poem in front of me and fold it, putting it my handbag. I might make a pot next. I need something for my spare change. But where's Maya? I take a glance around the room.

'Looking for someone?' Helen asks, nudging me. I catch a glimpse of a little person on all fours in clear stealth mode. Maya. Like a cat. A ninja cat, dumping tubes of glitter into the collection of handbags stored underneath the table.

'This is why we can most certainly be friends,' Helen says, chuckling heartily and giving my daughter a double thumbs up.

Chapter Fourteen

Tom,

You really can be such a humungo dick sometimes. Of course I have friends and actually I did go out and I celebrated my new job with Lucy and I went clubbing and had sex with a man called Mario who had a really giant knob and I came like a billion times, so really, piss off with your girls in bikinis and your travel and you showing off thinking you're all spiritual and enlightened and putting Instagram pictures of you on beaches in tie-dye writing stupid quotes about peace and sunsets. I hope you go swimming and a crab swims up your actual bum.

Grace

It's one week until the memorial and people are descending on Bristol in their swarms. It feels like a convention. Tom would love a convention in his honour. We should have hired out a university hall and had special guest speakers. Dress as your favourite version of him: hippie-surfer Tom, noughties-dance Tom, waistcoat-teacher Tom. Tom-Con. We could have merched it out properly.

The guests flit in and out of my life, they drop in for tea and tag me in their social media posts. At times, it's a little too much so I hide in my room, in my Huggly with my girls, and we watch *Moana* together. I can't hear another story; I can't drink another cup of tea while someone holds my hand. That's not a safe or comfortable way to drink hot beverages in any case.

Then a Friday happened. Cue chaos. Yes, the family have descended on the place with all their accompanying children, partners and husbands. My parents have rented a massive Airbnb to house everyone. It's like some familial experiment to see who will be the first to storm out. I feel we should be starting wagers. Lucy will be the first to pick that fight. Meg will be the first to leave. If I didn't have a home it'd be entertaining to stay there and witness it all unfolding. My mother has made a detailed agenda. There will be walks, there will be dinners with an exact meal plan, a cooking and washing-up rota, and a games night when the world could very well implode in a sea of Monopoly money.

Except today when, for one afternoon, my mum and dad have taken charge of all the grandchildren and me, Meg, Emma, Beth and Lucy are headed to a spa for an afternoon. This was Meg's idea. Obviously, we could have gone to the lido again but after our act of sabotage I fear they may have our faces on a poster on the wall so we've opted for the Nirvana spa on the outskirts of town. It's big on a tropical motif, despite being ten minutes from the M4.

Meg and Emma like a spa. They like the idea of relaxation and sitting still in a hot room to open up their pores. Beth, who is currently pregnant with baby number two, is more worried about whether she'll look like a pink beached whale. Lucy just wants to know if there will be alcohol. I worry about what sort of ailments one can pick up from a Jacuzzi. In my mind, I'm thinking foot fungus and things one can catch inside one's cooch. I don't do spas. I don't do sharing my relaxation with other random people when I could easily do that in my own bathtub and with added extras that would be frowned upon here. Like a tube of Pringles and a cheeseboard.

'Seriously, Lucy?' Emma asks.

We've set up camp along one side of a swimming pool that's surprisingly dark and underlit. It feels like a pool in a Bond film where the floor would open up and they'd release sharks to feed on all of us. To the left of us are two older women who are bundled in white towels like Christmas puddings. They are obviously here for the peace and quiet. I resist the urge to inform them they won't be getting much of that here. Mainly because of Lucy, who has shown up today in the tiniest of bikinis that owes a lot of its construction to both crochet and strong knotting. Emma has gone safe with a one-piece and Beth is just wearing whatever fits – hoping she can use her bump as a flotation device. Meg has gone one-piece fifties style, which lifts her in all the right places, while I picked my trusty high-waisted two-piece. It means if I bomb into this pool, things will stay where nature intended.

'Lucy, I can literally see your crack,' Emma says in judgmental tones.

'Lucky you!' Lucy replies cheekily. 'Don't be such a prude. Where did you get that number? You look like you're about to swim the one hundred metres freestyle and beat your PB.'

'Girls, not now…' Meg whispers.

Emma scowls as Lucy lies down on her sunlounger, bending up a leg like she's taking in the sun. She would lie there naked to absorb all the relaxation if she could. Meanwhile, Beth is already asleep, as proved by the string of drool pooling from her lips. She seems to be the very opposite of what Lucy is presenting. First time pregnancy and motherhood hit her like a ton of bricks but, this time round, she's embracing the curves and the excuse to nap whenever she wants. There is a glow in her warmer than the infrared sauna across the way.

'Beth is asleep,' I say, pulling a towel over her like a blanket.

'Leave her be. I think she's been trying to get her GCSE kids sorted before she goes on maternity leave. She was like a narcoleptic on the drive up. She'd wake up to eat crisps and then fall asleep again,' whispers Emma.

I stroke her head.

'I'm not asleep. I'm just boiling in this heat, like a jacket potato,' Beth mutters with one eye open.

'Then take off your robe,' I say, peeling the extra towel off her.

'I can't. I didn't shave. Bad enough waddling in here, I don't want to look like a hairy walrus.'

'I didn't shave either, it's not like anyone's looking,' Meg replies.

I often wonder how we came to be, the five of us. Meg and Lucy couldn't give a flying fox who sees their bits whereas the rest of us attempt to show a bit more reserve.

'Do you wax, Luce?' Beth asks, glancing over at her.

I think we all know the answer to that question. Lucy is in entertainment – she dances, acts and twirls around things. You suspect she needs it done for costumes and such but for other reasons too.

'I do. I have a lovely lady in Hammersmith who does it, her name is Petra. I like her methods.'

'She has a method?' Beth asks. 'I just wondered if it may be easier to just see a professional and get things tidied up before I give birth to another. I can't see mine at the moment.'

'She hot-towels the area and then gets me on all fours for access. Smoother foof that way,' Lucy replies.

Emma shakes her head. This is not what people discuss in spas. We should be talking about cleanses and where we buy our quinoa.

Meg laughs at the very thought. 'B, please don't. You'll have enough going on down there… You want enflamed lips with regrowth itchiness on top of trapped hairs? No…'

Beth seems reassured by Meg's words of wisdom while Lucy and I look on in interest. Another thing to separate us is that Lucy and I have not had babies – well, mine didn't come out of me – and it's always an education to learn how they came out of our dear sisters in such a savage fashion. They have intimate relationships with their bits now, often talking about their parts resembling the Channel Tunnel, which sometimes makes me glad I chose to adopt.

'And I was going to announce it to the room later on tonight but I'll give you a preview. We are having another boy,' Beth says, smiling broadly. Her smile is contagious. Another person to welcome to the brood, for us all to love.

'Oh, B!' Lucy squeals and leans over her towelled body to congratulate her.

'We found out before we came up here.'

Beth's long-term man love is a man called Will. The year they had their first child, Joe, was tumultuous but they seemed to have found their groove in the last few years. She certainly seems calmer this time round, like a baby isn't going to be a hand grenade in her life. She sits up and heaves a leg over the side of the sunlounger.

'Any names in mind?' Meg asks her.

'Don't even start… We're veering towards Jude.'

We're not appalled by this.

'Frankly, I don't think we've gone alternative enough with the names,' Lucy contributes. 'I want to go to a park and shout, "HEY! JULIO! LET'S GO ON THE SWINGS!"'

Everyone laughs.

'Just don't call him Tom… please…'

All the sisters suddenly mute their chuckles. That was not my intention. It was a joke. Please keep laughing. I pout my lips at having sledgehammered the atmosphere.

'Why?' Beth asks.

'I know two people now who've named their babies after him. I mean, he'd love having all these namesakes but…'

'It's his name,' Meg says. 'Like if I had a really yappy dog that dry-humped everything then I'd call it Lucy but that would be funny.'

Emma finds this particularly hilarious. Meg gives me a look from her sunlounger and winks at me. Thanks for saving that moment.

'You're such a cow,' Lucy says. 'If I had a cow, I'd call it Meg.'

'But you'd never own a cow so basically you've stolen my joke and the moment is gone.'

'Girls, girls…' Emma says, mimicking Meg from before. 'Well, I am thrilled, B. I can't wait to meet him.'

It is a thing, our brood of family. This empire we seem to be building and calling our own.

Lucy suddenly jumps up from her sunlounger. 'YES! Girls, the bitches who were hogging the hot tub have gone. Let's do this! I'm going to bagsy them.'

She canters off, getting the attention of a lifeguard who blows his whistle for running on the poolside. Don't swear at the staff, Lucy. He seems to let her off because that bikini offers little support for her ample assets. She sees another lady heading for the hot tub and stands her off, literally swan-diving into that thing and spreadeagling herself across it to safeguard it for her sisters. I won't lie. We see her do this a lot. Whether it's the roundabout in the park or a table in a pub, that girl can secure you territory like no other. She should be a wrestler or perhaps a foreign diplomat.

'Can you get barred from a spa?' Emma asks me.

'I don't think so but you guys can go back to London when this is all over. I need to live in this town.'

As Meg hauls Beth up, Emma and I are the sensible ones who make sure we've left no belongings behind. You can tell which part of the hot tub Lucy is sitting in from her face. Enjoying those jets, are we, Luce?

'You look stressed, hun. Are you OK?' Emma asks me, as she sifts through Lucy's pile of things. Sunglasses? Really? I think she's also just dropped a thong.

'There's just a lot going on. I'm not sleeping again,' I tell her.

She reads my face in the way Emma does, with due concern. As our family doctor, she worries about those basic physical and mental constructs that keep her sisters functioning.

'Do you need a prescription?' she asks me. 'How about that counsellor? Are you still seeing them?'

'Not any more. I don't know. It comes in waves.'

'And this month must be like a tsunami.'

She knows. Emma is like me in many ways. She went through an awful divorce about six years ago now with a man who was a serial liar and cheat so I think both of us can lay claim to having been through some of the worst life can throw at you. Our personalities sorted through the debris as best we could and we threw ourselves into other endeavours, but we understand what it is to climb out of the dark holes that can be pain and grief, clawing at the ground and just trying to wake up every day and breathe.

'Well, you know where I am if you need my help. Speaking of waves…' she mutters to me. 'Lucy, for the love of all that is healthy, do not do that please.'

Lucy is paddling in the hot tub, doing poses reminiscent of an unclassy Esther Williams. Please don't do a handstand in there.

'I'm not getting in there, I don't think I'm supposed to with the baby,' Beth says. 'I'm just going to dangle my feet. No one look at my bush.'

Emma, Meg and I disrobe and enter hesitantly. I never quite see the attraction of these things. It's always reminiscent of being boiled, like a vegetable. I take a seat and watch as Emma examines the water for things that shouldn't be in there, like pubes and panty liners.

'I had sex in a hot tub once,' Lucy boasts. 'It was on a yoga retreat with a man actually called Chakra.'

We are all curiously po-faced.

'Was his surname Khan?' Beth asks. 'Because that is a yoga-disco niche worth investing some money in.'

Meg and I crease up.

'Surely, it's easier to work out the places you haven't had sex?' Emma jokes.

'I've had sex in a hot tub,' Meg adds.

Emma looks slightly horrified. Lucy claps in delight.

'It was a holiday cottage in the Peak District. It was quite nice, to be fair. At least it was warm.'

'But what happens when they jizz?' Beth asks.

'It just dissolves in the bubbles, doesn't it?' Lucy says with mischief in her eyes. Emma retches, and I can almost see her mentally listing the types of physical germ types that fester in these waters. 'Are you telling us you've never had underwater sex, Ems?' Beth asks. 'Even I've done it in a swimming pool.'

'Like a public swimming pool?'

'No, because that would be illegal, but on holiday we had a villa with a pool once.'

Emma nods in reply, almost fascinated. She never shares sex stuff with us. She has a new boyfriend now and she won't even tell us what his johnson is like. Whereas I feel I know everyone Lucy has dated quite intimately. She once went out with a man with a two-tone dick. She never knew why it was two different colours but we called him Ombre. I don't even remember his real name.

'You are all feral, I can't believe we're all related,' Emma adds.

A waiter suddenly appears next to the pool with two bottles of champagne, glasses and a bottle of OJ for the pregnant one.

'Are you the Callaghan sisters?' he asks.

'Ooooooooh, Meggsy! How luxurious!' Lucy squeals. The waiter gives her the once-over and she winks back at him.

'This isn't me. I didn't order this,' Meg says, looking worried about the state of the bill after our afternoon here.

'No, it's from someone called Mr Kohli.' We all stare over at Emma. That's her boyfriend, Jag. He sent champagne? He can stay. Bubbles in bubbles. Emma smiles from her corner of the tub. In Jag, she has a boyfriend who repaired years of anguish caused by her ex. He gives thoughtful gifts, and we are all entranced by his extended repertoire of trainers, but best of all we love how he adores our sister, how he holds her in the highest esteem the way she deserves.

'Ems, he's now officially my fave,' Lucy says, glugging from her glass. Meg hands me a glass and I clink hers.

Emma shakes her head. 'He's such an idiot. Well, seeing as we're making announcements, I also have one. I think Jag thought I'd probably tell you today. I should at some point.'

'Did you two finally have sex somewhere that wasn't a bed?' asks Lucy.

I snort a little out of my nose.

'No,' she says, pausing. 'He asked me to marry him and I have said yes.'

Lucy lets out a huge squeal of excitement that sees the bottle of champagne tip into the hot tub. She and Meg scramble to undo the damage as Beth reaches down to embrace Emma's head and give her a huge kiss.

'You knew?' I ask Beth.

'I'm pregnant, I have rights. I cried. I woke up Will when she told me.'

'When did this happen?' Meg says, slack-jawed.

'New Year's Eve. It was very corny, one knee on the South Bank where we met. But I can't think of anything I want more than to be his wife.'

Meg wades over to embrace her while Lucy continues to make quite the racket, splashing about. I feel warmth. It could be the hot tub, it could be the champagne, but the warmth leads to tears. Emma sees them and comes over to hug me.

'That's not quite it,' she says hesitantly. 'We both don't want a big wedding so given we're all here... we've booked a venue for tomorrow. It's just a restaurant with lunch. Come along?'

We all sit there in silence.

'You what?' Beth says.

'We're getting married tomorrow. It won't be a huge thing, just someone with a big book, we'll say some words and then we've got a three-course meal.'

'Ems, I literally have a suitcase packed with maternity leggings. Joe has jeans and hoodies,' Beth says in horror.

'Same. Unless you want me there in a bikini?' Lucy says.

'How long have you known me?' Emma sighs. 'I got you all dresses, and outfits for the little people.'

We all pull faces. She had us in lavender for her original wedding.

'Jag chose them all, they're very "trendy"... don't worry,' she says, sensing our discomfort. 'I mean, I need bridesmaids.'

Reticence turns to smiles.

'You literally just have to show up. We sorted everything from London.' Emma turns to me. 'The only thing I was worried about

was whether I was hijacking Tom's memorial. I just thought…
or maybe I didn't. I didn't want to take attention away from that
or for this to be seen as insensitive. We just thought, as everyone
was here…'

All the sisters turn to me. At the heart of it, this is Emma's
organisation skills coming into play. This is economically a good
way to ensure we can get our money's worth out of the travel. Oh,
Emma. A wedding? I can't feel anything but love here.

'Ems, it means this whole week is also about something good.
And Tom would have really liked that. He wouldn't have wanted
this week to be a sad one.'

Emma sighs with relief.

'We've factored in Linh too so please bring her along.'

I nod happily. Lucy kicks her legs in the pool like a child and
raises her glass.

'Oh man, someone's getting married in the morning,' she chirps.
'So basically, this is like a hen do. We need this to kick off.'

'No, we don't. We can go back to the house and do face masks,'
Emma commands.

'I have a friend… we can get a stripper. It's a good company,
they can guarantee eight inches and more.'

'LUCY!' Emma shouts.

The sound of all their giggles and banter is like music to me.
There will be a wedding tomorrow. This is a huge surprise but also
such a joy. It shifts the focus, the hectic nature of the week, into
something else, and I am suddenly grateful for it. Emma found her
happiness again. This is everything.

'Excuse me, ladies. Unfortunately, we've had a complaint from the group over there that your party is making a lot of noise and disrupting the serene vibe we hope to create at Nirvana spa.'

The voice comes from behind me and I slink my shoulders into the bubbly water to escape. We're that rowdy lot at the back of the classroom. This may be the same man who told Lucy off for running poolside. I daren't turn around.

'I'm sorry. I just shared some good news and we all got a little overexcited,' Emma says.

'This is a hen do. She's getting married tomorrow,' Lucy explains.

'Yes, but that is also a hen-do group and they're behaving in accordance with the general feeling of the spa.'

Meg looks over at the behaving group all lying separately on their sunloungers. They have dip with raw broccoli florets and are reading sensible self-help books.

'Looks a riot. We will try and be more *Nirvana*, apologies. Namaste.'

That sarcasm is met with silence. I try and hide my face with my hands. Don't start something. I don't think you know what you're taking on, young man.

'Did one of you urinate in the hot tub?' he asks.

'Excuse me?' asks Meg, her face not entirely impressed.

'The shade of the water has changed.'

'I spilt some champagne by accident,' Lucy adds.

'Really?' he asks.

'What are you implying? How very rude. It's not urine,' Emma says, trying to maintain some order.

'How do I know that?' he replies, aggrieved.

'Come and smell it,' Lucy suggests.

'I don't think that would be appropriate, Madame.'

'Don't "Madame" me. You're accusing one of us of taking a slash in your hot tub?' Lucy comes out of the water at this point and stands next to him. I turn around. Please don't hit him. The bikini clings to her without much room for imagination. He looks at each and every one of us in turn until his gaze fixes on me. *I know you.*

'Jordan. You're Jordan,' I say.

It's Orlagh's boyfriend. However, the way he looks at me makes me think he has no idea who I am. Youth. We met in a bar where you wore impossibly skinny jeans with suede loafers with no socks. I was with a loud Australian.

'You told us you worked at a cinema?'

The sisters study my face. We'll blame the champagne, the general humidity for my forwardness.

'I did? How do I know you?' he asks me, confused.

'Orlagh Headley. My kids go to school with hers and you're…'

'You're Sam's new bird.'

'I guess. Grace.'

My sisters are uncharacteristically quiet as they watch this play out.

'I got fired from the cinema. I was caught stealing the nachos.'

'Oh. I'm sorry,' I say, not really sure how to respond further.

'Don't tell Orlagh,' he blurts out.

'OK. Maybe give us a break then? I'll promise we'll try and behave ourselves.'

I scan Lucy's face. The key word there is *try*. Have I managed to get us out of this mess? I am not sure but Jordan does a very strange thing of putting his hands on his hips, trying to ascertain what authority he has left standing there in his white polyester shorts.

'All right then. Enjoy. Ladies. Have fun.'

He strides away, Lucy snarling and sneakily sticking a middle finger up at him. Meg pushes one of my shoulders playfully. 'Look at you, finding your bargaining power at just the right time.'

Lucy lowers herself back into the tub. 'Well done, G. Did he just say he stole nachos? Who the fuck steals nachos?' she asks. 'It's not even real cheese.'

'I think that's why we were so quiet, we were slowly taking that in,' Meg adds, trying hard to hold in her cackles.

'How old is he?' Beth asks, seeming to question the legality of his relationship with Orlagh.

'He's twenty,' I say through gritted teeth. We all try and rewind our minds to think what it used to be like to be that age.

'So Sam's wife is shagging that and you're shagging Sam,' Lucy says, laying it all out plainly for us. Their faces say it all. There is no competition here.

'Or not. A school mum did tell me they may have broken up as he got crabs.'

Emma looks horrified. 'People still get crabs? Seriously? Those polyester shorts can't help. Lordy, the friction.'

We all look covertly in his direction.

'And sisters… this is why I wax. Everything,' Lucy announces. And with that, laughter. I hope not so hard that Beth loses control of her pelvic floor and actually does piss in this hot tub but it's sweet, super sweet. It's most certainly going to get us thrown out of here.

Chapter Fifteen

G, which sister wrote that last email then? I'm hedging my bets on Lucy or drunk Beth. Though I have seen Meg get drunk before and she is fond of that type of rhetoric too. I mean, the outside bet is Emma but who knows with your crazy crew. Do I miss it? I miss the clamour of all those Callaghan sisters. I hope you and Mario are very happy together. Remember to use lube if he has a big dong or the chafing will do you in. I look forward to seeing the wedding pictures.

T

'Gracie, what size shoe are you again?' Lucy says, bursting into my room in her pants and a bra, a phone to her ear. She opens my wardrobe doors and scurries around on the floor. 'It's mostly old lady Marks & Sparks heels,' her voice says, echoing through the walls.

I pretend not to be offended but it's the FootJoy padded soles; they really are a revelation in comfort.

'Bingo! There's something here in a nude. Bit dull but they'll do the trick. I'll see you there, Megster.' Her arse emerges from the wardrobe and she dusts the shoes down to let me know it's been a lifetime since they got an airing. It reminds me a little of when we were teens and we shared everything. I think there was a point when Mum also used to buy knickers in bulk multipacks and just pass them out among the group.

'Shoe drama?' I ask.

'The best sort of drama but all sorted.'

'Well, come here and make yourself useful.' I gesture over to her. 'Help me with these grips.'

I seem to have inherited Lucy last night. Mainly as she was trying to push a stronger hen-do agenda that Emma was not willing to partake in so I brought her to mine to avoid potential conflict. It was a chance for her to meet Linh but she also became another set of hands as we sat into the night getting the little details together. My mother was horrified at the unravelling events of Emma's impromptu wedding. *I'll just run a brush through my hair. I don't want fuss. Jag is literally wearing Vans.* So we've spent the last twenty-four hours panic-buying better fitting underwear and accessories, and my kitchen table is currently covered in supermarket flowers.

'I pressed your dress. You can wear it instead of strutting around half-naked,' I tell Lucy as she jabs grips into the base of my hairline.

'I do not strut.'

'Yes, you do.'

'The dress is a little dull, no?' she says, removing it from its hanger. I press my hands against the skirt of mine. I have to disagree. Jag went for a wrap dress in a navy. You can't go wrong with it. This man can stay forever, in my opinion. 'I was thinking…' she mutters, in a sing-song voice, adjusting her boobs.

'Never a good idea.'

'Maybe we should invite Sam to this thing… it could be a nice way to meet him?' she says, innocently but not. I can't think of anything worse than him being interrogated by my family.

'We have to be at the venue in, like, three hours, so no.'

'He's a bloke. He literally has to find a suit, wipe down his pits and rock up.'

'Still no.'

'Spoil. Sport.'

I grin at her through the mirror. She can find her fun elsewhere today, just not at my expense. She twirls in the mirror trying to work out if she can shorten her skirt.

'Anyways, where's *your* date? Do you have anyone on the horizon at the moment?' I ask her. We always ask Lucy that but we always know what the answer will be. There is no horizon. It's just a sea, full of boats – and Lucy has partied on every one, multiple times, with all the fish in the sea. I don't worry about her in this sense because she's in control of every vessel she commandeers. She often tells us she's not looking for love in any shape or form. She just wants to enjoy life and all its colourful waves and currents, loudly. If we look at her complex layers, I know she does it for validation, for attention, because being the youngest she was often forgotten. I think we left her in a Tesco as a child once. But it's in contrast to me. I'm quite happy staying on the one boat, wearing a lifejacket and ensuring the shipping forecasts are being kind. The sea is an unpredictable mistress.

'No,' she says, hanging her arms around my neck. 'I'm shagging a banker called Gareth. He makes me shout at him though and he has a thing for bondage.'

'Marriage material then?'

She does a strange movement like she may be shuddering.

'What does he look like, this Gareth? Is he at least fit?' I ask.

'He looks like a young Matt Damon.'

'That's good?' I say, hopeful.

'Oh… he's nice to look at but he's messed up in the head. Huge humiliation fetish. I make him wear my pants and then he ejaculates and cleans my flat while I shout at him.' I sit there slack-jawed. 'It's a mummy regression thing. It's fun but, after a while, it gets tiring being so mean. And all that flogging has given me a touch of tennis elbow.'

My jaw is still slack. Today is supposed to be about a wedding and the wholesome nature of love and now that's all that floods my mind. What does she flog him with? Remind me never to borrow her belts.

'Question… then why?' I enquire.

'Education, dear sister,' she says, her eyebrows doing a cheeky jig. 'I always thought it was funny that you guys went to university and then literally shut down in your twenties and turned into adults. We're still allowed to have fun. I encourage fun.'

'Is that why you did two degrees and a master's then – just to be able to justify that lifestyle?'

'Well, I also did that to get one over on all you bitches and become the smartest sister,' she answers, pointing to her forehead. She has a ridiculous point. I mean, Emma is the heart surgeon so she's the one I'd want standing over my aorta, but if I was stuck in a street fight outside a chicken shop in a foreign country, without a phone and a wallet, then I definitely know which sister would pull me out of that hole.

'So getting back to Sam coming to this wedding…'

I shake my head. 'It's limited capacity. In Emma's eyes it's not even a wedding.'

'He could come for the after-drinks part?' Lucy says.

'There is no after-drinks part. It's literally a ceremony and lunch. We've explained this to you many times, Luce.'

'But it's a wedding.'

'But it's Emma.'

'So snoresville. I bet you she's got chicken for the main. Bet you a tenner.'

'I'll take that bet. She'll be classy and go for lamb,' I retort, fist-pumping her. Two little girls suddenly run in wearing navy and gold dresses. I turn and smile broadly to see them take to my bed and start jumping so the netting of their skirts balloons up and down. The joy on their faces is a picture. On their feet, brand-new gold Converse, fresh out of the box – Jag definitely picked the outfits. Lucy can't quite contain her excitement and jumps up with them. My bed had better be able to take that, Lucy.

'You guys look AWESOME!' she screams. In the doorway stands Linh, her head resting against the doorframe. She wears an elegant trouser suit that she's accessorised with flowers and ornate earrings. She looks over to me and beams. *These are the reasons to stay alive, why we stay behind.* I can almost hear her whisper it into my ear ever so quietly.

*

'Why is Lucy limping?' Beth asks me as we gather in the foyer of this waterfront hotel in the city of Bristol. It's Emma all over. It's classy yet functional. You know it's a hotel with a good parking facility, pillow menu and that breakfast is included and not some add-on buffet extra.

'She fell off my bed,' I reply.

'Having sex?'

'No. She was jumping with the girls. Why would she be having sex on *my* bed?'

Unfortunately, this gives both of us a severe case of the giggles and Meg glares at us in reprimand as she tries to organise everyone before we walk down the aisle. For the smallest wedding in the world, Emma does seem to have the biggest entourage.

'OK, we need all the little people first. Hold hands. And then each sister in single file and then Emma with her two girls giving her away… Are we clear?' barks Meg.

Our nephew, Joe, salutes her cheekily and Lucy laughs.

'We need a bride, though, Meggsy?' Lucy says, heckling the co-ordinator.

'She's in the loo. And slow walking, one together, two together. Lucy, go through it with the girls. Gracie, go check on Ems.'

I go in search of our missing bride, turning to see the toilets signposted by the reception desk. These are fancy loos, with towels instead of dryers and mandarin and ylang-ylang hand lotion as a bonus. In fact, it's a very fancy hotel, though I'd expect nothing less from Emma, my organised sister-twin. She's posh but not posh, with good taste and a precision about her. She'd have thought about every last detail of the day, from the types of drinking glasses, the folds on the napkins (swans, fancy), to what socks the boys are wearing.

'Ems? Meg told me to come in and check on you,' I say, as the main door of the ladies closes.

I push at some of the doors until I get to the last cubicle and find her sitting on a closed toilet. I hadn't seen her outfit yet but it's what you'd imagine Emma would pick. It's a white tea-length dress with good tailoring and a clean neckline. No veil or lace but a flower in her hair finishes off the look. Pride swims deep in my veins to see her so graceful, so beautiful.

'Just having a deep cleansing breath,' she says.

'Take your time.'

'Or not, the registrar has to get to another wedding after ours,' she giggles, nervously. Her hand trembles and she clenches a fist to steady it. She's a surgeon by trade so it's strange to see her hand shake like that. I go over and wrap mine around hers.

'You all right?'

'Is this too quick? I had a feeling that maybe this was too quick. Jag always sensed my uncertainty and I think he thinks I feel uncertain about him. But it's not. It's getting married again, it's the girls. It all feels so quick.' She exhales loudly and slowly.

'We don't have to do this. We can tell the registrar to go and then just have a fancy well-dressed lunch,' I suggest.

'But…'

'It's all paid for…' I say, finishing her sentence. It does feel nice to have another fiscally minded sister as part of our clan. I pull her out of the cubicle as she looks into the mirror and adjusts the wispy bits of hair around her forehead.

'Do you love Jag?' I ask her.

'Very much so.'

I like how those very words bring her peace, how they fall out of her mouth with zero hesitation.

'Then don't waste any more time. Marry him.'

She knows where this comes from. Tom and I always said no regrets but, if I could turn back the clock, I'd have hesitated less. I'd have travelled with him, married him sooner. I'd have created more memories of him by my side.

'Is Mum fuming? I've not seen Mum.'

'She's fuming because she's not got a fascinator and Beth did her hair and made her look like Hillary Clinton.'

Emma giggles uncontrollably.

'This feels different to when I married Simon,' she says thoughtfully. I don't like her mentioning her ex's name today of all days. Hell, all us sisters still refer to the man as Satan for all the hurt, lies and absolute shittery he put Emma through, but I understand why he's in her train of thought.

'Because, deep down, you knew Simon was a cock?'

'Perhaps. I had that big poofy fairy dress on, remember? I thought I had reached some life's pinnacle of marrying another surgeon and that was my life done. Happily ever after.'

We both examine our reflections in the mirror. I guess we all think that at some time but life is never quite done with us. There's always a plot twist, a sequel, a bonus chapter. Five years ago, could any of us predicted that we'd be standing here now, doing this?

'Now, I feel a bit older, a bit wiser. Like I know what I'm letting myself in for.'

'You did get old…' I tell her.

She hits me playfully with her bouquet.

'You got braver too. You've allowed someone into your life again, been re-educated about what love is. You don't know how happy Jag makes us,' I tell her. 'If you were marrying another Simon, Lucy would be having words, you know that, right?'

'She'd already have stabbed him. We'd be taking it in turns to visit her in prison.'

'This is true.'

She turns to face me. She's the tallest of the sisters so is about three inches above me. When Tom died, Emma was the sister who was there that day. She held my body up as it collapsed to the floor; she explained everything to me in plain medical terms to help my understanding of how Tom was leaving us: how he would draw his last breath, how he would have been feeling. Strangely, I needed that, to think of things in that organic sense. Even when Emma was going through the pain of her divorce, she put that all aside to offer her knowledge, her support. I hope Jag heals you, Ems. I hope this next chapter is glorious.

'When did you get so wise, Gracie?' she asks me.

I look at her in confusion.

'*You're* the surgeon. I was reminded by Lucy today that she also has two degrees and a master's so she has all the smarts too.'

'Bull,' Emma replies. 'None of us went through what you did. I would take all of that away from you in a second, but look what a beautiful soul it's made you. You know more than all of us combined.'

My eyes glaze over to hear her say that out loud. The door suddenly swings open and Beth runs in, tossing her bouquet at me.

'This baby is literally juicing my bladder like an orange.' She scampers into a cubicle and we hear a long stream of wee hit the loo. 'And I don't know what you two are doing in here but Meg is going to put Lucy in a headlock soon and I'm too pregnant to get involved in that fight. Hurry the fuck up.'

Emma and I laugh silently, as she bends over and kisses me on the forehead.

*

'Do you take this woman to be your wife? Will you love her tender, leave her all shook up every night and never leave her with a suspicious mind?' Elvis asked us, his lip curled up, strutting a pose I hoped his jumpsuit would forgive him for.

'I do,' Tom replied.

'What about you, little lady?'

'Don't I get the song-title vows?' I asked him.

Tom grinned at me. If we were paying for actual Elvis then I wanted the full shebang. You don't come to Vegas and not get the full bells and whistles. Elvis had better be dancing later too.

'OK then… Will you promise to love this hound dog? Show him the depths of your burning love and not leave him lonesome tonight? Uh-huh-huh,' he asked me. I was pleased to get the extra uh-huh-huh.

'I do,' I replied, giggling.

I remember Elvis had phenomenal hair and a real commitment to a genuine quiff, but he had a slight paunch so was more burger-eating Elvis towards the end of his career. Let's get married, Tom had joked. I had brought him along as a plus-one to an accountancy conference in Vegas. It was a working holiday where Tom promised me we could go and see Cirque du Soleil as long as I let him wear a tux one night and pretend to play blackjack like he was one of Ocean's Eleven. We were at a breakfast buffet that seemed to cater for all food groups and mealtimes as there was a man in a cowboy hat next to us eating lasagne and salad at eight in the morning.

You're mad, I told Tom. *Nothing would give me greater joy than making you my wife*, he replied. I assumed he was still drunk. I was sitting there with a three-egg omelette and a cup of coffee, no make-up, and my hair pulled back from my face. *Nothing would give me greater joy than doing something completely spontaneous and random. Think of all the people we'd annoy back home. Your mother would never forgive us. We can have a party back home to please the elders. Come on. I'll buy the clothes, pick up some rings and a bouquet. We need witnesses. I'll find those too. Come on, Gracie, let's live a little. I want to get married by Elvis and hang out with you forever.* I smiled.

Tom ended up wearing a bottle-green velvet suit he'd picked up from some vintage shop near our hotel and he accessorised with white Converse. It was very Tom. He had style about him. He wouldn't have worn some bog-standard, charcoal regular-fit suit from Marks & Spencer. Just buy me something white, I told him. He went vintage with that too. It was a sixties shift with lace. Tom said he liked how it had history to it, like it'd been worn before by another bride. There was love in its threads. And dust, I joked, and what looked like a suspicious stain on one of the arms. The witnesses were two people called Jim and Martha who were from the Coventry branch of my then accountancy firm. I still send them Christmas cards. Jim wore a Hawaiian shirt and we all went out for a prime rib and shrimp dinner after, in a restaurant that had a half-mile-long salad bar I still rave about to this day. Tom used to jest that he only married me because only I could get that excited about unlimited croutons and ten kinds of salad dressing.

'Then without further ado, and in the power vested in me by the good state of Nevada and the power of the god that is Elvis Presley, you may now leave here, husband and wife. You may kiss this little missy here, my friend…'

'Thank you very much.' Yes, in my delirium, that sentence came out of my mouth in an Elvis style except it didn't sound like Elvis. I sounded like a Welsh person with wind. Tom laughed, so very loudly, and then we kissed. He dipped me as he did it and I shrieked. Martha took a brilliant picture on her phone and it was the one we framed and sent out to everyone back in the UK so they could shout at us. You did *what?* My mother still questions the legality of that day. God, that was a good day. Elvis sang 'Viva Las Vegas' and 'Always On My Mind'. We danced. In a room that was a velveteen dream, that matched Tom's suit, where there were people waiting outside for their turn. We were married.

*

'Jag and Emma. You've come here today, in front of your family and friends, to declare your love and commitment to one another through marriage…'

I come back into the room. All the little nieces are cross-legged at the front of the room, Jag's father is sobbing uncontrollably, and there is an emotion on my mother's face. I think it may be relief. Emma and Jag look joyous; it was the small ceremony they both wanted. I know that feeling all too well. To cut through all that wedding bullshit and just have you and him, standing there,

together, the focus on all the right things. Though I am pretty sure
Emma would have screamed blue murder if she'd been made to
wear a used and suspiciously stained dress.

'… And so I am very proud to pronounce you husband and wife.'

As sisters, we all explode into applause, Lucy more so than the
rest of us, and both Emma and Jag kiss sweetly and fold their bodies
into each other, him whispering something into her ear.

'YES, EMMA!' Lucy shouts. My mother casts her a look. We
are not rowdy people, Lucy. Lucy doesn't care. Meg wolf whistles.
Beth is overcome by hormones so sobs and shares tissues with Jag's
family. Oh, Emma. I can't deny that feeling inside me, that swell of
emotion. It's pride, it's happiness, but I'd be lying if I said I didn't
feel all those small fractures in my heart sting a little. Love is shit
like that. How it can spark the whole spectrum of emotion in a
second, how it has such tremendous range. I try to stop myself
from crying, from sobbing but I can't. A small hand reaches up
and wipes a tear that rolls down my cheek.

'Mama, are you OK?' Maya asks me. 'Are you sad?'

Her eyes look up at me and study my face.

'Far from it. It's a good day.'

Emma and Jag proceed to leave the room in a round of applause,
our small group following them, and I stand Maya on a chair next
to me as she rests her head on my chest.

'So what did you think?' I ask her. 'How did you enjoy your
first wedding?'

'Why does she have to obey him?' she asks. 'I don't understand
that word.'

'It means she'll do what he says.'

'Sod that,' she replies. Jag's mother, who is in earshot, smiles broadly.

'You don't think you'll get married one day?' I ask. I can't think back to a time when I was Maya small but I did remember we played weddings a lot when we were little. We used my mum's net curtains and sateen bedspread and she'd shout at us for dragging it down the stairs. Being the tallest, Emma was always the groom. Maya's look, however, reads horror.

'Can I marry you?' she asks me.

'No. That's not really how these things work.'

'Oh.' I seem to have broken some illusion in her head of what the future may look like.

'Do you think you'll marry anyone again?'

I shake my head.

'Well, I don't think I want to obey anyone so I want to stay with you forever, is that OK?'

I stop for a moment. Forever. I pull her close to me and embrace her tiny frame under mine. I don't know what that word means any more but let's promise to do that much. We can hang out together for as long as the fates allow.

'Is there food now?' she asks, pulling away.

'Yes.'

'I might get married then if there's food after. Like spaghetti?' she asks.

'Perhaps,' I say, studying the sparkle in her eye. God, this girl loves spaghetti. There are worse things to love.

I hold her hand and let her jump off the chair. Another rogue pair of hands hug me from behind. Cleo. We stand here for a moment, this assortment of arms, super-chic dresses and homemade bouquets.

'Where's Ba Linh?'

'She went to the bar with Aunty Lucy,' Cleo informs me, rolling her eyes. I hope she gets that eye-roll from me. I hope Lucy knows Linh is on three different types of medication that won't mix with what she has in mind. The girls glance at me and take a hand each. Look at us all matchy-matchy. Come on, girls, let's see where this goes. Let's hope to Elvis there's forever and spaghetti in our stars.

Chapter Sixteen

G,

So I'm told I'm going to be in Amsterdam when you're going to be in Amsterdam. We're seeing each other, right? Coffee? Spliff and a pancake? Is this going to be weird? I've told Astrid that I can stay in a hostel if it's weird but I suspect it could be good fun. Gracie C going on holiday. This is rare. I bet you're dispensing all your shampoo out into the little bottles and labelling them, aren't you? And putting an extra pair of knickers in your handbag. Why do you do this? Is it because you're scared you're going to wee yourself? I mean, naturally, this may happen because you'll be so excited to see me but try not to do that. I get in Tuesday. I hope we get to see each other.

T x

Emma Callaghan is married to Jag Kohli.

'You see, it's properly official because it's on Facebook now,' Lucy tells me, waving her device in my face. The wedding was two days ago now and, despite Lucy's attempts to borrow Meg's credit card, christen the union with sambuca and put a tab behind the bar, it was the civilised affair Emma and Jag had wanted. There was chicken for the main (tenner for Lucy) and a sensible treacle tart for dessert and we all parted ways at four-ish with dresses we could use again for other occasions. Looking at Lucy's phone now, I see the picture Emma has chosen for her profile and it makes my heart sing. Instead of the standard shot, it's some reportage snap of the moment Jag whispered something into her ear and she's creased over with laughter. And it's that Emma you don't see too often, one who has let her emotions into the open for the world to see. I hope her ex-husband catches this picture on social media. I hope it makes him cry.

'Is that what you're wearing?' Lucy asks me when she finds me in the kitchen.

'Yes? It's dinner with Astrid and Farah. It's hardly going to be a big night out,' I reply.

'Are you wearing make-up?' Lucy asks.

'Are you saying I need make-up?'

'I was thinking of going a bit jazzy, girls' night out?' she hints with actual jazz hands.

I shake my head. After karaoke and entertaining all the guests who've descended on Bristol for the memorial, I don't want another big night out. I want a dinner with close friends where I know I can wear trainers and won't be judged for it. Given the tightness of her dress and her platform boots, Lucy, however, has different plans.

'Go on, have a nice evening,' adds Linh, sitting at my kitchen table reading a newspaper.

'It will be but I want to be back at a reasonable hour too. Are you sure you don't mind looking after the girls and Isaac?'

Linh shakes her head at me. This sleepover had been planned weeks back and I didn't want to renege on my promise. Isaac showed up an hour ago with a sleeping bag and swimming goggles so the lad means business, but I am worried three kids may tip Linh over the edge. Speak of the devil, he runs into the kitchen.

'Hi, Linh! Hi, everyone!'

We all wave at him.

'I like your hair!' Isaac tells Lucy. He turns to Linh. 'And you're a very cool grandma. My grandma smells of ham. I wish my family looked like yours. You all look different, that's kinda cool,' he announces to the room, his hand inside a box of Cheerios, helping himself.

Linh watches him curiously. He still seems to be jogging to a song in his own head. It's possibly reggae, maybe disco. I really wish we could hear it.

'Isaac, I'll be going out tonight but Linh will be here. Is that all right? I cleared it with your mum already.'

'It's coolio.' He puts an arm around Linh. Lucy laughs to look at him, like she may want an Isaac. 'Me and the girls are just going to chill. See yas.'

He runs out again and I notice Linh's curious expression again. 'I can get one of the sisters to help out?'

'I can manage. When all else fails, I can put them in front of the television until they fall asleep.' She puts a hand to my shoulder. 'Go. I also need to binge-watch the next season of *Scandal* and I can't do that with you in the house.'

Lucy laughs. She's bonded with Linh over the past few days. Both of them share that passion for pushing the envelope, for not doing what people expect.

'Well, you have our numbers if there's a problem. I am literally twenty minutes down the road.'

She nods obediently.

'Is there anything you want before we head out?' I ask.

'Yes. Your sister is right, at least put an earring on,' she answers cheekily.

*

Astrid and Farah come as a double act. All us Callaghan girls went to the same school – Astrid was in my year, Farah in Lucy's, and we became connected through sisterhood, friendship but also when Astrid and Farah fell in love and got married. Lucy and I have seen that relationship from the ground up, from two awkward teens learning to traverse through new feelings, awakened sexuality, to university, jobs, travel and marriage. They live in Amsterdam. Yes, the very place where Tom and I reunited after a time apart. Astrid has never admitted it to me but I think she invited us both there on purpose to orchestrate some meet-cute where we'd fall in love again. *And would you look at that? We only have the one spare bedroom; you and Tom will have to share.*

The last time I saw them both was at their wedding while I was on my post-Tom travels. Lucy came along. We don't speak of that trip in too much detail though, because Lucy and I left their reception, got caned in a hash bar on some very potent brownies and we lost time. I mean, that's one way of putting it. We ended up in an extreme S&M bar where I threw up after watching something unmentionable on a stage that still sends shivers down my spine and Lucy got into a fight with a drag queen after she accidentally set fire to her weave. I also lost a shoe. That sort of thing.

'That was an excellent night,' Lucy says now, bringing that story back to the dinner table.

'It was not. I still haven't been able to work out if we're legally allowed back in Holland,' I remind her. We were cautioned by some Dutch policemen on mountain bikes wearing incredibly short shorts.

'By excellent, I mean memorable. Come on, I bring that story out all the time.'

'I imagine you have a plethora of them, dear sister.'

'Yes, but that one is the best. Did I throw your shoe in the canal?' she asks me.

'Fuck, you did. I can't even remember why.'

'That is the sort of high we all need to be at some point in our lives.'

I can never work out what Lucy's intention was on that trip. I was there to see my best friends get married but my sister was on some mission to help me forget, to throw me into some heightened state of being where I wouldn't be wandering around the streets of Amsterdam a sad crying widow. *I can't bear to see you that sad, Grace, so I am going to dry-hump this Dutch road bollard until you laugh and can't be sad any more.*

Astrid and Farah sit opposite us in this Asian fusion restaurant in hysterics. That night, while they were busy glowing as newlyweds, they hadn't realised the bridesmaids had snuck out, off to find legal highs and get reprimanded by the Dutch. They knew nothing until we'd returned to their house, me with one shoe, wearing a wig that wasn't mine, and slept for twenty-four hours straight on one of their sofas.

'I thought you had slipped into a coma at one point. We were holding mirrors to your mouths. We kept rolling Lucy into the recovery position,' Farah says. Her eyes glow green, warm like wasabi.

'Yeah, and we didn't have enough blankets so had to cover you both with bath towels.'

Lucy and I laugh. It was a crazy few days. If I wanted distraction I got it.

'And when you finally did wake up...' Astrid adds.

We all smile. It was because I had to take a call. It was from a lawyers' office in Saigon, someone who wanted to discuss some paperwork Linh had filed to ensure I was a legal guardian to her two granddaughters. It was the most sobering phone call I'd ever taken. I had the driest mouth so Astrid tried to feed me water through a straw. They all stood there while I sat ashen, tears rolling down my face. It was Grace back in her recent default setting. The sobbing became more intense. Lucy thought it was out of physical pain because I was so hungover. And then I told them. Lucy was frantic. *You did what now? You're going to adopt? Girls? They're sisters? I need to ring people.* I stopped her. All I remember was Astrid watching me, my body trembling a little, and she held me. *This is an amazing thing, Grace. Does that make us aunties?* I nodded. Lucy hugged them, welcoming them into her gang. I will forever be glad I got to share that news with these three people.

This evening we are sitting in a harbourside restaurant, carved out of some old shipping container, the early spring air threatening to steal the winter from us. It's a newer and funkier Bristol compared to the one where I spent my university years. I used to revel in the access to the Jason Donervan in the early hours but now the city is abuzz with pop-up cuisine, street food and people dangle their legs over the harbourfront supping at organic homebrews. It was a scene Tom and I came back to Bristol for, for evenings like this.

'I am going to order us some more drinks because I'm not nearly drunk enough,' Lucy announces, getting up. 'Farah, come with. There's a barman who's slightly fit and I need a wingwoman.'

Farah rolls her eyes and Lucy swings her legs over the bench. Jesus, Lucy, how much have you had to drink, because that barman has a shit beard like a bargain-basement Disney villain.

'You look really well, hun,' Astrid says as soon as they're out of earshot.

I put a head to her shoulder. Astrid rarely talks of Tom and his passing. To her, he was an acquired friend, someone she inherited after I went to university, but she welcomed him into our fold, which is very her.

'And how are you feeling about the weekend? All sorted?' she asks.

'Kinda. I guess it's all lined up, ready to go.'

She studies my face. You can tell she has mixed feelings about how this will affect me but she's here and that to me signals her strong empathy and the true quality of our friendship.

'Farah and I have news. We've been looking into surrogacy recently. I don't know, maybe something about what you did made us think.'

'Astrid! That is amazing. Really?'

'Really. It seems there are many options for a lesbian couple, though – adoption, fostering or we can go and choose some spunk from a clinic. We're just revelling in the choice for now.'

I reach out and hold her hand. 'You're not asking me to be your surrogate, are you?'

'Ha! No. I'd ask Lucy before you.'

'Charming.'

'Mate, we've got to keep that one busy or she'll find trouble. She keeps telling me she's bi now.'

'Yep. Mum says it's a phase. I don't know. To me though, it's just a long line of one night stands and anecdotes that she relays via WhatsApp and emojis.'

'It's Luce. I feel we could spend a lifetime working her out. But look how bloody happy she is. She embraces everything with such joy. It's inspiring if vaguely annoying.'

I don't deny that at all; absurdly happy seems to be Lucy's default emotion.

'And I'd say the same for you. It's good to see you so… well. When I saw you in Amsterdam last time, all that emotion was still etched in your face. You look a bit…'

'Less pained?'

'More Grace…' she says, leaning into me. 'Luce also said there was a school-dad booty call on the scene?'

'The gob on that girl. His name is Sam. It's just a thing.'

'Well, you be careful there, yeah? Look after yourself.'

'What with? My bits?'

She knocks her head back to laugh. 'I mean, look after your heart.'

I'll try. Our heads suddenly turn when we hear my sister's cackle from across the restaurant and see her lean into the bar in the way Lucy does. She ended up going full out-out which means she's wearing her good pants or none at all. But please, not that barman.

'She doesn't let up, does she?' Astrid says.

'Well, you have to admire how she takes the bull by the horns.'

'Quite literally.'

If I go near the bull pen, I will pet the bull cautiously until we've developed a rapport.

'I mean, she can do better than that barman, though? He doesn't even have an arse – it's waist and his trousers just hang there.'

'You're asking the wrong girl,' Astrid jokes. She looks around the bar space. It's a midweek crowd so most are here for celebrations or after-work dinner specials.

'How about him?' she asks.

'Astrid, he's wearing dungarees.'

'They're a thing now.'

'Yeah, if you're a Super Mario Brother.'

Likewise, I also scan the area. I immediately discount the men two tables down who are wearing dress shoes with jeans but take an interest in the studenty, artisan crowd, waving cigarettes around with wild abandon. The sort you know have poetry in their lockers. Lucy could get with the one in the checked trousers with the scarf. I'd approve of that.

'Or maybe Luce needs a middle-aged sad case to pull her into check.'

I turn and see a table by the bar where two people are sitting then swerve my head around again immediately. Astrid senses my discomfort.

'You know them?' she asks.

'Yeah. School-run parents.' I sneak my head around for another glance. No, they are not. That is definitely Ross Cantello, the notorious Carrie Cantello's husband, and next to him is Liz Boucher, Carrie's best mate. 'They're not together...' I explain, shocked.

'They look together,' Astrid says, who's in a position to snoop. 'They're doing the leg-pretzel thing under the table which I never understand. Unless there's a tablecloth there then it's pretty obvious you're trying to rub his knob with your toes.'

I snort a little on my mojito. Astrid can't quite look away now and I nudge her.

'What's the skinny on these two then?' she asks.

'Ross is a recovering alcoholic and his wife is a primo bitch, obsessed with Harry Potter. We've knocked heads before in a serious way. And that lady is the wife's best mate.'

Astrid winces. 'Wow. And there was me thinking you'd disappeared into some boring version of suburbia. That's juicy. I'm not sure I understand the appeal, though. I can see his nipples through that jumper. When will people learn to layer?'

I can't turn now, can I? This is too good. Proper soap-opera-level scandal.

'What are they doing now?'

'They're doing googly eyes. She thinks he's hilarious. "Oh, Ross... I can't wait to tweak your nipples later." There's also a lot of hair swishing. I take it she's married too?'

'Yup.'

'Hold up.' She stops Farah and Lucy, who are returning to the table. 'Girls, stand just there…' She grabs my phone on the table and takes a picture of them, not knowing we just want the background.

'Gotcha,' Astrid says, putting the phone down in front of me. Lucy and Farah look at each other curiously.

'Who are we stalking?' Lucy asks. 'Is it the barman? Forget him. I've seen him up close and he has Eminem lyrics tattooed on his neck.'

'No, it's some school-gate parents Grace thinks are doing the naughty behind their respective spouses' backs.'

Lucy's head swings round, examining the crowd. 'Oooooh, is it nipples and cork wedges?'

'Yes,' I say, pulling her back down to the table.

'You only wear a cork wedge in August unless you're in Marbella. It's the rules,' Lucy says, taking a long sip of drink. Wow, there are fumes coming off that. Negronis. I don't trust them because they're pure liquor. They are intent on hurting you.

Farah positions herself at the table so she can examine Ross and Liz more closely.

'They look the sort to have some interesting sex. I reckon they meet in Tesco car parks and she blows him in the back seat,' she says.

We all giggle at the comment. I don't even want to imagine that as I'll have to wait outside the Acorn classroom with them tomorrow. Do I feel sympathy here? Carrie was such a bitch to me that it might help explain why Ross plays away but is she a bitch as a consequence of his philandering? There are kids in this picture so that upsets me. But also the fact that Liz is attached to Carrie's arse most days, that she still holds onto some pretence they are best mates. That, to me, is warped.

'Don't giggle too loud. I can't have them noticing us and then my cover blown,' I say. This may not be easy with Lucy.

'That's a Travelodge affair, you know it. Quick twenty minutes where she does all the work then they take it in turns to use the facilities and she makes the bed afterwards like they haven't been there,' Farah continues.

Drink erupts out of a nostril as she says that. 'God forbid if his wife ever found out. She would murder him,' I say.

'Yeah, you mentioned that… You've knocked heads with his wife? How?' Astrid asks.

I take a deep breath, knowing I need to hold back some detail or Lucy will find her. And burn her things. 'She's a busybody, judgemental sort. The worst kind of school-gate bitch. We've had words.'

'Did you lamp her?' Lucy asks, a bit too excitedly. This is where Maya learnt her fight tactics, wasn't it?

'No. Because that would drag me down to her level.'

'But that's the point, you go down to their level, you silence the bitch and then you rise up again like the phoenix you are. It's what we Callaghan women do. It's what our name means,' Lucy informs us.

'Your name means "Silence the bitch"?' Farah asks, grinning.

'It means contention or strife. Mum did one of those ancestry things. We had Irish ancestors who were keen on a brawl, it's in our blood.'

'I think half your blood is alcohol, which is why you like a fight,' I say. 'I'm not getting involved. In any case, by the looks of things, I don't want to pile on that woman's woes.'

Lucy, Astrid and Farah all stare over at Ross and Liz again, their noses wrinkled. That would be a whole lot of drama to break down and I wouldn't know where to start. *Oh, Carrie. So you're quite hateful, we've known that for ages, and Ross is sleeping with Liz.* I see that going down well at the next harvest assembly.

'Well, you're a better person than most but we knew that anyway, Gracie,' Astrid adds, winking. 'So where to now?' she says with a hint of trouble in her eye. Farah downs her drink in one. Lucy bangs her feet like they're the sound of a drum roll. I knew they'd do this. Oh, we're just going out for a 'quiet dinner'. That night in Amsterdam was supposed to be a 'quiet walk' after the reception. I can't do another Amsterdam. The very thought is making me gag.

'Yes, bitch!' Lucy squeals, double high fiving her. 'The night is young and so am I.'

'You're nearly thirty,' I tell her.

'Piss off.'

*

It's 2.32 a.m. For the love of all that is holy, I need to lie down. I stop walking and lie on the cobbles, looking up into the sky. Hello, Tom? Are you up there? You're not because you didn't believe in any of that. You were a man of science with slightly spiritual leanings but it's nice to think your body makes up part of the cosmos in some way.

If you were here, it'd be useful. I remember we went out in Bristol once and you managed to blag a lift from a random man in a white van at three in the morning as none of us knew where we were and we didn't have any cash left. You were always the one still laughing, still standing at the end of the evening, still suggesting the night go on forever, until the sun came up. By that measure, you'd love this. The fact you're dead and it's basically an excuse for me to have spent a month beforehand getting horribly drunk with all these people we once knew. You'd approve of the drinking, of me getting out there and having fun.

But is this fun? I don't think my liver is having fun. We went to another bar after dinner. No, we went to three bars. I reach into my pocket and there's a salt shaker in there. Did we do tequila? All three of them are dancers too; they like to stand in a circle and throw shapes in a strange accentuated fashion. I danced. I mean, they had to drag me on the dancefloor against my will but I joined in. I jiggled to some funky house disco beat and watched them gurn and laugh through the flashes of light, occasionally stopping to hug me, pockets of sweat in the creases of their forearms. The alcohol helped. The fact I love all these girls dearly helped too. I think I had fun.

However, this part is not fun. Astrid and Farah have gone on a hunt to find us late-night snackage that I hope to god is something deep-fried and fatty, and I have been left here with Lucy, who has danced her way along the docks talking at the very top of her voice, which makes me worry for the state of her hearing.

'Gracie, babes. Do you want me to carry you?' she says, doing a muscleman pose. She's serious. How would we do that? Can I piggyback? The cobbles are hard against my back but I hope there may be a therapeutic quality to lying here.

'No.' Instead, I do a very classy move of spinning my body round like a windmill and throwing up over the side of the docks.

It takes a moment for my vomit to reach the water but, when it does, a group of men walking past cheer. This is not elegant. And now I know we definitely had tequila.

'Woah, Gracie. Don't fall in.' Lucy puts a hand out to stop me from rolling into the docks and comes to lie down next to me, twisting my hair so it's out of my face and not hanging down over the ledge. I can hear Tom laughing from here. She offers me her scarf to wipe my mouth and I use it to shroud my face.

'Leave me here. I want to sleep here.'

'Then you'll need company.'

There is silence as she allows me a moment to burp loudly into the night sky and remember how to breathe.

'I don't remember throwing up in Amsterdam,' I mumble.

'No, but I peed on a line of bicycles. Do you remember? I have a picture. I got on all fours thinking I was a dog.'

I giggle uncontrollably.

'To be fair, anything could have happened in the 'Dam and neither of us would have known what occurred. I had a handprint-sized bruise on my arse that night, did I ever tell you? It makes me think I may have got up on stage at that sex club we went to…' she says, confused.

I flare my nostrils at the thought. She holds my hand and I notice her eyes scanning the stars.

'I know you miss Tom, Gracie. I'm sorry I can't make things better for you. I can't be Megs and Emma and look after you in that way. Sometimes I don't know what I should be saying or doing,' she says, snuggling into me.

'You do make things better. You remind me to smile again. All Tom ever wanted was for me to go out there, full-bore, and live. You do that exceptionally well,' I tell her.

'I do, don't I? If there was anything Tom's death taught me...'

'Errm, you were like that when he was alive too...' I remind her.

'True.'

I retch a bit and Lucy holds my hair back once more. I'd like to say it's sweet and considerate but I think she also takes a picture of me at the same time as I lean over the docks again.

'Have we broken her?' a voice says suddenly. Astrid appears, eye make-up halfway down her face and looking particularly joyous that she has managed to acquire us kebabs. I see Farah gorging hers down, strands of shredded lettuce hanging off her lips like whiskers, and retch again. Lucy jumps up to see the food and they all stand over me, like they're looking down on a body and working out how to dispose of it. Just roll me over the side, girls.

'What's that?' Farah asks me, her garlic-sauce breath clouding the air.

The three of them all turn to something behind me, and I arch my head to the source of their glances.

'It's called *The Matthew*. It's a replica caravel ship from the fifteenth century,' I mumble.

'All right, Wikipedia,' Astrid says, peering down at me. I would look up but I can hear the sound of her chewing.

I only know this information as I once went on it on a school trip as a parent volunteer. One child got the wrong message and came dressed as a full pirate that day.

'Can you go on it?' Farah asks.

'Yes. You can hire it out for things. But…'

Too late. It's Astrid who starts jogging towards it and the other two follow with mischief in their eyes. I mean, don't mind me. I'll just choke on my own spew on the actual ground. Please don't go on the boat. There's a big locked gate there for a reason, girls.

'Girls, no,' I shout faintly, but it falls on deaf ears. I try and sit up. What are you going to do, jump onto it? Lucy is in heels. There's no walkway.

'Lucy, check for seamen on board,' Farah announces into the night air.

'Aye-aye captain! You know I like seamen.'

At least be original with the jokes too.

'Arrr, me hearties! Lucy's here to walk your plank,' Astrid adds, sounding less pirate, more Brummy. That's the joy of being drunk: the jokes are funnier, the voices are louder. At least be discreet pirates. That's not the way to turnover a ship. I think I can hear them actually singing sea shanties. Please. No. It's called trespassing. That thing is run by old people volunteers too. I met one of them. His name was Neville and he knew a lot about the sea. Don't get kebab on it either because it's replica and that looks expensive to replace.

Oh balls, they've found a way. I watch as they tiptoe on like burglars, the unfortunate acoustics of these docks meaning I can hear their every move and the sound of the ship swaying and creaking in the water. A group of people walk past me and I hear them audibly tut. Shit, they're going to get reported, aren't they? I'll spend the rest of the evening down a police station trying to bail them out. I stand up and stumble over to the stern of the boat.

'Lucy, get the fuck off. It's trespassing!'

Lucy's head pops up, her eyes darting in different directions like she's looking for intruders. She puts a finger to her mouth.

'Sssshhh, matey!'

'You're not a pirate.'

'How dare ye?! I am the mistress of the seven seas.'

To her credit, she's always done accents incredibly well but now is not the time.

'Don't touch a thing. Tell the others too.'

Her head disappears and my phone suddenly glows.

Yikes. I thought it best you saw this before the school gate goes into hyperdrive.

It's a message from Sam forwarding a screenshot from a What-sApp chat. There's a picture of me and Astrid in the restaurant. Astrid leans into me so the angle looks like we're about to kiss. The text under it reads: *Spotted! I don't know the popular term for these things any more? Bisexual? Pansexual?*

I can't even comprehend what I'm looking at.

What are you doing up?

I've been bingeing The Queen's Gambit like a sad case. Helen just texted it to me as she saw it in another WhatsApp group and didn't know what to do. I'm sorry. It's a really shitty thing of Carrie to do. She's such a bitch.

Not lesbian by the way. She's a gooood mate of mineee.

My fingers hover over the screen and I forward the picture Astrid took of Ross and Liz in the restaurant.

And this is who took the picture…

Wow. Seriously? Are they?

Possssssibly.

What are you doing up?

I'm on a nigt out. Currently tying to get my sister offfff The Matttthew.

Righto. And least you're with people and you're safe. Sounds wilder than my night. Am now obsessed with chess. Are you OK?

Because Carrie has told everyone I'm a lesbian? I'll live.

He replies with a line of laughing emojis.

How would you lure a group of drunk prrirates off a ship?

With rum and a pot of gold, no? Enjoy. Here if you need me. Love you xx

I stop to read those words at the end of the message. Oh. I mean, it's the early hours and I'm drunk but I didn't think we'd got to that stage yet? I don't know how to reply. I stare at my phone for a bit longer. You can love people in many different ways. I love chips but not in a romantic sense. It's an umbrella term. You can love your friends. I love those crazy bitches on that boat, for example. But before I have a chance to reply, a beam of strong light gets my attention. Fuck. Get. Off. The. Fucking. Boat.

'This boat is a national treasure!'

I don't know if it's security or the police. I see Astrid and Farah jump off the way they came in and run in the opposite direction, leaving a trail of kebab as they do. They left Lucy? Where the hell is Lucy? The man races after them and, for a brief second, I am glad they both are wearing trainers. Lucy's head appears.

'ABANDON SHIP!' I hear her shriek. I don't even know what sort of jump that is. I think it's a star.

'No. No. No. Lucy… Lucy!'

And then I hear a splash of water. You stupid bloody cow.

'Lucy!' And then a moment of panic. Lucy can swim. We had the same swimming teacher. Her name was Liz and she had a mullet. But Lucy is drunk. And wearing some pretty heavy platform boots to weigh her down. I can't lose Lucy. I should jump in. Please, Lucy. *How did your sister die? By trying to evade capture by jumping off a pirate ship.* She resurfaces in the way a shark might jump to catch a seagull for its dinner.

'FUCK! IT'S REALLY FUCKING COLD!'

I run over to a ladder that leads into the water and climb down a couple of rungs.

'Here, swim here! Can you swim?'

'I can't, urrrgh. Are there fish in here?'

'Yes, sharks. Swim, you stupid bloody bitch.'

She does a mistimed front crawl over to me. I don't want to tell her she's probably swimming through a disintegrated stew of my own chunder.

As her hand reaches the ladder, I pull her up and she lands on the docks in a wet heap, still laughing. I immediately wrap my arms around her, crying.

'Are you just drunk or are you sad I nearly drowned?' she says, her jaw quivering.

I take off my padded coat and wrap it around her as she shivers uncontrollably. She reminds me of a very sad version of Captain Jack Sparrow without the hat. She pulls something that looks like an old leaf out of her mouth. I hope to god it's nothing else. I try and warm her up, rubbing my hands up and down on her arms. If anything I now feel completely sober.

'I'm sorry,' she says. 'No one will let me in an Uber now.'

'We'll have to wring you out first...' I say, laughing, trying to stop her body from convulsing. 'But don't worry, I have spare knickers in my handbag.'

'Who carries spare knickers in their handbag?' she asks.

'Me. For moments exactly like this.' See, Tom Kennedy. Useful.

'Thank you for not running off with the others,' she says. 'Where's my other boot?'

I look down and indeed she has lost a shoe, á la Amsterdam.

'At least all our super-drunken nights out now have a theme.'

'They're expensive boots.'

'Well, I'm not going scuba diving to find it, you daft cow.'

In this street light I'm not sure, but her lips look to have a blue tinge to them. She's right, we won't be able to get an Uber, but it's lucky I know someone who might be up.

'Arrrrr…' she says in a faint pirate voice, a light tapping noise making me realise her teeth are chattering.

'I think you'll find the term is "shiver me timbers",' I say. 'Let's get you home, sailor.'

Chapter Seventeen

Tom, I will be in Amsterdam. I'll be taking the train from the airport to Centraal and then I will be taking a bus to Astrid and Farah's. When you say you'll be there too, will you be staying at theirs? I am sure it's big enough for the two of us. And it's not quite a holiday. I am combining travel with a trip to our Utrecht office. Do you have anything booked in? I want to go to Anne Frank House but I suspect that might not be your bag. I look forward to seeing you then. Where to next after that? Do you need anything from the UK?

Grace x

'I didn't know what to do so I put her in a hot bath and put some Dettol in it. How do I check for frostbite?' I ask Emma. She is super unimpressed that I have her up at three in the morning but she's a sister and so needs to be privy to these things, and I don't want to disturb Linh and wake the rest of the house.

'There'd be loss of feeling and discolouration in her extremities. They'd be a funny colour. I'm more worried about Weil's disease…'

I hear her switch a light on and chat to her husband stirring next to her. Her husband. That's new but good.

'What the hell is Weil's disease?' I ask.

'It's a disease you get from rats' piss in the water. Did she swallow any of it?'

'She was pretty drunk. Could she die?'

Emma senses that this is something which preoccupies my mind more than it used to so I can sense her guilt immediately.

'Do you want me and Jag to come and help?' she says.

'God, no. It's the middle of the night and then, if you wake the house, Mum and Dad will get up and it's not worth the drama.'

'She likely won't die but just check the usual symptoms – fever and if she goes yellow like a canary then that's her liver failing so get her to A&E.'

'I can't tell if you're being sarcastic or not,' I say.

'I'm just being thorough. A hot bath, lots of blankets and socks.'

'Should I wrap her in foil?'

'She's not a turkey…'

I laugh in reply.

'God, that girl is like a cat, how many lives has she used up already?'

'At least eight. Say hello to Jag for me.'

'Jag, Gracie says hello. He says hello back. Let me know if you need me.'

The line goes dead and I'm glad for a moment that Emma didn't delve for too much information. Like, how did I get Lucy home? Oh, I just rang my man lover to come and assist. He's downstairs now, drinking tea and filling up all my hot-water bottles, which is another reason I didn't want to wake Linh. Luckily, Lucy was too out of it to ask too many questions but she did manage some innuendo about being wetter than an otter's pocket that raised an eyebrow in the rear-view mirror.

I lightly push the door to the bathroom, where Lucy is floating quietly in the warm water, her hair drifting like seaweed. She'd look like Ophelia were it not for the tattoos and the nipple ring. The whiff of Dettol fills the air and I think about what Emma said about her liver failing. I pour another capful in.

Lucy opens her eyes. 'No more Dettol. It reminds me of when we were younger and someone would have a tummy bug and Mum used to hose down all the bed linen.'

'Wrong smell, that was Zoflora,' I say, putting my hand to her upper arm to see if she's warmed up yet.

'What did Emma say?' she asks.

'She said if you go a funny colour then I need to get you to hospital.'

'That's reassuring. I still feel frozen inside.'

'That's because of your ice-cold heart. Sam is downstairs making hot-water bottles and tea.'

She looks at me for a second, raising her eyebrows.

'Stop that.'

'He's better looking in real life, which is reassuring. And I liked how he brought blankets… that's forward thinking.'

I bend down and turn the hot water tap on again to top up the temperature.

'At least you were too delirious with cold to be too embarrassing.'

'I'm warming up, though.'

Maybe I should just leave her frozen; she'll be less trouble that way. The door suddenly swings open and a little figure is standing there, bleary-eyed, one pyjama leg rolled up, the other down. Crap. It's Isaac. I immediately pull the shower curtain across so he can't see Lucy's naked body.

'What are you doing?' he asks. 'Who is in the bath?'

I'm not quite sure what to say. He'll have no concept of what the time is so I can just lie and say it's Linh. I'm not sure how I will explain why I'm standing over Granny in the bath, though, giving chat.

'It's my sister, Lucy. You met her briefly this evening.'

'I did. She had nice hair.'

'Thank you,' says a voice from beyond the curtain.

'What are you doing up, little man? Can I walk you back to the room?' I ask.

'I need to wee.'

'Oh. Right. Ummm… you have a wee and I will go outside and, whatever you do, don't look behind the curtain, OK?' I instruct him plainly. Please don't look behind the curtain. My reputation at that school gate is bad enough.

'Sure thing, Grace Face.'

I see that has caught on. I tiptoe out into the corridor and listen to him weeing through the door.

'It's late for a bath,' I hear him say.

'Well, Grace was helping me wash my hair. I need help some-times.'

'You can't wash your own hair? How old are you?'

Please, Isaac. No questions. Lucy, don't reply. I hear him flush and stick my head around the door again. He's standing there, tempted by the curtain.

'Right, washing hands and off to bed you go, please. Here, let me help you with the soap.'

He looks at me curiously and at the pile of sopping-wet clothes on the floor.

'Why did she lie to me?' Isaac asks.

'Lie to you about what?'

'Why is she in the bath, it's the middle of the night?' I look at his confused face and don't quite know what to say. Do you tell a young impressionable child that a grown adult tried to invade a ship and fell off said ship into the docks? I don't think that's good parenting.

'It's because I'm a mermaid.'

I stop for a moment to hear the voice beyond the curtain. Isaac's mouth opens in shock. From pirates to mermaids in one evening, that's good work.

'I went swimming in the docks. I came back here to wash up and Grace lets me use her bath to wash my tail. Sometimes my human legs fail me and I need to be in water.'

'Can I see your tail?' he asks.

'NO! If you see me in my mermaid state then I can die.'

'Your sister can see you.'

'That's because she's family.'

I stand here not really knowing how to contribute to this fairy tale, bemused at how he's buying into this but not the idea that she couldn't wash her own hair.

'And you must keep this a secret, Isaac. Promise. Pinky promise it with Grace.'

He nods his head furiously and sticks his little finger out. Oh. OK.

'Now, go back to bed, Isaac.'

I hear his footsteps literally sprint through the corridor to the girls' room and I pull the curtain back to reveal that Lucy has covered her parts with all our washcloths.

'I look forward to him waking up in half an hour now when he has nightmares about there being a large fish person in my bath.'

Lucy shrugs. 'Possibly less scared than if he'd seen me naked, though, right? With all my piercings?'

'This is true. Just don't snag my nice Muji washcloths on your taco ring, OK?'

*

I've left Lucy upstairs in my well-loved Huggly and several layers of hoodie and thermal joggers. Meg made fun of the Huggly but look at Lucy now. It may just save her life. She's lucky she's in the house of someone so averse to the cold but also runs a comfortable line of clothes meant for working from home. I've also left her sweet tea and given her three hot-water bottles, expertly filled up by Sam, who's now sitting at my kitchen table, cradling a mug and urging me to also hydrate and warm myself up. I don't look particularly well, given a couple of hours ago I was spewing over the edge of the docks, but he doesn't seem to mind my tired, sallow face and frazzled hair.

'Thank you, knight in shining armour.'

He doffs an imaginary hat to me.

'You'd do the same for me,' he surmises.

'You know, I think I would. I owe you.'

He takes a long sip of his tea and then looks at me. 'I'll bank that for another time.'

I try and wind my mind back to whether he means in a fiscal sense. Or is this a sexual thing? As lovely as he has been this evening, I really don't think I can summon up that mood.

'You know I'm sorry I haven't seen that much of you since we went out with Ellie… I've been slammed,' I explain.

'It's cool. I get it. Busy times and then your sister got married.'

'Yeah. I wasn't sure whether to invite you. It was a small thing anyway and I don't think I'm ready to introduce you to the whole clan yet.'

His eyes widen as I say this. Introducing anyone to your family, never mind one as intense as mine, is quite a relationship milestone. I didn't mean to scare him. But he did say he loved me by WhatsApp though and ended with a double kiss. At the same time he also sends me pictures of his cock so that's by the by. I guess what lingers is the sense of whether we're going to go next level with this relationship. Orlagh knows, and there's also a little tribe of kids to factor in. We always agreed this is casual but where are we going?

'I mean, I miss you but we've been in touch with the odd message, meme. I think it's also been good for me to figure some things out on my own too,' he says quietly into the twilight.

'Such as?'

'Orlagh broke up with Jordan. She's been living with her mum but she's been messaging me a lot, thinking about reconciling perhaps?'

My heart flutters as he says that. I had an inkling. Not that I want to compete with his ex-wife but I worry for him. They are flutters of pure panic.

'And every time I get a message, do you know what I think?'

'You're taking a fucking liberty?' I say.

He laughs loudly, then adjusts his volume to ensure he doesn't wake up the rest of the house.

'I just think, *you're not Grace.*'

It's my turn for my eyes to widen.

'Because you're… in love with me?' I whisper slowly.

'God, no… I mean… What I want to say is… you're a really decent person, Grace. You're kind. Orlagh is not kind. What she did to me was not kind, in any shape or form. And when it comes down to it, you just ask yourself if you want someone in your life like that again.'

My flutters subside. He's worked it out for himself. I think of Emma for a second. Her first husband was a complete and utter bellend and look at her now, lying next to a new husband, a man we all adore and root for in every way. It can happen but Sam needed to work that out for himself.

'Well, I am glad. And thank you… I don't deal with compliments very well.'

'I know. I'd say something nice to you in bed and you'd hide under the duvet.'

'I've done it for years. Tom hated it.'

He smiles. It's not like he doesn't know who Tom is but I think he was aware he was always competing with someone else when it came to me, someone who wasn't even there for him to swim into at a local lido.

'So, what do you think you'll do then?' I enquire.

'I think I need to be single for a while, exorcise the ghost of her, learn how to co-parent.'

'That sounds wise.'

'I think I'm going to take up rowing. Is that weird? Does that make me sound like I'm having a complete middle-aged breakdown?' he asks. 'I thought, let's do something that Orlagh wouldn't let me do. Embrace my freedom for a bit.'

'Go for it. Watch out for Weil's disease though. You can catch it from river water. Keep your mouth closed,' I advise.

He nods. We sit there quietly, sipping our respective drinks. There's a feeling I can't quite put my finger on. This may be it. Whatever this was. A brief romantic interlude to fill the time and heal our wounds. Yet I don't feel sadness here. I can't be sad. Neither of us are ready for relationships. He just has to start rowing.

'And the whole "love you" thing. What I meant to say was, Orlagh broke me when she left, she really did. And then you came along and made things better again. So maybe not love in the traditional way, but what you've offered me is friendship and companionship in a really lonely time and, however this ends up, I will always love you for that.'

I am not sure why but the honesty of his words, the sweetness of it all, the very early hour, make me tear up. He looks mortified that he's made me sad.

'I'm not sure what I just said. It's very early and I watched too much of that chess show.'

I laugh. 'It was perfect. You've been a wonderful person to have by my side. I'm glad we've got to know each other. I really am.'

These are strange declarations to be making at such an hour, and none are singing with romance, but we both know what we're doing here. It's a break-up of something that never quite was. But what is lovely is that I've acquired myself the loveliest of friends from our strange arrangement. Someone I can call at 3 a.m. to deal with a beached mermaid, but also someone who knows he could show up at my door at any time and I would be there for him. Not even in a sexual way. *I'd show up for you, for sure.*

'You were almost like some sort of sex therapist. You could make a lot of money doing that,' he says.

'I believe that's called prostitution.'

'Forget I said that.'

I chuckle under my breath.

'Orlagh might always hate you, though. I am sorry about that,' he says, wincing.

'Oh, I can deal with her.'

'And what are you going to do about Ross Cantello and Liz Boucher?' he says, obviously invested in that drama.

'I mean, I could go in on Monday and ruin some lives, put that photo on some T-shirts or post it anonymously through Carrie's letterbox.'

Sam nods, impressed by my level of subterfuge.

'Or... watch that drama unfold on its own. Carrie's not my favourite person but, if that happened to me, it'd be crushing. There are kids involved. Perhaps the best thing to do is leave well alone.'

He smiles. 'And that's just decent Grace all over. Are all you Callaghans like that?'

'No. My eldest sister wanted to go shit on the Cantellos' doorstep. And you met the youngest who fell off the boat.'

He laughs again.

'Thank you, Sam.'

'My absolute pleasure.'

I look at my watch. Crap, it's almost four in the morning. I haven't been up this early since I was a student. 'It's late. You can stop here if you want, take a sofa?'

'I might just do that. And thank you, what we had was kinda fun.'

'It was. Is this going to be weird seeing you at the school gate every day even though I've seen you naked?' I ask.

'I was thinking that. I mean, I've seen your lady garden.'

'Can I appreciate the way you referred to it as something so lovely?' I say, grinning.

He shrugs. 'I don't think it'll get awkward between us, ever. I like you too much for that.'

And there it is. Except I haven't lost you at all. I want you to get on that rowing boat or whatever people row – a canoe? And I want to push you off the jetty, wave you off into a clear blue sky, sun streaming down, and see you paddle away, from me, and from that bitch ex-wife of yours into the world again. He stands up and does the very decent thing of getting our mugs and putting them into the sink to rinse. I also stand.

'Come here,' I tell him and pull him in for a hug. He's still a very good hugger until I feel a bulge pressed against my thigh.

'Is that your…' I say, confused.

'That's my phone,' he says. 'You've seen my knob, you know it's not the shape of an iPhone X.'

*

Back upstairs, I go into my room and see that we seem to have created enough of a mini incubator situation that Lucy has pinked up nicely. No signs of liver failure or frostbite and, for a moment, I feel what it must be like to be Emma, to have cured someone and delivered successful medical care. Maybe I'm in the wrong profession. Remind me to tell Meg in the morning that my Huggly is a wonder of thermal medicine.

'Why are you stroking my face?' mumbles Lucy, her eyes still closed.

'I'm checking to feel if you've regained a decent core temperature.'

'The best way to do that is to stick a thermometer up my arse. If you can get through the four layers of leggings you put on me.'

I spoon her from behind. It's like hugging a giant fleece bear. She grabs my arm and pulls it around her.

'Where is lover boy? Did you give him a cheeky blowie downstairs to say thank you?' she says. I elbow her in the back but I doubt she actually feels anything.

'With the house full? No. Actually, I think we may have broken up.'

Lucy flumps over like a giant marshmallow to face me.

'Shit, really? Was that because I trashed his car upholstery? I can pay to have that valeted and shampooed. I'm sorry, Gracie…'

I don't know whether to eke this out a little. I could have a lot of fun with Lucy's guilt and get her to do some chores for me in the morning to earn her penance. But, deep down, I know she just cares.

'It was very civilised. We make better friends, what we had just…'

'Filled a hole?'

'Or two?'

She guffaws and I put a hand over her mouth to shut her up. She gives me a huge hug and I embrace her tightly back.

'Are you sad?' she says, her head resting on my shoulder.

'Nah, how can I be with you as my sister?'

'That is obviously the best way to answer that question.'

'Go to sleep now. We have to be up early,' I say.

'But why?' she moans.

'We have to fling you back in the bath so Isaac will still think you're a mermaid.'

She giggles. I pull a bit of duvet over me and close my eyes, her arms still around me.

'Do you still kick?' I ask.

'You know I do… Grace Face. You know that's a thing now, right?' she mumbles softly.

'It isn't. It really isn't.'

Chapter Eighteen

For my life, Gracie. New York is MENTAL. And do you know what's most mental about it? It has zoos. In the plural. Like, it's this enormo city busting at the seams but, hell, we NEED ZOOS. Let's throw some penguins and a fucking lion in the middle of this metropolis. I went to the Bronx Zoo today with Doug. We walked around with giant pretzels as big as our faces. I've decided I like a zoo. I know you don't because you say the animals look sad and should be roaming free on savannahs doing their Circle of Life thing but have you seen kids at zoos? They're so fricking happy. Like properly enchanted. It's contagious. There was this three-year-old today who saw a gorilla and he lost his shit. My wish is to always be that excited about life.

I enclose a Bronx Zoo lemur fridge magnet with this note. I chose it because his tail is at a strange angle so it looks like his wang. I hope you love it. I hope you still love me.

T x

*

EVERYONE is here. And when I say everyone, it does feel like the whole of my address book and Facebook contacts list is in Bristol descending on this memorial that will happen tomorrow.

What do we wear? Is there anything I can do? I'm ovo-vegan in case there is food. I miss Tom. I'm so glad to be in town. How close are we to London again? Can I see Big Ben from here?

The texts roll in thick and fast. I reply to all of them with smiley emojis and just hope they can work these things out for themselves. I am not one hundred per cent sure how I feel about this whole thing yet. I teetered on indifference when it was first touted to me but now I just want it done with. In the same way you feel about a birthday as you go further into your thirties maybe. Let us all come together and then put everyone back in their corners of the world.

Today, in an attempt to try and entertain the masses closest to me, I've decided to take advantage of my zoo membership and drag everyone out to see some penguins so we can ooh and aah over them instead of thinking about tomorrow. I've also dragged my whole family here, mainly so they can spend some time out of their Airbnb where things are starting to unravel. I say unravel, it's mostly Mum doling out plenty of asides referencing Emma's quickie wedding. She's also perpetually worried that all the tiny people are going to wreck the joint so she won't get her deposit back, and totally underestimated the scale of catering necessary so is producing lasagnes the size of football pitches every night. That's a lot of béchamel. So it's fresh air and animals for all today and also a chance to welcome a few more visitors to the party. One of whom stands by the entrance, the same way he's always stood since we were students, hands in pockets, looking completely lost.

'UNCLE DOUG!' Cleo screams as she runs towards him. He bundles her up and gives her a massive cuddle. It's a bloody joy to see him so I bring him in for a hug too.

'Gracie Grace…'

'Dougie Doug. You made it.'

'Of course.'

Maya wraps herself around his thigh and he pretends to fall over like he can't quite handle their collective hugging.

'So this place is still standing?' he asks me, looking up in awe at the sign. We used to frequent the zoo as students in some attempt to be ironic or get through a hangover so it feels good to bring Doug back to a Bristol haunt of old. It was either this or the Lizard Lounge, a local notorious nightclub where Doug once threw up down a girl's cleavage. I'm not sure we need to meander down such nostalgia this time round. I hand him his entry ticket.

'It certainly is. Here, admission is on me. I've just let my family through. Joyce is wandering around in there too with Linh. It's a family affair.'

He smiles to be identified as such but he was always more like a brother to Tom and certainly the most favourite of honorary uncles.

'And Tom loved a zoo…' I add. I think that is why I come back here, despite my reservations about them; they always make me think of that excitable, curious Tom I once knew and loved.

'That he did. I remember I took him to Bronx Zoo,' Doug says, crouching down to tell the girls. 'We were with the monkeys and someone thought he was a tour guide so he spent ten minutes telling this group of tourists some amazing made-up facts about macaques.'

Cleo and Maya giggle hysterically. It's a new story to me but one that doesn't completely surprise. I have a feeling that's what this weekend will be all about: tales for days about that boy but ones with monkeys are always welcome.

'You sound slightly American?' I ponder.

'Well, permission to slap that out of me if needs be.'

'Will do.'

'You're Doug…' a voice says as we get through the turnstile. I turn to see Beth, who waddles over via the gift shop. She's an indiscriminate hugger so goes in to greet him.

'You're a sister?' he asks.

'I am. Didn't we go to a Massive Attack concert together?' His eyes suddenly read familiarity. Doug met all the sisters briefly at the funeral but he always is very confused by the sheer number of us. I mean, we outnumber the actual wildcats in this place. I remember that concert; it was back when I was a student and Beth visited me for the Bristolian musical experience.

'You're here?' I ask her. 'Are you trying to escape?'

'No, silly. I needed the loo… again,' she says, resting her hands on her pregnant belly. 'But permission to hang with you guys for a bit? Everyone's obsessed with the aquarium and it's a bit dull.'

I nod as Cleo and Maya excitedly lead Doug away to the leopards. I like how they've literally imprinted themselves onto him, keen to show him their manor. I like how Doug doesn't really have a choice.

'This was one of your more inspired ideas, by the way… putting wild animals between Mum and Lucy,' Beth mutters, her eyes closed to feel the spring sun on her face. Either that or she can sleep and walk at the same time. She nestles into me. It's a moment of quiet on one of those glorious days where the sun almost glows blue.

'Has it got really bad in the rental then?' I ask.

Beth's tired face says it all. From what I hear, it's a mixture of people stuck on devices and shouting at each other, like a scene from a stock exchange. When the stock has dropped. And the bankers haven't slept properly for days and are climbing over each other in a frenzied mass of bodies.

'Mum won't let us play *Just Dance*. She says our dancing is all too bad, it will end in disaster when we break things.'

'Savage.'

'She's also offended that I'm putting ketchup on everything.'

'Everything?'

'It's a craving. There's obviously vitamins in there that the baby needs.'

Out of all the sisters, Beth is the most neutral – she's slap bang in the middle and connects us all – but there is also a wonderful sense of chill and warmth that radiates from her. She roots through her handbag, a jumbled assortment of receipts, hairbands, baby wipes and what looks like an adult sock. This is where the genes differ. She hands me a Fruit Pastille.

'How long have they been in there?' I ask.

'They don't go off.'

'I believe they do.'

'Just eat one, you fussy cow. Now remind me, did I sleep with Doug?' she continues, her voice lowered. 'After that concert…'

The voices of my girls and Doug drift over as they try to search out some elusive lynx. 'How am I supposed to know? I wouldn't have been there. And why am I only finding this out now? You slept with Doug?'

She seems amused at how the questions pour out of me. 'Possibly. We were very drunk at that concert. My memory is like porridge these days. I definitely slept with someone in Bristol. It wasn't Tom.'

'Well, I'm glad to hear that much. You sound like Lucy…' I tell her.

'No, Lucy remembers everything. She'd be able to tell us how long it went on for and the exact angles of his cock when erect,' she says, descending into giggles. 'Don't make me laugh. I'll have to go to the bloody toilet again.'

We stop for a moment to look at the red pandas, poised on their logs, waiting to be photographed and admired.

'Want to hear some gossip?'

'Always.'

'Mum and Meg had words last night,' she continues.

'I'll assume they weren't good words.'

'Maybe I shouldn't tell you. But Mum had had too much Chablis and basically said the memorial was a really shit idea. She tore it down.'

I'd swing my head around in shock but a red panda over the way has made eye contact with me. It feels rude to break its gaze. To be fair, it's not a surprise. It sounds just like something our mother would say; she's not one for holding back what she thinks. A tiger might be a natural comparison but she's more like an elephant. She loves her herd. She'd stampede anyone who gets in their way with particular force. I was there when she broke Emma's ex-husband's nose on that Christmas day when her marriage fell apart. God, he was a class-A dick. There was actual blood. It was excellent. It was big Mama Callaghan energy.

'And what did Meg say?' I ask.

'She'd also been on the Chablis so they had it out. She called Mum insensitive, possibly a bitch. Emma chipped in. Then Mum talked about how, when she died, she didn't want fuss, which was lovely and macabre. And then we all played Scrabble and Lucy trumped all that drama by putting down the word "flange". It was a fun evening.'

I squeeze her hand. You can imagine she was the referee no one really listened to.

'But why would she say that? She won't make a scene, will she? On the day?' I ask.

'No. I don't think so. I think she just wants to protect you. She doesn't want you to feel all that grief again, all that sadness. None of us do.' She reaches down and holds my hand. 'It's classic Mum, though, eh? I find she likes to throw herself in the path of all these crashing emotions.'

I smile to hear it said like that. While Meg and Lucy always fought my mum's protective streak, I always thought us three in the middle tolerated it a little better.

'True. But she can't be there all the time. Her girls are out in the big wild world and sometimes shit things will happen. She just has to be there to pick us up when it all goes wrong,' I add.

The red panda, gnawing on a bit of bamboo, looks over at us philosophising. *Girls, keep it light. We're at the zoo. Just take a selfie with me and move on.*

'Dad is good at the picking-up,' says Beth.

'That he is. So are you.'

'I am?' she says, mildly surprised.

'You used to bring me doughnuts when Tom first died. Single jam doughnuts in bags. There really is nothing comparable to that as a gift.'

She pouts, knowing I'm trying to divert her attention away from the serious chat. 'But I do worry about you. Being here in Bristol, alone. I worry you don't have us around to help with the picking-up.'

I think what it would be like if the gang were at my beck and call, all of the time. The babysitting perks would be tremendous but we'd earn a reputation on some mafia-style level. I turn to face her.

'I'm not alone. I've never been alone.'

The thing is, I know that if things ever get particularly bad then I have all of them on speed dial. They'd drop what they were doing and they'd come to be by my side. This. This week of them tolerating this strange holiday/living situation is evidence of that. *We're here, Gracie.*

'Oh, we're also all wearing something yellow on Sunday. I thought I'd pre-warn you because we might turn up looking like a troop of canaries.'

I smile. Beth looks to my wrist at a yellow friendship bracelet I bought off a street market vendor in Vietnam. It was Tom's favourite colour. Yellow was his thing.

'I'll look like the fucking sun,' Beth tries to joke.

'Radiant.'

'Round.'

'Thanks for the goss, though. Good to at least know…'

'Well, that's my job. Sister spy in the middle.'

Kristen Bailey

'Then who am I?' someone says from behind us, grabbing us both at the waist and trying to sandwich herself between us.

'The mistake on the end,' Beth says, kissing the top of Lucy's head.

'What are you guys up to?'

'Just having a wander. Do you know where everyone is?' I ask her.

'Scattered. All the kids wanted to see different things. I've given them all scavenger-hunt tasks. They have to tally how many animal willies they see in a day.'

Beth turns to glare at her. 'You know Joe is, like, two?'

'And? It's all biology. Also, I have no barometer for these things. You forget I was the youngest of five so I was told everything way too early. Like, I knew about periods when I was six so if anyone is to blame for the way I am…' she points her finger between us, 'it's all you bitches.'

'How did you find out about periods?' asks Beth.

'Well, it was the loo with the faulty lock. I walked in on Meg and saw her changing her pad and I thought she was dying. And she screamed at me to get out and then ripped some pubes out because the pad had wings. I thought she'd been stabbed.'

'In the flange?' I say.

She shakes her head at Beth. 'Flange is an architectural word. Look it up. All your minds are in the gutters, it's so sad.'

Beth's bosom and belly jiggle from laughing. 'So what you're saying is, we turned you into this,' she says.

'It was part of being the youngest – everything was passed down, the clothes, the knowledge. The only thing I was able to carve out for myself was my winning taste in music.'

Beth puts her hand to the air. 'Nope, that was all from me, so really… you are just some poor imitation of us all.'

Lucy sticks her tongue out at us both. 'Wait, is that Doug?' she asks.

'You haven't slept with Doug too, have you?'

'No. He was at the funeral. Who's slept with Doug?' she enquires.

Beth pretends she needs something at the very bottom of her handbag as Lucy's eyes shoot between us.

'Wanger!' she suddenly says. For a moment, I think she's talking about Doug but turn to see that red panda. That panda has a wanger. And all of us tilt our heads to watch him jerk himself off, quite casually, not really caring who's watching. Lucy, I think we may have found you a BFF.

*

'And these are native to Venezuela and Brazil,' I say, mumbling in the darkness. 'Isn't that interesting, Joe?'

I stand there in the gloom, pushing my nephew's stroller back and forth. The zoo was far too much for Beth's toddler son so I've taken on the job of pushing him around and keeping him asleep. If that sounds like a chore then it isn't because this spares me the riot that is the penguin feeding. Has it been a nice day so far? The girls are ecstatic to have a crowd around them, no one has thrown Lucy to the wolves yet, or for that fact my mother for commenting how all the drinks are severely overpriced. So, for now, the cool darkness of the reptile house is providing some respite.

'And this bad boy here is from Guyana,' Doug tells me. I also have a Doug with me, who, today, has provided the perfect escape when family members have become a bit too full on. 'There's actually someone coming from Guyana tomorrow, do you know? His name is Barrett. I've told Joyce I'll pick him up tomorrow from the airport. Apparently, Tom met him under a waterfall on some trek and lent him fresh socks.'

Sounds about right. I continue to push Joe's stroller and move on to the next snake, which doesn't seem to want to make an appearance. Or maybe he's that big twig?

'I sometimes walk around this place and realise I only know where half these countries are because Tom went to them. São Tomé and Principe. It's one of thirteen countries on the Equator, did you know that?'

'Was that where he went dune surfing?' Doug asks.

'No, I think that was where he went scuba diving and stepped on a lionfish,' I say.

I hear Doug chuckling in the darkness. All that travel was Tom's greatest achievement. He kept tallies, religiously checked his passport to count for stamps and visas, and he'd study maps when we were together, plan trips. He'd watch YouTube videos of trains and treks, work out the cheapest and best ways to get places. He had such an intense wanderlust to get out there and see the world, to experience it and breathe in some different air, watch the sun circle another sky. I used to get him to tell me all his stories at night when I wanted to go to sleep. Tell me about that time you went to Namibia, the story with the bus, and he'd give you gorgeous nuanced details of dirt roads, landscapes that looked like they were painted onto skies and heat so hot his tongue stuck to the roof of his mouth. They were the best stories to fall asleep with.

'He got about, eh?' Doug says.

'That he did.'

Doug wanders over, putting his hands in his pockets like he does. Like he's shoving all his emotion back in those pockets or else he'll be a little bit lost. I never know how to make things right for Doug. He lost his wingman. I feel that so empathetically yet I also never want to tell him how to grieve; that journey is his own. I urge him to sit down on a bench next to me.

'Joyce asked if we were free tomorrow morning. She said there was something on and she didn't feel she could face it. She was a bit vague,' he says.

'I can be free. We can do it together?' I suggest.

He high fives me, in a very un-Doug kind of way.

'OK then, Americano. That's new.'

He looks at his hand and opens his fingers up and down.

'Yeah, it's the guys from work. It's all we do – high five and call each other "dude". Tom would find it lamely hysterical.' He's not wrong. 'Is there anything else I need to do for the day? Please use me so I can feel helpful. Are you talking? Joyce tells me the Aussie ex-girlfriend is reading a poem,' he continues, slightly horrified.

'Yes, Ellie has written something for the occasion but, no, I'm not speaking.'

I guess it would be customary for the widow to do so but I never have. Even at the funeral, I couldn't eulogise my own husband. I wasn't sure what people wanted to hear. He was taken from me before his time. Every ounce of my being ached. Cancer could go fuck itself. My words would have seethed with anger, I'd have finished it with a mic drop – not even that, I'd have thrown that mic like a javelin and stormed off. That would have been the eulogy, a winning tribute. I am trying to gauge if that's judgement or disappointment in Doug's look.

'You should say something...' he says softly. 'You can imagine Tom looking on at you and having a laugh because it would make you feel so incredibly uncomfortable.'

The comment makes me chuckle. That it would.

'I like how Tom did that, constantly,' Doug carries on. 'He'd push us out of our comfort zones whether we liked it or not. Do you know one thing he did for me before he died? He used to give me pep talks. When I was browbeaten and life and love had got the better of me, I used to call him, and wherever he was he'd sit down and put the world to rights. He was like my own personal life coach. He'd literally shout at me for not having any belief in myself. I think he gave me one of those speeches in the middle of a crowded train. Anyway, he recorded one for me before he died. I keep it on my phone for the hard days.'

I tear up slightly, my hand gripping my nephew's stroller.

'I have anxiety attacks sometimes that I'll lose it so I've saved it to about five devices. It's irreplaceable. Did he do one for you?'

'He did,' I whisper, taking a deep breath. 'It's him reciting the words of "Always On My Mind".'

It was our wedding song. It's a three-minute sound recording of him reciting it like a poem. He laughs in the middle. He takes a long pause at the end before he switches the off button. I save it for the very bad days, the ones when I feel like I'm forgetting him, when nothing but the sound of his voice will do. To say it out loud, though, seems to numb my face, that all too familiar emotion rising to the surface of pain – real physical pain. It can be like that sometimes, grief. It seems to play like a song where the high notes come crashing down to absolute lows and you don't know how to scale back up them again.

Doug senses it immediately and wraps his body around mine. It's warm and familiar. He'd do this all the time when I went to visit him in New York. After I got run over by the rollerblader, had my phone stolen, got off my tits on drugs and then ate the bad hot dog, we used to sit there in Doug's flat looking at reruns of *Seinfeld* without saying a word. He knew there was no city big or bright enough that was ever going to help me. I just needed canned laughter, four walls and big Doug hugs. Oh, and bagels. I got through a lot of bagels.

'I've upset you, I'm sorry, G,' he whispers. 'Let's hang out while I'm here. I want to see you, chat and walk around this old city again with one of my bestest friends. I'm renting an apartment in Clifton.'

'You're renting a flat, Doug. You've gone American on me, again.'

'Never. Also… and don't hate me for this…'

'Yes?'

'I think I may have slept with your sister, the pregnant one. I mean, I didn't get her pregnant. This was a while ago and I knew I'd slept with one of the sisters, but is it terrible that I never knew which one?'

He pulls a face at me and I laugh loudly, the sound echoing around that empty reptile house, possibly waking up the geckos.

'That's awful. You must buy me a fridge magnet to make it up to me.'

'Will do,' he mutters, observing a young girl who speeds into the reptile house past us. His eyes follow her as she makes an ungodly noise, trying to test the acoustics of this place. 'By the way, if I haven't said it already, stellar job with those girls of yours. They're kinda brilliant.'

'That they are… It's not from me.'

He gives me a strange look. 'I think you'll find that it is. I always knew you'd rock the mum thing. I mean, you could have a glass-licker, like that one over there.'

I turn around to see Doug gesturing at the noisy little girl who raced in here before. Don't do that, honey. Tree frogs are in that exhibit and tree frogs are poisonous as fuck. How do I know you, though? I've seen you before licking glass at… school.

'Oh, Grace… it's you.'

The hairs on the back of my neck literally straighten like darts. Carrie. Really? How apt I would bump into this woman in a reptile house. It's like that speaking snake from Harry Potter. But before I can say a word, I see her eyes scan down to Joe and over to Doug. It's too late to dash over and hide by the giant Perspex iguana, isn't it?

'Carrie…'

And suddenly, a wave of guilt, or maybe bile, rises to the surface as I see Liz behind her and realise I know something Carrie doesn't. You're here too? Two snakes. I don't quite know what to do.

'I didn't realise you had another child,' she says, peering into the stroller.

'No, this is my nephew.'

And this isn't some other random lover of mine, this is my Doug. I don't say that out loud. But I am super glad it's him sitting here and not any of my sisters.

'And this is my… brother.'

Doug nods, maybe not in agreement but in a way that tells me he'll play along. 'Yes, I am Doug. I'm here for the weekend to see…' I make eye contact with him to let him know that these two gossips don't need to know anything about the memorial. '… my nieces and this lovely zoo. They have leopards.'

'Oh…' Carrie says, still scanning, wondering if Doug might be a bit socially inept. Seriously, scan over there and watch your daughter before she licks a bin. Doug can sense the atmosphere but it really is too much to break down with just the blink of my eyes. She's a bitch. There was biting, Doug.

'Well…'

'So…'

It's a back and forth of single words. How do I tell you that the biggest snake in here might be your best mate?

'Anyway…'

'*You* need to show me the monkeys, sis…' Doug says. Christ, he's a shit actor.

'That I do, bro…'

He laughs, just as Joe wakes up to see us both and realise that we're not his parents. Definitely time to leave. We put our hands up to wave, awkwardly, and I push the stroller away as quick as humanly possible.

'What's the beef there then?' Doug mutters as soon as we're out of earshot.

'Big salty school-gate beef. I'll tell you over a coffee…'

'That I assume I'm buying?'

'Of course…'

But as we get to the plastic swing doors, I stop for a moment, still hearing Carrie's voice echo around that dark, still space. I think of my mum, my sisters, but, most of all, Tom. When do you jump in the path to stop people getting hurt? When do they deserve your kindness, your help, your protection? Despite how bloody awful they can be, maybe that answer is always. Tom would say, always. It's just the way you go about it. He was the sort of person who would talk to his best mate wherever he was, lend complete strangers his socks. He'd fix this in some way.

'Doug, can you push Joe over to the kiosk? I just need to do something.'

'And not let me watch?' Doug replies, almost disappointed. 'Do your thing. If it descends into a brawl, protect your face. I'll be your alibi.' He wanders off, laughing. I hope Joe doesn't think he's being kidnapped.

I slink back into the shadows of the reptile house and wait for a moment, watching the kids and adults move and stare between all the different cages and tubes, their faces all backlit by the pale fluorescent light. When she's on her own, I finally make my move.

'Liz…'

'Grace?'

We are standing over a Komodo dragon that doesn't even flinch. He just stares into space wondering the purpose of his existence. I hope what I say next will add some excitement to his day.

'Tell Carrie about what's happening with Ross. She's your friend. Do the right thing by your friend…'

The colour in her face drops immediately, almost in the style of a chameleon. I think the Komodo dragon is smiling.

'You saw us that night, on the docks.'

'The night you took a photo of me and my friend and told everyone I was pansexual.'

Panic consumes her eyes. 'That was all Ross. It doesn't mean anything with him. Are you going to tell people?'

'No. Because it shouldn't come from me. I'm just seeing it from Carrie's angle,' I explain. 'The longer your affair goes on for, the more hurt, the more grief she will feel. No one deserves that.'

No one. I pout my lips and decide at that moment to make a semi-grand exit into the shadows, backing into a bench. Classily done, Callaghan. Liz stands there, confused, and watches me as I scuttle away. Was that the right thing to do? Who knows? My mum would have told Carrie. Meg and Lucy would have raised merry hell. But Tom would be proud, I think. You've said something. You've tried to make that better. As I exit and break out into the sunshine again, I flinch and see Doug standing there by some giant boulders with a confused toddler and two giant cardboard cups.

'Latte, two sugars.'

I exhale loudly, grabbing the cup from him.

'Did you slot them and feed them both to the boa constrictors?' he asks.

'Of course. I'm a fricking ninja, me.'

He grins at me widely. 'Those girls get it all from you. Trust me.'

I don't know how to begin to reply to that but I take my cup and tap it against his.

'Now macaques. Joe and I checked the map, they have those here. Let's go and make up some facts about monkeys.'

A squeal comes from the stroller. I hope that's excitement.

'Lead the way.'

Chapter Nineteen

'Your balls can get cancer?'

'Well, yes. The biopsy from the lump in your right testicle is cancerous, I'm afraid. But in your case, I'd like to do more tests. The pain you have in your back and abdomen worries me so we just need to do these scans for our peace of mind.'

'But I'm not even thirty. And you're talking of removing one of my balls… like, do you just lop it off?'

'Not exactly. But you will still have full function of the other. Are you Mrs Kennedy?'

'I am.'

'Well then, I'm glad you're here. Tom will need plenty of support.'

'Are you sure it's cancer? Maybe it's just a cyst? Maybe I am growing a third testicle and I am a marvel of medical science.'

'Is he always like this?'

'Unfortunately, yes. I apologise in advance.'

It's today. I'm sitting on the edge of my bed, a towel wrapped around me, hair dripping onto my naked skin, the picture I keep by my bedside in the corner of my eye. It's our wedding photo. I kept that dress despite the stain on the arm and the fact I'll probably never wear it again. I could don that today. With a big shroud over my head? I don't know how casual to keep this. Joyce sent a picture of her outfit for today. It's bright and floral and I know Tom would have seen it and told his mum she looked radiant but, as an aside, he would have told me we could see that print from space. Next to me is my Huggly. Could I wear that? Maybe over my wedding dress? This was all a terrible idea.

'What would you wear?' I say to the photo. 'If I was the dead one?' He'd lovingly dust off the velvet suit. I'd hope that under the jacket he'd be wearing a T-shirt with my face on. He would actively avoid black, that's for sure.

How are you? Are you OK? One of us can come over and help if you want. I'd say all of us but if we all come round then that might be more trouble than it's worth. I could come? Maybe Ems? Let us know.

Babes, Farah and I love you so much. Let us know if you need us xx

Grace, I am back in Bristol. Do you need me to pick anything up? What do I wear? X

Stupid question and sorry to disturb but is there parking at the school?

My messages are full of conversations like this, telling people just come along, dress casual, bring an umbrella as we're outside, and don't eat lunch because Joyce pressed the wrong button and we have five hundred sausage rolls coming instead of a hundred.

'Mama, are you OK?' Cleo says, peeking her head around the door. She's dressed in a polka-dot shift with leggings. I marvel at how her hair never moves or changes shape and falls beautifully around her face. I usher her in the room and hold her close to me.

'Mama, you're dripping on me...' she says, matter-of-factly.

I laugh, sitting back. 'Sorry. I just can't figure out what to wear. You look smart. I like this dress on you.'

'It's because it's a shift. Shift styles suit every body type.'

'Who told you that?'

'Aunty Emma.'

Of course she did. Cleo studies my eyes and puts a hand to my cheek. She has a wonderful habit of being able to read my thoughts, of knowing when she has to snap me out of them. She walks over to my wardrobe and runs a finger through my clothes, pulling out a Christmas jumper and some leggings.

'Wear this.'

'Or not?'

'People said Uncle Tom was fun. He'd find this really funny.'

'I could wear those antlers on my head too.'

She swings her head back and giggles.

'Or you could wear your disco dress? I like the disco dress.'

The disco dress was an online sale purchase. I didn't see the thumbnail properly and thought I was buying a lampshade. I've never quite had the heart to give it away as the girls like to wear it on occasion and have dance parties in the living room.

'I could get Aunty Lucy to turn on her phone and you could shimmy. You could play that song you like to play for us… the ha-ha-ha-ha one.'

'"Stayin' Alive"?'

'Yes.'

The irony is lost on her but it makes me chuckle uncontrollably. This could be a fitting way to eulogise Tom, through the power of disco.

'Or what about this?'

It's a grey jumpsuit. I used to dress in that thing all the time, my go-to outfit for dinner or drinks, the ultimate dress-down and dress-up outfit. Needless to say, I haven't worn it in a while, looking at the dust that seems to have gathered on the shoulders. It's because it was a Tom outfit. Let's go grab a drink, on it went with a denim jacket and trainers, let's go to dinner, let's get out the statement earrings and a trusty ankle boot.

'Grey goes with yellow. I think it would look nice,' Cleo says sweetly.

'I think you might be right.'

She looks excited she may have helped and jumps on the bed to join me again. I take in her face. She would have been two when her parents died and she never mentions them any more. Not with sadness at least. We talk about her memories of them, and Linh is good at providing stories. We try and piece together a vision of them so the girls can learn about their foundations. It's not a fairy tale, it's not a lie, it's a story that led us both here, to this moment. *You helped me learn to live, to love again.* You will never underestimate how much I keep that close. Cleo stares at me, knowing I'm still deep in thought.

'Do you want me to do your hair?' she says, putting her hand to mine and raking her fingers through my knots. 'I could put clips in it? And my glittery Alice band?'

'I think I'm good, little one. Thank you.'

'You are very welcome.' She smiles then claps her hands. 'Now chop-chop...' she says, doing her very best impression of me.

*

'Callaghan!' Doug waits for me outside the entrance of the school, an arm in the air to alert me to his presence. He didn't go yellow but I like how New York has affected his styling. When I knew him in Bristol, he was overly fond of a hoodie and stained tracksuit bottoms that had holes in awkward areas. Today, there is some smart tailoring going on. He comes in for a hug as I get close.

'Looking lovely, as always.'

'Smooth. But thank you.'

'Now tell me, this didn't always look like this, did it?'

I shake my head. The Latymer Academy. Tom loved this place, the kids, the work. There was stress involved in secondary education but he had a plethora of stories about the kids. I'd never seen him as excited as when he was marking a piece of work and he'd been able to teach a child the right use of an interesting rhetorical question.

'I feel old looking at this place.'

I put an arm around him. 'Well, we are.'

We walk over to the entrance to the school and there stands Mr Harrison, Tom's old headteacher. He was always very gracious to me. He came to the funeral and wrote such lovely words on behalf of the school. He's also six foot seven, which makes me wonder how he manages with the majority of doorways and buying trousers. He must surely sew extra bits on the ends of the legs.

'Oh, Grace… so lovely to see you. You look wonderful.'

'You too, Mr Harrison. This is Doug Murray. He was a very good friend of Tom's who's visiting from New York.'

They shake hands as I look out into the courtyard. Everything is set up, glasses lined up with bottles of wine stacked behind, chairs for about a hundred people and a stage with a podium and a giant picture of Tom's face. Joyce went with the LinkedIn salesman pic then. I smile to see it. *Hi, I'm Tom and I can help you get a great deal on a conservatory.*

'So, I am so glad you came down early for this. Did Joyce explain what was happening?'

'She didn't actually,' Doug explains. 'I thought I was here to put out chairs.'

'Oh…' Mr Harrison says, thoughtfully. 'Well, as long as you're all right to speak into a camera?'

He starts walking through the school as we follow him, Doug shifting me a look. I thought we were here to receive the catering. Camera? This isn't good. I haven't gone full make-up today, I've not prepared for this. Is it live? If it is then I need to ring people to tell them to switch on the television. Doug ambles through the school corridors curiously. I can hear a hum of voices behind two closed doors and they suddenly open. Oh. OK. There in front of me stand about one hundred boys all in their PE kits. We're here to watch a basketball match? A competitive bout of dodgeball maybe? There are cameras set up and some screens dotted about the room too. A lady with a clipboard scurries over to introduce herself.

'Hi, I'm Bethan! I'm from *Points West* with the BBC and we are so glad you could be here today. When Joyce told us you'd be coming down, we were so thrilled.'

Joyce, Joyce, Joyce. Has she completely ambushed me? Doug looks around the room.

'And you are?' Bethan asks him.

'Oh, I'm a friend. So you're doing a news report on the memorial later?' he asks curiously.

'Well, yes, to celebrate the opening of the new wing, but we've also got some representatives from a testicular cancer charity and some of the teachers and boys from the sixth form are here. They're going to run through an exercise of teaching the boys how to feel for irregularities in their own balls.'

Oh. Doug bites his lip and eyeballs me. That's a lot of testicles. I mean, this is important, so very important, and a productive side effect of Tom's death, but I am confused as to why I'm here. Do they want me to watch? I'm not a teacher but I think this goes against safeguarding protocol.

'So you want us to...' I double-check in case she thinks I'm an authority on this. Obviously, I wasn't at the time.

'Oh, we just wanted some soundbites. It'll be such a good, informative feature...'

I nod. Maybe in the corridor, though? Right? A few of the teachers and students look over to me. What are they going to do? Are they all going to do it at once? Or are they lining up and someone is going around with a rubber glove? I bite my lip for a moment thinking that I'm glad Doug is here and not Lucy. This shouldn't be funny. Oh, that's what the screens are for? A camera in the corner of the room captures an inspection of a group of boys.

'So, avocados. Does anyone know why they're called avocados?' says a voice behind the curtain.

Whose bollocks look like avocados? I'm not an expert but I think the point at which they're green means you have a problem.

'Avocados hang in pairs on trees, one slightly lower than the other, so they are the Aztec word for testicles. It also explains why your penis may hang to one side more than the other to account for how your balls hang.'

I hear boys snigger behind the screen. This information is peak pub quiz knowledge.

'So you're looking for a smooth contour. You may be able to feel certain ducts within the ball sack that carry sperm – these are not lumps but you want to feel for any lumps in the general shape; roll them around in your hand between your fingers. They should feel like long eggs…'

'I'm not dressed for this,' Doug says out of the corner of his mouth.

I try to hold back my laughs. 'Neither am I.'

'Is that a lump?' I hear a voice say. I am a tad nervous for one of the lads for a moment.

'That's a hair follicle. Hair is totally natural. A lot of hair, in your case.'

Doug has to turn around to have a moment.

'What are these then?' asks one boy.

'Are you sexually active?' the doctor asks.

'Yes.'

Oh dear, someone get that one some antibiotics. Behind a screen, I see a row of shorts around ankles. Oh Lord, that man's head of geography; Tom disliked him because he used to lecture everyone about their carbon footprint and rode a bike to school that had six mirrors. He's going to get his balls out in the school gym. He waves at me. I wave back. I really don't know how I feel about this. Balls. They're the ultimate boy joke, up there with farts, willies, wind and jizz. They're such ugly-looking things too. We barely even give them a second thought. Which is probably where we went wrong. Look at this, Tom Kennedy. They're all checking their knackers on your behalf. You must be bloody loving this, wherever you are. I see Bethan approaching me with a roving cameraman who sets up his equipment in front of us.

'So I'll just ask you some questions and then we'll get this off to the editing suite. Relax, it'll all be quite easy.'

'So how do I check my prostate?' I hear a voice say from behind a curtain. I'm no doctor but I believe that's tomorrow's segment. Definitely bring gloves for that.

'So it's a special day at the Latymer Academy today,' starts BBC Bethan. 'Nearly four years after one of their teachers died tragically from testicular cancer, the staff and students are gathered here today to celebrate the opening of a new wing of the school built in his honour. A ceremony this afternoon is being preceded by a clinic session led by a charity which is encouraging the male students here to check their testicles regularly… And with us today is Grace Kennedy, who was Tom's wife…'

Crap. That's me. Nice segue, Bethan, from the vision of hundreds of testicles to me. I don't know how to tell her I no longer take

Tom's name. Yikes. Run with it. She doesn't introduce Doug but he stands close to me for the support and probably for safety from all the exposed cojones in the room.

'Grace, what are your thoughts about today?'

The whole day? Or just this moment where I'm playing witness to all these kids paying tribute to my husband by checking out their mansacks? I hope they got written consents from the parents.

'I just think it's great,' I say. 'This is so important and if Tom would have wanted anything to come from his death, it would be for people to think more about their health at any age.'

Doug smiles. Wow, that was quite eloquent of me, plus I didn't cry.

'How old was Tom when he passed away?'

'He was twenty-eight.'

Bethan shakes her head in disbelief, in sadness.

'And can you tell us any more about the symptoms that alerted him to his illness?'

'Well, I think the problem is that he thought nothing of them. He had some lumps in one of his testicles and then fatigue, stomach pains, which is when he finally went to a doctor.'

'So if he'd gone to a doctor earlier then he might still be alive?'

I freeze for a moment. When someone dies, you think in hypotheticals all the time. It's the very beauty of hindsight. We used to play-fight a lot and I'd pretend to kick him in the balls. Sometimes I made contact. Maybe it was my fault. Maybe he wore his trousers too tight. He liked to drink carbonated drinks; he was a sucker for Diet Coke. Was that what caused his cancer? And yes, I'd have gone travelling with him when we left university or visited him more, or left my ego at the door every time we fought or tried to psychoanalyse our relationship. As soon as I saw that lump, I should have dragged him to a doctor myself under some false pretence. Oh, we're just going to talk about vitamins. Even when he was ill, I should have told him to fight harder, try every drug going; I should have done more to make him stay.

'Possibly,' said Doug, sensing my unease. 'But I guess cancer is a roll of the dice like that. Tom was just desperately unlucky. I'm Doug. I was his best friend.'

'And what do you think about today, Doug?'

'I'd say Tom would be happy to have this as his legacy. If he can stop anyone getting ill or losing a loved one then that would be enough. For all these lads to be here with cameras in the room. Well, that takes a lot of balls... not balls. I mean, we need the balls here to do what we need to do. Like, courage, that's a better word...'

'Do you check your balls, Doug?' Bethan asks, digging him out of his hole.

'Obsessively. Like, not all the time. But I do it a lot. Not that I set my watch to how often I do it but I do it regularly.'

Bethan switches her microphone back to me to save Doug going any more crimson. 'And later, the opening of the new wing... what are your thoughts on that?'

'I think Tom would feel very proud. He loved this school very much. I can't wait to see it.'

'And that is a cut for now, I may come back and find you in a moment,' she says, before they head off again.

Doug turns to me. 'You know none of what happened to Tom is your fault? Right? Never think that.'

'You know me.'

'Just don't. He'd hate that. I hate that. You were the best thing that ever happened to Tom Kennedy. He'd be so proud of you and your girls. I know it.'

'He'd be proud of you too, Dougie. He always was. His dorky best mate living it large in New York. How you still look out for his girl…'

'You were my mate too, Gracie.'

'Is it bad I want to cry?'

'Bethan would love that, it'll make great footage. You crying in a room full of bollocks.'

'Don't say the word "footage"…'

We stand in the corner of that room like naughty schoolchildren, not really knowing what we're doing. I imagine Tom in this hall during an assembly, doing his laid-back thing on a plastic chair, the kids looking up at cool Mr Kennedy. I wonder who replaced him. I hope he's a worthy successor. I hope he pays better attention to his health but I hope he teaches with the same joy Tom did.

A young man suddenly walks towards us. Please don't ask us to come in for a closer look.

'Hi, are you Mrs Kennedy?' he asks. The boy is in a strange in between stage of adolescence where his facial hair is sprouting in strange patches on his chin like it's having a territorial battle with his acne. The high-rise blush in his cheeks makes me think this approach is out of his comfort zone and he can't quite look me in the eye. Maybe he's the one with the super-hairy balls.

'It's just… Mr Kennedy taught me when he was… you know… here.'

'Oh, that's lovely. What's your name?'

'Kieran Perry. Mr Kennedy was my form tutor.'

Were you the one who gave us the good Tempranillo one Christmas? That was good wine.

'I just wanted to say… he really helped me when I was at school. I'm dyslexic and he used to stay behind at lunch and help me with my work.'

Doug and I beam. That sounds typical Tom.

'And… like, if I get the exam results, I've got a place to study English at Manchester and that was really all him…'

We all pause for a moment, my eyes glazing over. The boy did have legacy and it's standing right in front of me. Oh, Tom. I hope if you are haunting me then you're seeing this boy. You're seeing something that went very right in all of this. I suppose half the boys are here for the banter but there are others in this room who loved and respected you too.

'So I just wanted to let you know and… it was really good to meet you.' He reaches out, takes my hand and shakes it.

'You too, Kieran. Good luck at university. My sister went to Manchester. It's great up there.'

He smiles and turns to go back to his friends.

'Oh, Doug… if they all have stories like that then this might break me. We may need to leave.'

'Right, we also need to find you a sink…' he says, smirking.

I look down at my hand, realising what Doug means. Did Kieran just grope his tackle and then shake my hand? Seriously? I fricking hope that's not a pube in my palm.

Chapter Twenty

Tom, I don't know what this letter is. I think it's a last-ditch attempt to tell you not to leave me. Don't go travelling. Stay with me. Here. We can rent a small flat in Bristol and just keep living here like slightly older students. I'll do my accountancy training with the uni and we can get you on a teacher training course and then buy some house with a yellow door and get a cat called Juno. I'll even let you have a shelf for all your Star Wars *crap. You've given me all these reasons for why you want to travel, why you need to get around the world but the bottom line is I don't want to be without you. And you can call me sad and poke fun at that all you want but the thought of being without you devastates me.*

I love you, you absolute bastard. Please stay.

I love you, G xx

'Is this comfortable?'

'Well, I am dying so I'm not sure how you'd describe comfort at this very point in time.'

I puffed the pillows around his head. In those last days, he wanted a fortress of them and the hospice provided generously. It was a wonder they had any left for anyone else. I used to put the brushed cotton covers on as he liked them and I curled up at the bottom of his bed like a cat. They had wheeled in a cot bed for me but it creaked every time I rolled around and, in any case, I wasn't sleeping very much by that stage.

'You're very droll.'

'Even in the face of impending death. I will take that as the ultimate compliment. Can you put that on my headstone? *Funny even when dying.*'

'I thought you wanted to be cremated.'

'Just put it on a plaque, in a place where it can be seen.'

'Like in the loo.'

'Yes, as you take your morning dump, you can remember how funny I was, until the very end.'

I propped the laptop up on the table.

'Are you thirsty?' I asked him.

'For alcohol.'

'That would mix well with your morphine.'

'You're such a spoilsport. I watched an episode of *This Is Us* without you today when you went to get coffee.'

'I can't believe you. I can't watch now. I'll have missed a whole hour.'

'You can catch up when I'm dead.'

'Is there a point when that stops being funny?'

'No… Just lie here, watch it with me. Please, Gracie.'

He patted the side of the bed and stuck out his bottom lip. At that point, he'd lost a lot of colour and the fullness to his face but the eyes never changed. The illness never took away that twinkle in his eyes. I curled up in the same position I always did and we watched that show until we both fell asleep. Except he never woke up. That was how our last moments played out.

The next morning, Emma arrived with some coffee and fresh clothes for me and a nurse came in to check on him. I just thought he was asleep. He had slipped into a coma and that was the last time we spoke. I didn't believe her. Emma caught me as I fell to the floor. He's not gone. We didn't get to the end of the season. We don't know what happens. This was not how it was supposed to end.

I think of this moment now as I look at the plaque attached to the wall of the new wing they've built in Tom's honour.

The Tom Kennedy Wing
In Honour of Tom Kennedy
Teacher, Colleague, Friend
1990–2018

Should read: *Funny Even When Dying.* Joyce did good work, though; it's stately in both font and finish. The wing itself is modern and I'd say it's up to Tom's exacting standards. They haven't brought back the blackboard but I like the sofas and the bright murals that adorn the walls. One shelf holds books with the word Tom in their titles: everything from *Tom Gates* to *Tom Sawyer* to *Tom Jones…* and *Goodnight, Mr Tom.* Nicely done. There's a picture of him as you enter, with words underneath. I'll go and read that in a while.

I hope it's not in Comic Sans. *It's a font for clowns and kids*, Tom used to say, not even realising the irony that he was kind of both.

The ceremony has been going on for fifteen minutes now and I feel like I'm not here at all. It's like I'm just looking down, on autopilot, because if I think about any of this too much then I'll collapse in a heap. I need to stay upright for the girls, for Joyce. I can't break down and make a scene because today isn't about me. It's about Tom. I push down all that feeling to a place where I can just put one leg in front of the other and function. Smile. Don't take in too many words, just smile. After a month of scattered meetings with all these international visitors, they are now in the same place, in this courtyard. They all hold programmes and plastic glasses filled with warm wine. I don't even know half of them, some are faces I remember from the funeral, but I don't know you. Or you. And there's a band. They're all in school blazers and I feel for the young lad trying to balance his tuba. Could we get him a chair?

'His smile fixed in the stars ad infinitum.' Ellie's voice meanders in from the podium. 'That means forever/How I remember/My heart in a tether/Forever and ever/Whatever the weather/Special and clever...'

Wearing head-to-toe leather? I don't know why that line comes in my head but I use Maya, who is sitting on my lap, to hide my smirk. Ellie has been up on the stage now for five minutes. She introduced herself as one of Tom's great loves and I watched as my four sisters looked set to charge the stage. That would have been a sight. I mean, Beth is at a nice rotund stage of pregnancy so she'd have aided the attack.

Through her words, Ellie stops to dab at the corners of her eyes and, as much as I jest, and as much as it pains me, I know there is depth to the emotion. We shared him at one point in time. She loved him too. Her grief is valid even though her poetry kind of sucks. Would Tom like this? He'd like the sentiment of being adored but this poem is as long as the *Iliad*. Limericks would have been more his jam.

I have to do this, don't I? Just focus on this strange internal monologue of rationalising everything so I don't think about my dead husband. I think we did well with the wine choice. We didn't go with wine out of a box as that's definitely not what Tom would have wanted. *I don't want a hint of cardboard when I'm necking wine.* But I see the giant pile of sausage rolls, next to a more meagre one of mini spring rolls. That's an obscene amount of sausage. And then I think back to this morning with all the boys in the hall with their balls out. What a day.

Naoko is here. So is Robyn, who slept with Tom in Japan. If she cries and reads out a poem then I may have words. All the Japanese contingent is here, Astrid and Farah sitting behind them, cousins and aunts, friends and neighbours. Even Sam and Helen drift around at the back of the crowd. They came. You didn't even know him. But you know me. Thank you for being here.

I hear clapping and Ellie returns to her seat. I should clap too. Maya knows, doesn't she? She can feel every sinew of my body awkward and tense. I can tell from the way she takes a thumb and rubs it on the inside of my palm. She's always done that; it's always worked. I squeeze her fingers back, her skin soft and silky. I can also see someone else who knows exactly how I feel. Mum. Please look at someone else. She looks like an owl, transfixed. Like that

stuffed owl on Carrie Cantello's mantlepiece. Dressed in yellow.
That's not your colour, Mum. Don't laugh. Don't cry. Don't notice
how your mum is just staring at you, hoping, praying her daughter
is not going to break. Don't think anything. Just get through this.

Joyce is up to talk next. She's been sitting next to Linh. They've
always got on, bonded by that shared grief of having lost children
before their time. Linh grasps her hand tightly. Joyce got a huge
kick out of sending Doug and I down on ball-watch before. It was
wholly intentional as she wasn't sure she could do it and didn't
want to scare us off. She climbs the stairs slowly to the stage and
adjusts the microphone.

'Oh my god, I just can't believe how many of you are here today,'
Joyce says, the microphone crackling. 'He'd be so happy, so proud,
so very pleased.'

Don't look at her. Just don't take any of the words in. You can
do this, Gracie.

'I just didn't expect to be so emotional. I mean, I was having
wine and all these people were coming up to me, talking to me
about Tom and telling me all your stories. I can't tell you how proud
it makes me that my son touched your lives in some way. As his
mother, that makes me so…'

It's Maya who looks up to me first when it happens. Joyce turns
from the microphone, her bottom lip trembling. She tries to bite it
to control it but she takes a sharp intake of breath and exhales it in
a quiver, rubbing at tears with the base of her palm. Mr Harrison
offers her a tissue.

'Mama…' Maya says, terrified to see her Aunty Joyce so sad.
Joyce sticks a tongue out of the corner of her mouth, almost as if

to lap up the tears that trickle down her cheeks. You can do this, Joyce. Please do this. But she steps back from the microphone to have a moment. Linh looks over to me and I smile back.

'Maya, can you sit with Ba Linh so I can help Aunty Joyce?'

She beams up at me. 'I can come with you?' she says.

'I can too,' Cleo adds.

My heart twinges for a moment as they both cling to me. Let's hang out together. Forever. But this? I need to do it alone.

'I love you both… so very much. But stay here, littlies, OK?'

They nod and I trot up the stairs to the stage, silence filling that small courtyard space as Joyce stands there, trying to compose herself. I go up and embrace her.

'Hey.'

'God, I'm a bloody mess. This is fucking embarrassing,' she mutters. I pick a crumb of tissue off her cheek. 'Please say something, anything.'

I walk up to the microphone, my arm locked in hers, and look down towards the crowd. What is one hundred people? Is that the number of people Jesus fed with the minimal amounts of fish and bread? I have an inkling that could be more. But I feel like I'm about to talk to a stadium's worth. It's never been my forte in any case, to talk, to persuade a crowd with rhetoric and jokes. That was always Tom's job. That was a good opener, if I could remember what I just thought. I see Lucy move seats to go and support Linh and throw her thumbs in the air, a half-smile gracing her face. Don't look at my mother. Don't. Because she's crying. Meg's crying too. And Beth. We'll forgive Beth because of the hormones but the rest of them are of no use to me whatsoever. Useless.

'Hi.'

That'll do. Just tell them about the sausage rolls and take your leave, Grace.

'I'm Grace. Which is a really stupid thing to say because half of you know I'm Grace. Well, that person is my mother so I really hope she knows who I am.' My mother cry-smiles at that point and I see my father's hand slide into hers.

'I was Tom's wife.' I play with the wedding ring on my finger. 'It's been three years since he's been gone and it still feels strange to say that in the past tense. To say he's not here because I think all of you here today are testament to the fact he's never quite left us.'

Preach, sister. You can do this. Exhale.

'In the past months, the one thing I've learnt is how that man got about. In the nicest possible way, of course.'

Was that funny? I hope that was funny. I see shoulders moving up and down so I will take that as a yes.

'That was him all over, he had the biggest and most adventurous heart, and I am really happy many of you got to meet him and share in some of that. I'm glad he taught here and people remember him so fondly too. Teaching was a real passion of his so this is such an honour. He would bloody love this, a building with his name on. Because most of you will know he liked an element of occasion, a sense of grandeur. I think it was reflected in a love for fancy dress. He would go all out. Did anyone ever see his Henry VIII?'

It was for school. He made me dye his hair. He wanted to do the pubes too for authenticity. It stained the sink. I wonder how much detail I need to go into. A hundred people is a lot of people. They all sit here, waiting for me to say something, to close this.

There's that same camera that was there this morning. There are my girls. Maya waves at me.

'I didn't prepare anything for today. I didn't think I was going to speak. And now look at me...'

He would love this. If he were here, he'd be leaning against that pillar over there to the back, arms crossed and wearing some battered old trainers. *Come on then, Callaghan, spit it out. Tell us what you know.* Joyce grips onto my arm that much tighter.

'Loss is such a weird thing, isn't it?' I pause for a moment. 'It's broken my heart a thousand times over to not have Tom here any more. But... to have had him in my orbit for what time we did have was... perfection. And it's terrible but those aren't even my words. Those were Tom's. In a letter given to me after his death. A letter that asked me to keep moving, that told me all his final thoughts, a letter that asked me to replace him with someone worthy, like Drake.'

I see my mother turn to Emma to ask, *Who on earth is Drake?*

'I read it at least once a month. I hear him reading it to me. I ache with every word, I ache with loss. In that letter, he enclosed a ticket and he asked me to travel, just like he did. I did just that. I was really awful at it. I'm not adventurous like him. I'm really bad on planes actually. Really bad. But he knew exactly what I needed to do. I had to trace his steps, find all those other people who'd been in his orbit too. And slowly, those people all fell into my life. We were all brought together and a once empty heart slowly refilled again.'

Linh looks at me and nods.

'And now that heart aches with many other things... pride, gratitude' – I take a deep cleansing breath – 'and love. I guess people do that. They come in and out of our lives. There will always be loss. But by that same measure, we also gain. I know that because of my girls, my family, my many wonderful friends. I know about love because I was loved by the best person there was. It was a pleasure, an honour and a gift to be his wife. It really was. So… yeah… thank you all for being here. And thank you, Tom…'

The Tom I imagine standing at the back of the room shakes his head. *You're just plagiarising that letter to a tee, eh? No imagination.* I'm honouring your words, you tool. They are still the best words I know. The tears roll freely now. Am I making sense? It's very quiet. A majority of people I know are sobbing lightly. I should have gone with humour. I don't know whether to say more. Or less. Or raise a glass. Or just continue hugging Joyce. Her fragile face glows differently now. I've never said any of that out loud before. It was all some mashed-up monologue in my head, emotions that coursed through my veins.

'Too much?' I whisper in her ear.

'Perfect. You sod, telling me you didn't know how to speak in front of people.'

'You sod, for crying like that and making me come up here.'

She laughs and holds me tightly. No more words now. That's all there is to say. I look down at my girls who are watching me intently. Suddenly, a band strikes up to the right of us, in front of the building. Please don't ask me to sing. It's *Tom's Theme*. They kept in the flute. I need to pretend I like this, don't I? I am glad for the boy with the tuba being given a moment to shine at least. Tom is still there, leaning against the wall. God, at least stand up straight, man. This is all for you. Don't smirk. I know there's a kid in that crowd who's possibly a beat behind the others, someone who possibly needs retuning, but that's for you. I just stood up here and spoke for you, to you, about you. You dick. Some reimagined apparition of Tom looks at me. Some happy version of him I hope has had a shower and put on clean socks. Go on, say something.

Who ordered all those sausage rolls?

You have to ask?

He looks at me for a moment and smiles. I smile back.

Well done, he mouths.

For what?

For surviving. You will be fine, Gracie. You'll be just fine.

He turns to listen to the music, nodding over to the kids on their plastic chairs. *Don't look at me, look at them. Look how great I am that I now inspire music. Look at all these beautiful people. Look at you.* I glance over and back at the place he was leaning. But when I do, he's not standing there, he's gone.

Chapter Twenty-One

Hi. It's Tom here. Major Tom. The one from last night. In the club. Just in case you were too drunk and don't remember me. We kissed and we ended up in my room and you left a sock behind so I'm enclosing it here because socks should always remain together, right? I'm no good at being cool so I'll say I like you and I am going to the Watershed tomorrow because there's a special screening of 'Juno' and I bloody love that film. If you wanted to come along? We could get cheesy chips. I'm in Block A, Room 316. Drop by? Say hello? I have a sandwich toaster if that is going to help seal this deal xx

'I've never seen Granny Fi cry before…' Maya says, as I tuck her into bed that night. 'Her nose went very red. Was she all right?'

I nod, cupping my hands around her face and kissing her on the forehead. We all had a bit of a sob today, didn't we? Aunty Beth cried so much, she was worried she'd broken her waters (turns out it was wee but we won't talk about that). It was that sort of afternoon; the tears flowed, all laced with this strange cocktail of emotions that enveloped the event. However Tom made you feel, it was a time to express it, an open forum for us to get all that emotion out into the world before we wiped those tears away and went back to what we were doing. Maya studies my eyes.

'I don't know if you're happy or sad, Mama,' she mumbles.

Who knows? Another set of Cleo-sized arms reaches around my neck to ambush me from behind and prolong this night-time routine but I'll admit to not minding so much. I pretend to eat her fingers and hear her giggle, hanging off my back. It's a moment of quiet and normal that makes me sigh deeply. I can't explain the last few weeks but this is what I'd like to go back to please: this new normal of us three against the world.

'All I know is that you two girlies make me very happy and proud. You were very well-behaved today,' I mention.

'That's because Ba Linh gave us sweets.'

'Of course.'

A worry strikes through me for a moment that they were party to all of that today, though. Maybe I wasn't careful enough, protective enough. Was it all too much? But my mind is taken back to a time when I was first introduced to both of them. Just two little girls I met on my travels, connected to myself and Tom in some way. They were so chatty but limited to Vietnamese and bits of French so we gabbled away nonsensically and they played with my hair and I remember that glow, that way we were attracted to each other like magnets, some small semblances of love growing at the roots. A night when we all fell asleep together in a row, huddled next to other like cats. We were all tainted by grief but it didn't seem to define them. I remember how amazed I was by that, the sheer wonder of their resilience. It wasn't even armour, it was youth, it was the fact the worst thing had happened but there was still a path out of that for them, a path that led them to me. *I do bloody love you two. It's deep and maternal but it's so determined to do the right thing by you.*

'I'm sorry if it's been a bit busy here in the last few months. I think things might calm down now.'

Both of them look at each other. 'We liked busy. It was fun meeting all those people and seeing all our aunties and uncles. We want to do it more.'

'Really?' They nod enthusiastically. 'Are you saying our normal lives are boring then?' I laugh.

Cleo comes to sit on the edge of the bed. 'It was nice seeing you going out and having fun. Sometimes we worry you just stay at home all the time and drink wine.'

I laugh. 'I sometimes also drink other drinks.'

'Yeah, like tea, and you put face masks on and watch your shows,' Maya says.

'When you talked about travelling today, you said you weren't good at it... Why?' Cleo asks.

'I wasn't like Tom. He could throw on a rucksack and put on his trainers and go anywhere. I'm a bit more...'

'Scared?' Maya says.

'That's part of it. I just think travel, on your own, can be strange,' I explain. 'I saw so many wonderful new things but really all my memories of my travels are to do with people. It's people, not places, that make every day an adventure.'

Cleo grips onto my hand tightly. 'Does that mean we're your adventure?'

'My bestest one.'

Maya sits up on her knees. 'Well, can we make our adventure bigger? Maybe instead of memorials, every year we should go to somewhere new. For Uncle Tom. Just the three of us… make you better at travelling.'

As she says it, I see a look of mischief behind her eyes. That's definitely not from me – maybe her parents, maybe Linh, maybe Lucy, maybe her very own brain – but it makes me so very happy.

'That's a pretty awesome idea. I guess it'll be better than me sitting in this house…'

'In your Huggly.'

'You have Hugglies too. They are awesome.'

'Yeah,' Maya says, laughing. 'But you wear yours all the time… You look like a big woolly mammoth…' I tickle her and she collapses onto the bed, Cleo joining in.

'Well, this looks like fun.' A figure at the door gets our attention. Linh stands there, looking at this three-headed mass of limbs all entangled, and walks over to sit on the edge of the bed. Cleo jumps into her arms.

'Can we visit Ba Linh more too?' Cleo asks.

'I think we can manage that,' I say. Linh studies my face and there are knowing looks between the both of us. I think she understands today was therapeutic for me, that I feel lighter, more at peace with my own emotions.

'Well, we are all out of milk so I was going to send Mama to the shops and maybe I can tuck you both in?' she says.

I nod and watch as she crouches between both beds. She never reads stories, she tells them, and I adore this, the very artistry of it. I stand for a moment to hear some words in the faint light of the hallway before I head downstairs. Linh has promised to stay for another month. We'll finally go to Brighton in the week so she can visit her friend. I can't wait to take her on the bumper cars at the pier. But I also want to link arms with her and look out onto the sea, catch a new horizon.

Today felt like a wake, but not a wake, a party but not. Once the last sausage roll had been eaten and that boy had packed his tuba away, once they cut the ribbon to the new wing and I read the words under Tom's picture, we all gathered in small parties for photos and selfies and the exchange of more stories. People drifted out of that place to go back into their corners of the world. They stacked the chairs, they turned off the lights. By that point, I was exhausted. I had used all my words. Linh saw it too so, when people proposed more drinks, dinners and such, she allowed me to use her as an excuse and we came back here to the quiet of my house. I fed the girls rice and chicken and I bathed them and allowed for some form of reset. It's almost like it never happened.

At the bottom of the stairs, I put on my coat, beanie and trainers and slip out the door. It's not a complete look but it's milk. I should really get some bread in too so I'll head to the bigger supermarket and take a stroll down Whiteladies Road to digest the day. I said all those words, didn't I? I remember when Tom died, I didn't even tell a grief counsellor that much. But maybe it was because she wore very coral lipstick and I couldn't really focus on how she was trying to counsel me. It wasn't a natural colour.

My feet take me to the main road and I turn right into the main streets. What am I doing? It's Sunday and it's late. Nothing is open. The traffic flitters up and down the road and the only light seems to be from restaurants and cafes. Looking up, I see the large grey expanse of Richer Sounds. Talk about something that has outlived my days in Bristol, it's this music store. Do people still buy speakers the size of buses? Obviously they do in this city.

I stand here for a moment to think about a time when Tom and I were trying to make our way back from a nightclub and took cover here because of the rain. A moment when he told me he'd give me a piggyback all the way to our halls of residence, definitely a good thirty-minute walk, in the rain, uphill. He managed ten steps. I can't for the life of me think of the number of times I trod this road as a student in the first year, up and down, across the Downs and over to my halls. To lectures to nights out to back again, a carrier bag of groceries in the crook of my arm, cheesy chips with garlic mayo in the other. I once ran it in heels because I was so drunk and thought I possessed the superhuman power to do so. I was fun, once.

Before I know it, my feet have taken me down towards Cotham Hill, past takeaways and pizza shops that have remained the same, even if their names have not. A jute shopper tucked under my arm, I walk until my feet reach the streets that hold the university buildings. It's literally a street of houses that all belong to different departments. The streets here are quieter, still. In term time, on a weekday, say about 11 a.m., there's a throng of people that bring it all to life; it's filled with earnest, hungover students with their rucksacks and textbooks tucked under arms.

By the time I've got to Park Street, the traffic and crowds have picked up a bit more and I seem to be driven by momentum, some nervous energy hanging in my veins like electricity. I mean, it's mostly downhill, right? I can find somewhere that sells milk and bread around here. There will be somewhere open. But I just keep walking. It's why I like Bristol, that walkability factor, how you can just float around this city and be sucked into its little shops and corners. It's always felt like a city with pockets. Pockets of magic.

At the bottom of Park Street, it makes sense to walk just that bit further. A little trek more. Past the waterfront on to King Street, which is tucked just behind it. King Street is cobbled so I'm glad for the trainers, to be fair. As you walk down it, there's a Chinese restaurant which again seems to have stood the test of time, something we'll accredit to the fact it's built in the style of an actual pagoda. Renato's also keeps going (low ceilings, great garlic bread) and the Old Vic pub, which over the years has upped its modern status with a big glass-to-steel-ratio exterior. And then to my right, there it is.

It's now a place called Kong's. It wasn't always this. It was a really bad nightclub that we used to frequent back in the day. We paid stupidly cheap prices to go in, get drunk and stagger back home again. It was where I met Tom. We were next to each other at the bar trying to flag down a bartender. I'd seen him in my halls but was put off by the fake-confidence. Was he the one we had to call the ambulance for because of that tequila night? The communal fridge cheese thief? Or the one who used to hang a fishing rod out of his window and literally 'fish for gash' (not my words, obviously).

'You're in my reading group, right?' he said.

'I'm in your halls. In your block. I study accounting and finance.'

And for one small moment, the club went dead. Dead with some awkward, embarrassing silence that this would be all there was to say to each other.

'Abby?'

'Grace.'

'Well, I'm Tom.'

I couldn't tell if he was hitting on me or just turning on the social chum act, knowing I was ahead of him in the drinks pecking order.

'So which Tom are you?' I asked. 'By my counts, there's six Toms in our halls. Tom Godfrey, Casino Tom, Tiny Tom, Major Tom, Tripod Tom and Greek Tom.'

'Major Tom.'

'Was that name self-proclaimed perhaps?'

'It's because my dad is David Bowie.'

It was a lie and an awful pick-up line.

'My dad was a huge Bowie fan,' he carried on, 'and used to sing that song to me when I was a baby.'

I remember smiling when he said that. I did notice it was in the past tense. It seemed sincere, genuine.

'Better than Tiny Tom, I suppose?'

He turned to face me.

'You have experience of Tiny Tom?'

I did but I didn't let on.

'Tiny Tom is called that because he's only five foot five and looks like a Dickens character in that flat cap he wears. Tripod Tom on the other hand…'

'Likes photography?'

'May as well have three legs.'

'I won't even attempt to go there…'

I think of that first conversation as I'm sitting here with a bottle of craft beer at the bar. With my jute shopping bag. I literally went out for milk and bread. It would have been in this very spot, right here when it first started, when the sparks didn't fly as such but they were there, glowing like embers.

'Quiet night tonight,' says the bartender now, attempting to start a conversation with me. I can't quite read the look on his face. Is that concern? It's the big coat, hat and shopping bag, isn't it? I don't quite fit the cool vintage sweatshirt/arcade-game vibe of this joint.

'It is Sunday,' I say.

'That is true.' He has impeccably groomed facial hair. He's also wearing braces but as a style statement not as a means to hold up his jeans. They look fiddly? Plus, if you were sitting down to go to the toilet, wouldn't they trail in the bowl? I can't ask him that, can I?

'I knew this place when it was a nightclub,' I tell him.

'Crap, that was years ago. You don't look old enough.'

'I'll take that as a compliment,' I say, taking off my hat, hoping static is my friend. 'There used to be a dancefloor over there.'

'I believe it also had a cow-print wall, didn't it?'

I laugh. 'YES. And the ceiling used to drip onto the dancefloor. I could never work out if that was from the toilets or not.'

He pulls a face at me. 'You'd hope not. Taking a walk down memory lane, are we? I've never seen you in here before.'

'Kind of. I met my husband here.'

He studies my face to gauge what that means.

'Divorce?'

'He died.'

'Shit. That is awful. I'm very sorry.'

'People always say that. Don't be. I was very lucky.'

He smiles and nods. He takes out two shot glasses from a shelf. 'Look, I won't pry any more but this is on me. Take your time this evening.'

I bow my head in gratitude, reaching out over the bar to take the shot between my fingers. Sambuca. I'd recognise that aniseed smell anywhere. It scorches the back of my throat and hits the top of my stomach like magma.

'What's your name, by the way?' I ask him.

'I'm Tom.'

I laugh. 'You're frigging kidding me, right?'

'No? Crap. Was that your husband's name?'

'It was.'

He winces. 'It's quite a common name. It'd be weirder if we were both called…'

'Ronaldo?'

'Well, yeah… That would be serendipity knocking on your door, for sure.'

We share a look for a moment. What would your nickname be? Braces Tom? Trendy Tom? Major Tom's taken, I'm afraid. He's even stolen the song lyrics as the caption on his photo in his new wing. He's far above the world now but that will always be him.

'I'm married, just in case you were…' he says, seeming slightly terrified by my prolonged glance, like I'm fishing for a new Tom.

I reply by knocking my head back in laughter, though I'm worried I've now offended him.

'It's all good. I'm here to drink, not find new husbands. But tell me, Tom… what time do you close up here? Can I ask a favour?'

*

'What are we doing here, Gracie? Why have you got a jute bag?' Meg asks as she and her husband, Danny, run into the bar entrance. Alongside them are Emma and Jag, Lucy to the rear, and a very pregnant Beth and her Will. They emerge from an array of Ubers, curious, with an air of worry about them. My text was a bit random. It just came with an address. Maybe I should have added more detail.

'Are you all right?' Emma asks, taking in the state of me. My spirited walk has done nothing for my appearance and I'm part sweaty but also exceedingly balmy underarm. Lucy comes up and hooks her arm into mine; she's without a coat so I lend her half of mine.

'Is everything OK?' Beth says. 'When you went off after the ceremony, we were all a bit worried about you. You looked wiped out. We wanted to give you some space.'

They stand there waiting to hear the punchline.

'I want to dance.'

Meg and Emma furrow their brows, wondering why this requires their participation. Lucy puts a hand to the air, possibly stretching in preparation.

'This is the nightclub I met Tom in. It was a bloody dive back then but we met by that very bar. And I just strolled down here today, just to take it in. Relive a moment or something. Anyway, I then met the barman and his name is Tom too and he said we have this place until midnight.'

'We're dancing here?' Emma says, her self-conscious persona coming into view, assuming we're all going to be bopping around my jute shopper. 'Just us?'

'There are others.' I gesture to the back of the bar where Astrid and Farah are sitting at tables. Others are dotted around: Naoko and the

Japanese teachers all with drinks that aren't cider, Ellie and Ryan playing arcade games (loudly), and Sam and Helen. They've come with gifts today: stories of how Carrie threw a Harry Potter mug at Ross after she found out about Liz and took out his two front teeth. No news on whether Liz's face is still intact though we'll find out at the school gate tomorrow. Tomorrow. When the world goes back to normal.

The sisters all study my face for a moment as I half-jog on the spot. 'Yeah, I just have to keep moving for a bit,' I say.

Gracie? You OK, hun? Is she losing the plot? We'll stay here, of course, and try and partake but is this a sad Grace thing? It is the same look they gave me when, after Tom's death, I told them I was going to travel. Around the world. On my own. Like a world-tour-of-grief thing. Is this what people do? Meg's eyes scan to the ceiling. She also doesn't understand this music. There are no lyrics.

Lucy claps her hands together to rally them. It's dance. She doesn't question the why. 'Girls, you know we're doing this,' she says, clearing a space, her shoulders rolling into action. She don't need no music.

'But we have to get off early tomorrow for the drive back…' Meg says, her teeth gritted.

'What's an hour or two later?' her husband, Danny, says, winking at me.

'And you… B? You up for it?' I say.

Beth looks completely aghast. It would seem she was pushed out of the house in a onesie and Uggs so stands there wondering if she's even allowed to be seen in public.

'Well, the baby needs the exposure to the Bristol music scene. Just don't expect any big dance moves from me,' she says. I hug her. 'I know this also sounds shit but do they do tea here?'

Lucy takes my jute shopper and puts it in a nearby bin. 'It's bad enough bringing Emma into this place, ditch the old-lady shopper, yeah?'

Emma scowls at her as she and Jag head to greet Doug, who looks at me and lifts a beer bottle in my direction. Tom from behind the bar dims the lights and makes the music a little more in keeping. Disco. How apt. I put two thumbs up at him. I think back to a time when this place used to be packed to the rafters, throbbing to the bass of a Barry White anthem. From somewhere, I hear Lucy shrill and excitable. Jag drags Emma by the hand to a makeshift dancefloor. He has moves we did not know about. A hand falls to my shoulder.

'Are you OK?' Meg asks me, looking me straight in the eye.

I shrug my shoulders. 'Who knows any more? You are dancing, right?'

'I'll need a couple of shots first to keep up with Lucy.'

We look over and she's being borderline inappropriate – forming some sort of twerky sandwich between Astrid and Farah. I make a note to look out for them later, keep them off any boats in the vicinity. We laugh and Meg pulls me into a hug.

'Can you help me with something actually?' I ask.

'Anything…'

'I think I want to write a book.'

She smiles. 'I can do that. I can help at least. You got a name for it yet?'

'Nah… it's quite a story though. It starts in a club. In Bristol.'

EPILOGUE

'I am sorry. I am so sorry. I didn't see that. Please let me buy you another drink. Or order one from the air hostess, ladyperson. Oh dear…'

The woman scans down to the two little people next to me, eyes big and curious. They aren't naughty per se but I got them on this plane with all the skill of a gangly ape, juggling bags and blankets and sippy bottles in narrow aisles, so as soon as I'd put them down and ushered Cleo into a seat, I backed into the lady behind me and her drink. Urgh, I am awful at this already and I'm only a week in. What was I thinking? I know. My husband has died and so I will adopt two girls from his past life at the request of their grandmother because, of course, that is a totally natural state of affairs to adopt two children you've only known for a matter of months. I've romanticised this far too much in my own head. I haven't even parented on land before and now I'm going to do this in the air. They've never even been on a plane before. I should have roped in a sister to help. Asked their grandmother to come with. I did actually. But she refused. *I'll come out in a few months to visit. You need to do this on your own. You will be fine.* I marvel at how she has such faith in me. No. I can do this. I can do this myself. I am a capable young woman. Look at them with their tiny bushbaby eyes. Shit. What am I doing? I wasn't very good at travelling to start off with. I mainly got drunk in all these countries I went to, lost a shoe in Amsterdam and got suspected salmonella in New York. Little Maya stands on the seat and puts her arms up for me to carry her. I hold her close.

'Breathe,' the woman tells me.

'Sorry. I... it really was an accident.'

'It was water, I'll live,' she says, trying to catch Cleo's eye. 'I tell you a secret. I sometimes ask for the bulkhead seats as I know families will be sitting here. I like meeting new babies.'

That statement calms me for a moment; at least she's here out of choice as opposed to being stuck with two kids on a twelve-hour flight from Singapore. She holds her hand out for Cleo to shake but Cleo buries her head into my stomach.

'How old are they?' the woman asks.

'One and three. This is Maya and this is Cleo.'

'Wow, nice to meet you, ladies. And where's Daddy?'

Cleo tries to catch my eye.

'I'm afraid he passed away. I'm actually not their mother either. I mean, I am or this would be weird. Um, I adopted them. So yeah...'

The woman stops for a moment, her eyes tearing up. 'How old are you?'

'Oh, I'm twenty-eight.'

She's silent. I can't process if I've said the wrong thing. There is a vernacular here that I need to learn about. Have I made the girls feel rejected or alerted them to their own trauma? I am your mother. I am a mother. You wait until you hear that I'm a widow.

That will be the real conversation-killer. I try and cover the silence with attempting to sort the girls. This is the wrong thing to do. They look terrified. Maya literally clings to me like a koala. I can't even bend down to get my bag. Where did I put the passports? The wipes? Both children gaze up at me like they want me to tell them exactly what will happen next. I really don't know, girls.

'Well, that might be the best story I've ever heard,' the passenger says, studying my face. 'What a pair of lucky girls you are to have a mother like this.'

Cleo smiles as Maya nestles her head into the shallows of my chest. I don't know what to say back. She hardly knows me.

'I'm Lauren,' she says, handing me a packet of wipes I've left on the arm of her seat.

'I'm Grace.'

'Well, first rule of travelling with kids is the sweets. Who wants a sweet?'

*

'Mama, 37D. Are we sitting together?' Cleo says to me, her little rucksack on her back, head arched to read the numbers on the overhead lockers. Sandwiched between the both of us is Maya, who I try and move that bit quicker so we don't cause a queue.

'Of course, sweetie. Just a few more rows and we are… there,' I say in a plodding sing-song accent.

I haven't been on a plane since that day when I brought these two home. Since I met Lauren. She's a Singaporean expat, who now lives in London with three adult children and six grandchildren, so that plane trip was possibly the most valuable one to kickstart my adventures in parenting. When Cleo's ears started hurting on the flight, she taught her how to make them pop and was more than happy to hold Maya while I wolfed down food and legged it to the loos for a wee.

And you know what? We talked. When the cabin got dark and everyone was plugged into screens and attempting to sleep, Lauren gave me all sorts of wisdoms. She told me children can never have too much of your time and, when in doubt, bananas really are the best thing you can give a kid. And when we got off the plane, she tracked me down on social media and she still sends me Christmas cards. God, I wish she was here. Having not been on a plane since that day, I start to worry if that points to a lack of adventure. I can argue we were getting used to being a family, I was adjusting to motherhood and real life without Tom. But Cleo was right. It's time to get back out into the bigger world again and that, unfortunately, starts on economy class with an interesting plated meal involving a piece of cheese in plastic that will be impossible to open.

'HERE!' Cleo suddenly yelps and she scuttles into the middle seats. I've gambled in the hope that the flight won't be too crowded and we can bag an extra seat for us to spread out but we'll see what the flight gods give us. The girls' excitement is tangible as they fiddle with tray tables, Cleo taking off her shoes and literally emptying the contents of her bag to put in the seat pocket, like she's moving in.

'THEY'RE PLAYING MUSIC!' Maya says. Her bag isn't even off yet. But the earphones are in so she can ascertain if the in-flight entertainment will be to her liking. The speed and aptitude with which she fiddles with the buttons on the touchscreen is mildly alarming.

'LOOK! THERE'S A MAP THAT TELLS YOU WHERE WE ARE! WHY AREN'T WE MOVING?'

I put my bag down and take the earphones off her.

'That's because we're still on the ground, hun.'

She giggles, nestling into the seat and trying to find her seatbelt. I look around, praying that extra seat stays available to us. This wasn't like travel the last time. Last time it was a trip into the even bigger unknown, armed with new crisp passports and paperwork, and some of my baby gear was fresh out of the packaging. Now, organised Grace is on the plane, all the girls' spare clothes in separate plastic bags in my rucksack and the passports have their own folder. I even sorted out the sweets as I know Maya won't eat the green ones. Don't tell Meg I do that.

'Good evening, ladies and gentlemen, welcome to today's SQ322 flight from London Heathrow to Singapore. We are still boarding all passengers at the moment but a reminder to put all your luggage and belongings in the overhead lockers and ask our in-flight crew if you need any help or assistance today.'

Tom would love this. We're flying out to Singapore for a week and then we're headed to see orangutans in Borneo, culminating in two more weeks in Vietnam to see Linh. Is this my adventure of choice? Of course not. I may have given the girls a bit too much freedom with the decision-making but this is our plan. We are going to cuddle monkeys. And not bring one home. And also see our wonderful Linh. I won't lie. There are elements of this trip which petrify me. Safety concerns and mosquito-based illness are high on that list but there's also something about getting out into the world again, the excitement on these girls' faces, which lifts me. Let's do this. With a shitload of insect repellent, though, of course.

'Hey, I think I'm also in this row.'

I look up to find a man with a ponytail towering over me. Crap. That's my extra seat plan scuppered then. I smile as he glances over at the girls. I can't quite work out if he's impressed or not. I'm lucky. He doesn't seem like the business sort – he's casual with big earphones around his neck and dirty trainers, but also lines of tattoos up and down his arms. He reminds me of someone but I can't quite make out who.

'Yeah, sorry… I must be in your seat, I'll budge up.'

I shift my things over, realising it'll be just me and him now for the next twelve hours, acting as some barrier between me and the girls. Please be kind. Please be a Lauren. I think what I'll have to do if I need to wee now. I can't leave the girls within reach of a total stranger. I just won't drink for the next twelve hours. But then I'll get blood clots. That happens, doesn't it? We'll have to go to the loo at the same time. I'll wake them up. Or ask the air stewardess to help. Shit. Why am I panicky? I look over as the man puts his bag into the locker and a slice of flesh sticking out from where his T-shirt rides up shows me the tattoos are a whole-body thing.

'Did you want to put anything up here? While I'm up?' he asks.

I shake my head. 'No, thanks for offering, though.'

He comes to sit back down and Maya climbs onto my lap.

'I'm Maya. What's that tattoo on your tummy?' she asks.

I guess now is as good a time as any to find out if he likes kids or not.

'Umm, wow. It's a tiger.'

'Why a tiger?'

'I thought it'd be cool.'

'Tigers are cool. They're cooler than goats.'

'That is very true, Maya.'

'Sorry about her,' I interject. 'Just tell her your life story now and then she'll leave you be.'

'Don't apologise. My name is Max. Max and Maya – we could be a really good pop group.'

This impresses Maya less, who seems a bit dubious at the thought.

'Maybe but you'd have to lose the ponytail,' she says.

We are lucky this makes him laugh, quite hard. He takes out his hairband and shakes his mane out. He's one of those annoying men who has a wave to his hair, something that takes me hundreds of pounds' worth of product and equipment to achieve.

'You not a fan then, Maya?'

She shrugs. I've always liked the way Maya does this. She likes to give people the once-over, work them out and, like her sister, she does not hold back from telling them what she thinks.

'Are you going on holiday?' she asks.

'I am. I am going to see a friend of mine who lives in Singapore and then we are going to Koh Samui.'

'That's in Thailand,' Maya says. Max seems impressed by her knowledge. 'We're going to Kota Kinabalu to see monkeys.'

'Wow, very cool.'

'It is. And how old are you?' she asks.

'I am thirty.'

'Are you married?' she asks.

'MAYA!' I turn to Max. 'I'm sorry… she's not done that before. Maya?'

He chuckles. 'Well, you're very forward for one so young, but I'm not married.'

'I wasn't asking for me, silly. I was asking for my mum.'

I don't know what colour my face turns now but it's between red and reddest.

'I really am sorry,' I explain. I'm going to have to sit next to this man for twelve hours. This is why Emma suggested I give the girls a light sedative for this flight, wasn't it? I squirm in my seat a little.

'Is your mum looking for a husband?' he asks, trying his best to spare my blushes.

'I don't know but I like you. You look like that man from that film. The swimming man.'

'Who?' I say.

'The swimming man who's like a mermaid but not.'

'Aquaman?' he says. 'You think I look like Jason Momoa?'

She nods. We both laugh. He doesn't look anything like him. I might need to get this girl's eyes tested but I think about Tom for one small moment. Does Max do film work? Because I've written a book and he'd be kinda perfect if he doesn't mind taking some of that hair off and maybe wearing a prosthetic chin. Is this man good-looking? I have no idea at all. But my daughter is going to dig into her Haribo now, get out some gummy ring sweets and possibly make this official. Let's talk first. We have time. I may have to think about that hair though and see how big his tiger is.

The plane suddenly rolls to a start and the chime of a bell signals we have to put on our seatbelts. I reach across to ensure the girls are strapped in, leaning down to check bags are stowed safely, and make eyes at Maya. *You are terrible at setting me up with people. Don't do that. Not on a plane.* But she smiles sweetly, her body almost fizzing with excitement as she hugs her toy monkey tightly. I grip at Cleo's hand and she gives me a similar look. Let's do this, eh? I sit back and Aquaman catches my eye.

'I didn't catch your name,' he says.

'Oh, I'm Grace.'

'Best I know your name before I marry you, eh?'

I laugh. 'Very true.'

'I suppose there is no Mr Grace?'

'There is not.'

'Well, I'm Max. I like your yellow bracelet, Grace.'

'Thank you,' I reply suspiciously. 'I like your… hair?'

'Thank you. I grew it all myself.'

'That is impressive.'

I don't even have to look but I sense a very small person eavesdropping as we talk, a massive grin plastered across her face. I reach into the seat pocket and give her the safety announcement card, trying to focus her attention elsewhere. The plane lines up to the runway, a charge of the engine taking hold. I hate this feeling. I don't know if it's fear or excitement but I sense it in the pit of my stomach, in the back of my throat as the air sits waiting for me to either exhale or swallow. Maya holds onto me tightly, tiny fingers clasped around mine, almost like wire. I think I might feel good, or some version of it. I might be ready. Time for a new adventure.

A Letter from Kristen

Dear lovely reader,

Hello again! Or maybe you're new? Either way, thank you so much for reading – you really are a superstar and I feel so incredibly lucky that you chose to read my book. If you want to keep up to date with details of my writing, just sign up at the following link. Your email address will never be shared and you can unsubscribe at any time.

www.bookouture.com/kristen-bailey

I really hoped you laughed and cried with Gracie and enjoyed reading her story. I say enjoyed. This is the first book I've ever written that felt like an emotional sucker punch so I hope it wasn't too much. I think Grace will be fine – she has her gorgeous girls and she's just met a fit, tattooed man on a plane who looks like Jason Momoa so the future is brighter. I hope, out of everything, you were able to find the light and joy in her story.

You'll also be glad to know that her sisters all have their own books. *Has Anyone Seen My Sex Life?* is about Meg, *Can I Give My Husband Back?* is Emma's tale and look for *Did My Love Life Shrink*

In The Wash? if you want to learn more about Beth. Nothing would give me greater pleasure than if you were to go and spend some time with the other Callaghans. And keep an eye out for Lucy's story coming out in the very near future. That one may need to come with a warning.

Oh, Grace. I always knew what your story was going to be about and I always imagined that character of Tom so vividly in my head but I didn't know where your story was going to go, how I was going to make things better for you, who was going to come into your life and give you the hope you needed. I did know I wanted to dissect the different ways we experience loss in our lives. I've lost those I've loved but then I've also experienced the end of a relationship, the loss of a friend, the different stages of my life rolling to a finish.

I knew I wanted to write about people coming in and out of this play that is life – some people we get to keep, others we don't. So, in that way, travel seemed the best way to anchor this story. If anything, that's been my life for the past twenty years. I was one of those people who went travelling when I left university. I was not a Tom. I was a Grace. I wasn't the greatest of travellers (I'm very clumsy and gullible…) but I'm still quite transient. She gets around, y'know? In the best possible way, of course. I make friends, I lose friends, I move on and around the world. Those places and people all become separate chapters in my life. To that end, a lot of the characters and places in this book are very real. Please look Shunan up on a map. It's brilliant. I've moved on from those beaches, clubs and karaoke lounges but they all made up part of the journey so I'll always be forever grateful, especially to all the people I met along the way. Some I met by complete accident and some I'm still lucky to have in my life. Grace may indeed be right. For all those places I went to, it was the people who made it the best adventure.

While Grace's tale is one of grief, I also wanted to pay tribute to the love story she shared with Tom. I heard grief described in the most wonderful way recently: 'What is grief if not love persevering?' And that's the very core of this book: love, and the many ways it manifests itself. Whether it be lost love, long-distance or through marriage, family, motherhood, or friendship – love is all around, actually (I quoted Hugh Grant there – that's the most nineties romcom thing I will ever say…). I think I've just realised that in the past year too. This book was written in 2020/21 when, well, it was quite hard to love the world. Love was there but you couldn't even reach out and hold it… so to me love is really important, more than ever. I hope, dear reader, you have it in your life, in abundance, and recognise its power.

OK, enough with me being all soppy! I will sign off here. Before I go, I'd be thrilled to hear from any of my readers, whether it be with reviews, questions or just to say hello. If you like retweets of videos of people falling off things then follow me on Twitter. Have a gander at Instagram, my Facebook author page and website too for updates, ramblings and to learn more about me. Like, share and follow away – it'd be much appreciated.

And if you enjoyed *How Much Wine Will Fix My Broken Heart?* then I would be overjoyed if you could leave me a review on either Amazon or Goodreads to let people know. It's a brilliant way to reach out to new readers. And don't just stop there, tell everyone you know, send to all on your contacts list. Even those school mums who you don't actually like – you know the ones.

With much love and gratitude,
Kristen xx

         kristenbaileywrites

         kristenbaileywrites

         @mrsbaileywrites

         www.kristenbaileywrites.com

Acknowledgements

At the time of writing this, my wonderful editor, Christina Demosthenous, has just been nominated for Editor of the Year by The British Book Awards and I am going to stand up here at my desk, applaud and cheer like CRAZY and say this is richly deserved. She'd better win or I am going to write some angry emails. I owe her everything. She was the one who found me, who makes my writing shine a bit more, and ensures I control my very sweary mouth. In the rubbish year we've had, she still remains the ultimate cheerleader, critic and caregiver – and I am so grateful for her support and unwavering enthusiasm. Behind the scenes at Bookouture, a huge thanks also to Sarah Hardy, Kim Nash, Lauren Finger, Rhian McKay, Rhianna Louise, Sarah Durham and all the team who work tirelessly to make my books happen.

There's a lot of people to thank in this one so this is going to read like an Oscars speech without anyone playing me off the stage. However, I am anxious about missing people out so here goes: first off, here's a rolling tribute to all in no particular order (though Brendan goes first as he demanded it).

Special thank you to Brendan O'Cadhain, my native New Yorker on the ground who walked me through the many zoos of

NYC, educated me about tater tots and informed me he can eat mozzarella for breakfast. I am sorry, my friend, but the fact you hail from those shores and don't like pickles is an absolute tragedy. I owe you a big pack of Newports.

Graham Price, I always mention you in my acknowledgements but you really are such a gem of a mate. *Graham, I need the name of an indie band that's a bit up its own arse?* And then you text me back the perfect answer. You're like a thesaurus of good ideas. Thank you also for letting me read your travel diaries from your time in Saigon. We need to work on your handwriting though.

Japan. I spent seven months working in Japan in 2014 with the now defunct NOVA school of English. What a seven months they were. I want to shout out to Lee, who I shared a flat with and who was the person who picked me up from that small train station in Shunan and showed me the ropes. Jose, Darren, Ben, Rachelle, Elly, Glenn, Chris, Mike M, Mike S, Susan (Seiyu, Say Me), Curt and Madoka. I am not sure if we taught much English but, boy, we ate all the yakitori and we had all the fun. To quote Glenn, it still amazes me that so many fine vocalists could end up in Shunan together.

Bristol will always be my spiritual home. I spent three glorious years there as a student and, as a city, I love it madly, so it was an obvious thing for me to set a book there. Since leaving, all those wonderful friends I've made have gone in different directions – some I see once in a blue moon, others always like my Facebook pictures whatever the weather. Without wanting to sound like I'm having a midlife crisis, those really were the best days and I thank that huge cast of characters who were a part of them. Specific thanks to

Frances and Helen, who both clarified many details for me about our many nights out. It was Henry who walked into the harbourside. (Henry is alive, just in case anyone was wondering…) And where did we spend a lot of those nights out? Steam Rock. Lordy, I loved that place. I have no regrets about squeezing you into this novel despite the fact you closed down in the early noughties because that is the place I did all my learning, all my dancing, all my drunken snogging. Love and thanks to uni stalwarts Bethan, Anna, Shammi, Selma and Tim, too. And special mention to Joe, who, despite all the odds, was the one friend from uni who survived them all.

When my sister's eldest son started school for the first time, I told her to hang onto her pants. 'But all the mums seem so lovely?' she said. I told her to wait. Three months down the line, she started sending me screen grabs of the actual fights happening on WhatsApp. I write a lot about school gates and that's because the drama writes itself. You guys need to calm the fuck down and park your cars better. But a thank you to the school-gate mums who've become friends, who I would down wine with any day of the week. I'd name you by person but I suspect that would start more drama. However, I'd like to thank Meghan Conway. She'll know why.

And here's just a list of people who I love for a variety of reasons: they read my books, they share all my book spam, they're at the end of a phone, they've let me steal their names, outside the bubble of being a writer they're just really good eggs and I thank them for their friendship and support: Charlotte Klahn, Matt and Hanah Loveday, Barrie and Claire Funnell, Sara Hafeez, Claire Hillier-Brook, Kelly Adey, Drew Davies, Catherine Miller, Elizabeth Neep, Will Simpson and them folk at *The Writing Community Chat Show*.

Over the year, I've also met the LOVELIEST book bloggers on Instagram and beyond who've supported my books and been such a gorgeous community to come to know. Big book love to you all.

And now, the big players…

I need to thank my mother, Lauren, who the eagle-eyed among you will have noticed gets a little mention in the epilogue. That's my mum. And she does sit in the bulkhead seats because she loves a baby and I've yet to meet a baby who doesn't love her. My mum's the ultimate traveller. She began life as an airline stewardess in the mid-seventies so that kick-started the adventure but the wanderlust has never faded. She turned sixty a few years back and she's still cramming in the trips, WhatsApping me stories of how she nearly got mugged in Moscow and sending me pictures of men in thongs on Copacabana Beach.

In fact, I've been to all the places mentioned in this book but I've never been to Vietnam. That was not a problem though as my mum did, three years ago, and the way she described a banh mi could have very well been a whole chapter in this book. My mum is also South East Asian and moved to the UK in the late seventies when she met my dad. (Barrett from Guyana – did you spot him too?) She raised global kids and in that I mean she always makes us try every food, learn every capital city and have empathy and respect for people's stories, backgrounds. That to her was the ultimate education and one I don't thank her nearly enough for. She is one of three sisters, Linda and Maureen, and between the three of them, they are peak strong sister energy. Man, they have stories for days. Linh is an amalgamation of them all but you'll see shades of Fiona Callaghan and all the sisters in them.

Next, my little people. Thank you, kids, for enduring me as a mother. I am hard work (especially when I'm on deadline and I'm cooking you plain rice for dinner) but I hope you are having fun. Grace's story touched on her raising two kids as part of a mixed-race family and that echoes my experience completely. I have Asian roots but my youngest daughter was born platinum blonde. I once had a security guard follow me around Primark because he thought I was kidnapping her. We have a unique experience as a family but, for all our physical differences and the melting pot of cultures we represent, we are the best unit and my kids have taught me nothing but love, about belonging and the transformative effects of motherhood. Thank you, bambini. Now go and do a cup run.

I also wouldn't know what it is to understand love were it not for Mr Bailey. When I first met Mr Kristen, we spent a lot of time doing long-distance and wrote a lot of postcards to each other. The relationship bounced between Shunan, Bethnal Green, Hong Kong, Osaka and Singapore. This was pre-Facebook, pre-fancy phones so it was all vaguely romantic. Since then it's been a marriage and a love where we've continued to sometimes live abroad, have many babies and undergo every challenge together, and, believe me, there have been many. Life isn't easy but love is when it's with you. Permission to go and pretend to retch at this bold admission of emotion.

And then to the final part of these acknowledgements. I guess, when you write a book about loss, it will make you think about the grief you've experienced in your own life. So it'd be remiss of me not to mention my godfather, Malcom, and grandmother, Lydia. Both were larger-than-life characters in my world. I've mentioned I'm mixed-race and this meant I was always surrounded by a colourful and amazing catalogue of stories from places very far away. Uncle Malcom and Nana were two of the best. Memories of listening to my grandmother's tales of the war and growing up in Singapore are still etched onto me, and are at the beating heart of how I write and why I tell my stories.

And then there was Grace.

Grace was the last sister I named as a character. No names actually fit. I was going to continue down the *Little Women* avenue – maybe Jo, Amy – or lean on Austen – Marianne or Elizabeth – but then Grace came along. Grace was perfect. Grace Green was someone I actually knew once. When I left university, I took a job as a nanny for a wonderful family while I tried to figure out the rest of my life. I was twenty-one. That family were the Greens and I had two wonderful years of looking after their three brilliant little girls, Grace, Florence and Millie.

I stayed in touch with the Green family long after I left and, from afar, I saw three cheeky little loves grow up into beautiful young women. They always made me so incredibly happy and proud. However, the landscape changed one day when Nicola, their wonderful mum, messaged to tell me Grace had been diagnosed with leukaemia. I remember visiting Grace and her family around that time. I was pregnant with my youngest and I remember being in complete awe of her. She was so young but serene, so assured in the face of everything. When my youngest was born, the whole family sent gifts and a T-shirt about sisters that always made me think of them.

Grace had a brief respite from her cancer the following year but an aggressive relapse meant she passed away in 2016. She was twenty-four. I still keep in touch with Nicola and her husband,

Nigel. I still love that family very dearly. I take pause whenever I see a picture of Grace – it's not a sad pause. I can't be sad when I had the privilege of knowing someone as special as her once. It's an honour to name one of my beloved sisters after her – it feels like a fitting tribute, a way to remember her. Thank you, lovely girl, for the loan of your name, your spirit, your grace. I will always be in awe of you.

I know far too many affected by cancer these days and my research for this book meant I came across so many different stories from people that were both sobering, devastating and humbling. Below are the details for two cancer charities that I will be supporting on publication day and I hope that you might be able to visit their websites, learn about the important work they do and see if there is any way you can help them too.

Thank you. Love, always xx

www.anthonynolan.org/
https://orchid-cancer.org.uk/